Tammy L. Harrow

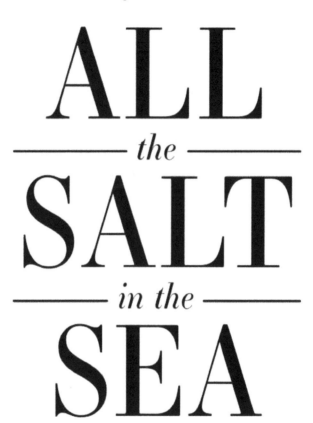

ALL
the
SALT
in the
SEA

All the Salt in the Sea
Red Adept Publishing, LLC
104 Bugenfield Court
Garner, NC 27529
https://RedAdeptPublishing.com/

This is a work of fiction. Names, characters, places, and incidents either are the product of the author's imagination or are used fictitiously, and any resemblance to locales, events, business establishments, or actual persons—living or dead—is entirely coincidental.

---

1. http://StreetlightGraphics.com

*To the lovers, dreamers, and those who deserve more than half
a life.*

"Everything you've ever wanted is on the other side of fear."
George Addair

PART 1

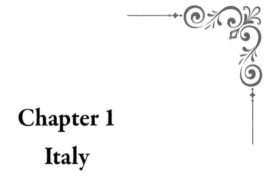

Chapter 1
Italy

Buses, cars, and mopeds jockey for space along the two-way mountain road to Positano. Without warning, vehicles stop in the center of the roadway, forcing the bus I'm on to screech to a halt. Oncoming vehicles round the bends and block the way. My driver curses in Italian each time, then he backs down and around the mountain without regard for the blind curves. Around me, wide-eyed passengers with worried expressions clutch seatbacks and each other. Fear emanates from my fellow travelers as they peer out windows and back at each other.

The ride from Sorrento takes nearly an hour. The old me would have been terrified, but a numbness has settled over me. Without the usual anxiety, I am fearless. Floating in limbo, in the dull space between life and death, has its perks. I rock and sway with the swerves and jerky movements of the bus, indifferent to life. On the right side where I'm seated, I can see over the cliff, hundreds of feet to the bottom. Mangled at the base of a mountain in the crumpled ruins of a bus would be a shameless and blameless way to die. The air is warm. The cloudless sky is a shade of cerulean blue. If one could paint a picture of a perfect day to die, this would be it.

Life as we know it back home in St. Augustine was a lie. A house built on shifting sands could never be anything but temporary. Now that my daughter is practically grown and Alex has lost whatever emotion he once held for me, my time there is over. He isn't aware yet, but I know his truth. I left the pills, each tiny wish, lined up on the bathroom vanity like small soldiers awaiting orders. He brought them home to me for weeks, little offerings to help us both. Leftover prescriptions from his patients, I suppose. Without saying a thing, he placed them in the medicine cabinet beside the others, maybe hoping I would swallow them all at once to honor his unspoken words. But I couldn't. Not even with half a bottle of the Opus One he'd been saving coursing through my veins. Somehow, in the deepest throes of darkness, I imagined the poetic justice of climbing into our marital bed and washing down the pills with his cherished bottle of twenty-five-hundred-dollar wine.

But I didn't. I left the pills, burned the goodbye notes I'd written, then bought a one-way ticket to Rome, where I stayed holed up in an outdated room in Trastevere, staring out condensation-covered windows and waiting for sunshine that never came. For days, I sat shivering in that room amid low-hanging clouds weighted with rain while watching a spring sky spit at the window. In the frigid building, the thin blankets did nothing but scratch at my skin. The exterior stone walls appeared to be a foot thick, yet the interior was thin enough for me to hear the neighbors argue then make up for hours. Their headboard knocked in rhythm against my wall. When the silence or noise became too much, I turned on the television and listened to the rapid-fire Italian, searching for any semblance of familiar words I'd learned from my grandmother years ago. I recognized very little.

Distance brought no relief. Traveling thousands of miles from home should have cured me or, at the very least, lessened the anxiety and sadness. But I felt the same as I had in St. Augustine. Rome did nothing to unbreak me. As another attempt to hang on, I bought a ticket to go farther south. Alex would be home by now, no doubt disappointed because of my cowardice. He would be angry that I left.

Ruby, my daughter, will be in Peru for a few more weeks, backpacking with her best friend's family. I emailed to let her know I'd gone away to my grandmother's hometown. At the end of summer, she'll be gone for good, off to college in Boston to start a new life without me. An aching twist in my stomach brings back the carefully scribed last words I wrote to my daughter. I asked her not to blame herself and reassured her that what I was about to do had nothing to do with her and that there was no way she could have seen it coming no matter how hard she'd searched. I explained the curse that had been passed down from my mother. I promised her that she wasn't afflicted and that every day I'd looked into her bright and curious eyes and seen no sign of it. Then I shredded the letter into tiny pieces so she would never know.

Halfway up a mountain in Positano, the bus stops, and I step out with the crowd. They dissipate, leaving me alone on the edge of the cliff. Tiny white boats jet out along the sapphire sea toward the island of Capri. Forests of bougainvillea in pinks and purples surround me. The flowers make their way up the mountainside, on the walls, houses, and onto every vertical surface. Bulging lemons hang from thin-branched trees in brightly colored pots.

My grandmother's hometown is even more picturesque than her description. I make my way down the hill in the direction of the crowds. Each of my steps is a little lighter than the last. Café tables filled with chatty diners line the road's edge. Symphonies of sounds fill my ears. Foreign chatter and laughter, the sound of clinking forks on plates, and wine glasses coming together in toasts. I edge closer to their happiness in hopes it will spread to me. Shoppers stroll in and out of boutiques with bulging bags as I walk along aimlessly.

The air is warm yet crisp with sweet scents from a nearby bakery. Farther down, at the bottom of the hill, the smell of salt, seaweed, and a hint of decaying fish hits me. I follow it, rounding a corner and stepping off the sidewalk and onto the beach. Soft sand gives way beneath my feet, and I take in the air. Saltwater is everything. The briny smells of the salty sea remind me of hopeful times. Of vacation, freedom, and endless possibilities. As the essence of our existence with the ability to both sustain and take lives, the sea brings both comfort and terror.

I take a seat in the sand and remain there for hours. Boats come and go from the shore. Fishermen cast their nets. Being in a place of such beauty lightens me and lessens the tension in my neck and shoulders. Leaving this world without coming here would have been a damn tragedy. Inside me, a shift begins, a slight metamorphosis of sorts that I can't yet fully comprehend.

Later, a small bus delivers me to Montepertuso, a residential area miles above and away from the tourists of Positano. At La Trattoria, a family-run farm-to-table restaurant, I hope to find Francesca, the best friend of my departed grandmother. An iron gate and pebbled walkway lead me to a wooden porch. The cliffside structure overlooks the entire town, with hundreds of pastel-colored houses cascading down to the sea below.

Twisted ropes of garlic, herbs, and peppers hang from bamboo ceilings throughout the open dining area. The unmistakable scent of a wood-burning oven mingles with roasted tomatoes, garlic, and oregano. These aromas, the very essence of Italian cooking, transport me back to my childhood. I allow the memory to play on. I am back in Franklin, Tennessee, standing in the kitchen beside my small and sturdy grandmother as she ties an apron around my waist then her own. Minutes later, our forearms are covered in flour, our hands sticky with dough. We roll out long strands of her famous gnocchi before cutting and indenting it with forks. I watch her and try to do as she does. Otherwise, she'll make me start over until I get it right.

"You mess it up, just like Francesca," she yells in the accent she never lost, yanking away my dough before tossing it into the trash.

She hands me a new piece. "Gentle *these* time." She kisses the top of my head as a way of apologizing for being such a perfectionist.

As teenagers, Francesca and my nonna spent summer days making the gnocchi and ravioli to sell to a trattoria in town. "If we do it wrong, we must take it back."

I have no idea if Francesca is even alive, but I need to at least try to be in the presence of someone who loved my grandmother as much as I did. Then I'll figure out what comes next.

A twenty-something woman with dark wavy hair greets me. "*Ciao*. Welcome. I am Luciana, and this is Stefano, my brother."

He waves and flashes a million-dollar smile with perfect white teeth. Stefano's hair is brown and stiff, gelled up in all directions. He reminds me of a naughty surfer waiting for trouble he won't be able to resist.

"Are you ready to be seated?" Luciana asks with a serious expression then places her hands together as if she's about to pray. There's a warmness to her. I like her straightaway.

I nod. The smells from the kitchen stir an appetite I haven't had in weeks.

"All the food is grown, prepared, and served by our family." She points to a smiling couple a few feet away, standing in front of a table near the kitchen. "That is Mama and Papa."

The parents have the same dark hair as their children. Mama's and Papa's is peppered with gray.

"There are no menus," Luciana explains as I'm seated. "But you will love everything here," she says matter-of-factly. "The only choice you must make is *vino rosso* or *bianca*."

I order the *rosso* and sip it while waiting for the food to arrive. The men in the family speak limited English, and Mama speaks none at all. Stefano and Papa go from table to table, shaking hands, patting backs, and chatting with guests.

Plates of broccoli, peas, potatoes, and spinach—all organically grown—are brought to my table. Mozzarella and prosciutto are followed by dishes of assorted fresh pastas, including mozzarella-stuffed gnocchi and ravioli that taste like my grandmother's. I close my eyes and savor each delectable bite of tender pasta as it melts in my mouth. The salty brine only fresh olive oil can bring comes through in the sauce. Bits of ripened tomatoes burst in my mouth.

Chatter, laughter, and clinking wine glasses echo throughout the room. They bring dessert platters out next. Overflowing with tiramisu, chocolate-dipped pâte à choux, and my favorite, baba au rhum, a sweet bread with a rum-flavored syrup, appear. As if that weren't enough, shots of traditional Sorrento limoncello, a delicious bittersweet lemon liqueur, is served with dessert. The limoncello both burns and soothes my throat going down and leaves my palate confused and longing for more. The food brings me comfort I haven't known since before my grandmother passed many years ago. My lips curve into an unexpected smile.

My phone is turned off and will stay that way. I won't allow Alex's lies to reach me here. Lunch is over, but I'm not ready to leave or to tell the family why I've come.

I study the language guidebook hidden in my lap to find the term for room recommendations. "*Vorrei affittare una camera da letto,*" I manage to say to Stefano, asking for a room to rent.

After a few moments of boisterous Italian conversation with his sister Luciana, he leads me across a little stone bridge to one of the rooms the family rents on the side of the multi-leveled restaurant. The view of the sea and mountains is identical to a photo that hung in our living room decades ago. In her final months, my grandmother sat in her ratty brown recliner with the teal-and-white afghan knitted by her own mother draped across her lap. She would stare up at that photo with a longing in her eyes I never understood.

"Here you go." Luciana's voice breaks my trance and makes me realize this is my moment.

I take a deep breath and go for it. "I believe our grandmothers were best friends growing up, and if Francesca is still with us, I would love to meet her."

Luciana's brows furrow. "Who is your grandmother?"

"Ruby-Lee."

"Oh," she says, her brows raised. "Sorry for your loss. Nonna was brokenhearted when she heard the news." She places her hand on my shoulder. "But she's not in very good health, and I am afraid talking about the past would just upset her."

I know I should understand her need to protect her grandmother, but I don't want to give up so easily. "I've heard many stories about our grandmothers growing up, and it would mean so much to me to spend a few minutes with her."

Before she can reply, Stefano appears, and they argue for a moment before Luciana turns back to me, wearing a forced smile.

"Please," I say. "I've traveled so far."

"She is out at a doctor's appointment but will return this afternoon," she says without expression. "I will ask her if she would like to speak with you and let you know."

Their arguing resumes, and even though I can't understand what they're saying, Luciana's narrowed eyes cut toward me, making it obvious I am to blame.

I SPEND THE AFTERNOON in town, where bougainvillea in various shades of pink covers tall stone walls. Lemon vendors with wooden carts full of fruit are set up in the alleys, just as they were more than a half-century ago when my grandmother was a young girl. Back then, she and Francesca peddled their own lemons and olives, trying to undercut the locals by selling their goods for a few cents cheaper.

I step in and out of shops, sampling offerings of bittersweet limoncello. None compare to La Trattoria's. After admiring a locally made soft white scarf, I buy it. Scents of fresh baked bread and buttery crepes waft from roadside cafés. Somehow, I still have an appetite. Because I've barely eaten in weeks, I indulge myself and exchange three Euros for a warm paper-wrapped crepe oozing with Nutella and banana. With the first bite, a memory of my brother, Tommy, springs forward. On an early winter evening, he's in the kitchen with both the refrigerator and freezer doors wide open. He complains that he's starving and begs our mother to make crepes.

"Please, Mama. I'll do anything you ask." He rubs her shoulders and smiles that perfect smile of his that worked on every girl he ever met, even our mother. He winks at me, as if it's a secret between us. Like everyone else, my mother couldn't say no to Tommy.

Stray cats follow as I wander through the alleys. While I stop to pet one, I look around, realizing I'm lost. I continue on without a care. Minutes later, I stumble upon an unadorned duomo, a rarity among Italian churches. The windows are small. The exterior stucco is yellowed and stained from age. The inside is remarkable, though. Dozens of chandeliers sparkle and bathe the cathedral in shimmering light. Life-sized paintings of saints hang around the room. Eerie eyes follow me. Thick stone walls keep the air chilled. I shiver and wrap my new white scarf around my shoulders.

Saying goodbye to Tommy shook my faith. Losing my grandmother sealed the deal. After her funeral, I didn't think I would ever step foot inside another church, yet here I am, standing before the altar, staring into a red-velvet-lined casket containing a replica of Jesus.

I imagine myself in his place, with my daughter looking down, wondering why she couldn't save me. Sadness flows, reminding me of the old demons, both mine and my mother's, that have haunted us for decades. Her depression was so severe that after my brother's death, she walked away from both my father and me, and she never looked back. Then my father did the same. He remembers it differently, though. "It was your choice," he said about my living with my grandmother.

My darkness comes and goes and often takes something monumental, like finding out my husband has a child with another woman, to send me into a spiral.

"My husband has a child with another woman." I whisper the words, tasting them on my tongue, expecting to feel something. But I'm hollow. His name is Jack. The name we chose had Ruby been a boy.

In a dim corner of the church, the smell of incense and sadness surrounds me as I contemplate a way to move forward in this life. I light a candle and speak to God for the first time in ages. The shame of praying to a God I've ignored for so long hangs heavy over me. My grandmother raised me better. She did all the right things. She took me to Mass on Sundays and forced me to appreciate the roof over my head and the food in my belly.

I apologize to God, though I'm unsure if he's listening, for what I almost did. I beg for forgiveness and strength and ask for help navigating this world and becoming whole again. Finally, I pray to Saint Jude, the patron saint of lost causes. Then I sit for hours in that darkened chapel, waiting for a transformation that doesn't come.

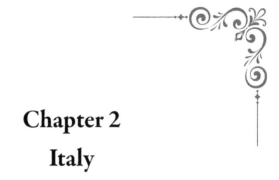

Chapter 2
Italy

Back on the mountaintop at La Trattoria, Stefano spots me and dances over. "Hey," he says, greeting me with an exuberant pat on the back before pulling me toward the patio. "*Mia nonna,* Francesca." He gestures with a wide smile and pulls out a chair beside a tiny wrinkled, gray-haired woman. A half-empty carafe of red wine and a full glass sits on the table in front of her. "*Mia amica,* Abby." He motions for me to sit.

She smiles a toothless, gummy smile and reaches her shaky hand to take mine. Deep creases frame her mouth. Her dark eyes are glazed with cataracts. Even at her age, she's beautiful. She looks up at me then back down to the thick photo album in her lap and points.

Luciana pulls up a chair, sits beside me, and folds her hands in her lap. "Our grandmother doesn't speak English, so I will translate."

Side-by-side, their wide dark eyes and narrow noses look similar. Luciana's long black waves cascade down her back, while Francesca's hair is pulled up, away from her face.

Francesca opens the book and points to a large black-and-white photo of two girls about the same age as my Ruby. She speaks, and Luciana translates her grandmother's soft, shaky words.

"This is my friend, Ruby-Lee. We called her Rubina, so the village boys did not tease her for her American name. She was as beautiful and rare as a precious stone, like her name. Her eyes were the color of sapphires, and…" She stops and reaches her wrinkled hand to my hair. "Her hair was red like yours." She grins, removing her hand and placing it back on the book. "We were raised next door to one another several kilometers from here." She gestures to the road. "But when her *nonno* in Sorrento died, her parents moved there to stay with her *nonna*."

Francesca turns the pages, stopping to point at images of my grandmother as a girl. She was so young and pretty.

"There were no buses then. So we wrote each other every day." She looks at me as if to make sure I understand, then she reaches between the pages and retrieves a small stack of yellowed envelopes. "These are letters Rubina sent that summer away. I want you to have them."

She extends her trembling hand. I take the letters and press them to my chest.

Francesca's eyes brighten. "At age fourteen, she lived with my family because her mama was too sad to take care of her and her papa had no money for food."

My grandmother never shared any of this with me, not her own mother's mental health issues or financial troubles. Her stories told only of an idyllic childhood. I had no idea her mother was afflicted as well. The family curse of sadness was handed down through generations, skipping beyond her to my mother and me.

Francesca turns the page. "And here we are again, happy together." She points to the two of them in the garden, their dresses pulled up to their knees. Their hair is tied up in scarves, and their heads are thrown back in laughter. I can see my nonna in the face of this young, joyful girl. Her eyes had the same sparkle, her smile the same warmth right up until the end.

Francesca's gaze meets mine.

"*Bella*," I say, stifling tears.

She removes the photo and hands it to me.

I press it to my chest as if it'll somehow bring my grandmother closer.

"You keep the photo," Luciana translates. "Nonna wants you to have it."

Francesca turns the page again and pauses, her own eyes tearing up. She kisses her fingers and presses them to the photo.

I wait.

"This is the last time I saw her before her family took her away to America," Luciana translates. "They left so her mama could get well. They were supposed to come back in one year, but they did not. Her papa got a job, and they never returned. Now she is gone forever." Francesca looks away as a tear rolls down her cheek.

Knowing we ache for the same woman, I find solace in her pain. I press my palm to the cool, papery skin of her arm to offer comfort.

"I think that's enough for now," Luciana interrupts. "My grandmother is not in the best health."

"I understand. Thank you also. *Grazie mille*, Francesca," I say. "I cannot tell you what meeting you means to me. The letters and photo—I will cherish them forever." I hold Francesca's hand in mine while waiting for Luciana to translate.

Francesca reaches out. Locking eyes with me, she strokes my cheek. "*Troverai qui la tua felicità*."

I try to translate her words inside my head, but happiness is the only word I know.

Luciana says, "You will find your happiness here."

I doubt that is true. "I hope so."

Luciana's smile reaches her eyes for the first time. "My grandmother says she is certain you will."

I say my goodbyes, return to my room, and remove a letter from the brittle envelope, careful not to crumble the delicate yellowed stationery. The words are scribed in Italian. Just holding them in my hands and being in this place makes me feel closer to my grandmother. An emotion, even regret, feels better than nothing. If I had been stronger, come sooner, and brought her with me, she could have spent precious time with her best friend, and I could have witnessed the love between them. Instead, all I have are old letters and shame. Why didn't I take the time to learn the language of my ancestors? Why didn't I ask questions about her parents, especially her mother? Is Francesca right—will I find happiness here?

As I place the stack of letters in the front pocket of my backpack, there's a knock at the door.

Stefano wears a mischievous smile. "Come, come," he says, jumping from foot to foot and pointing outside.

I'm skeptical, but his enthusiasm makes it hard not to follow along.

"Champagne for you." He motions to the tiny glass table on the patio, where a small, uncorked bottle and single flute rest.

Metallica plays from the bar area. The screeching guitar riffs make me cringe. Heavy metal music doesn't match the picturesque setting. Stefano bobs to the beat while strumming his air guitar. His eyebrows jump up and down as he belts out English lyrics in a thick Italian accent. He's lost in the moment and doesn't care that I cannot look away.

He stops mid-riff then enthusiastically gestures to the man leaning against the wooden fence rail facing the sea. I don't know how long he's been there. "Hey, Abby! *Mio cugino,* Daniel."

The man glances at me and nods, then he turns away, disinterested. I pivot around for Stefano, but he's gone. I'm unsure of his motives but take a seat and pour myself a glass of bubbly.

When Cousin Daniel glances my way again, our eyes connect for a moment. From behind, I take note of his chiseled triceps and tight pale-gray T-shirt. The way it defines his back muscles suggests he works out somewhere like a gym rather than a farm. His hair is dark and cropped short, his skin golden. I try to guess his age. Late thirties, maybe early forties. Why should I care? He walks toward, then past me, avoiding eye contact. Does he sense the deadness inside of me? Is it that apparent? Shoving my thoughts away, I sip champagne, taking in the view of the coastline, and wonder how it was possible hundreds of years ago to construct houses hanging from cliffs over the sea like this. How could they have transported the materials up the mountain to build these beautiful homes?

Glass rattles. Cousin Daniel is across the yard, organizing liquor bottles at the patio bar. He turns off the heavy metal and switches to an English-speaking alternative station. Daughtry's soothing sounds bring a sense of melancholy comfort, and I appreciate the gesture. Daniel nods my way then steps back to assess his work before rearranging the bottles again.

I try not to watch, but I can't help myself. He catches me, causing heat in my cheeks. *It's like I've never seen an attractive man before. What the hell is wrong with me?* I need to get out of there, so I stand to leave. Daniel opens his mouth to speak, but Stefano appears beside him and interrupts.

"Ayyy. Daniel, *cosa stai facendo*?" With a huge grin, he thumps his cousin on the back.

Daniel shakes his head and turns back to his bottles.

Stefano looks to each of us with a smile so big, it splits his face in half. I get it now. He's trying to play Cupid.

In slow, exaggerated English, he says, "Abby, wait. You come next door to restaurant at nine. Special night. Huh?"

I humor him. "Why so special?"

"Music and dancing." He swirls his hands in the air. "And magic too," he says, raising his eyebrows with a grin plastered on his face.

With a look of disgust, Daniel shakes his head and moves his lips, muttering something too quiet for me to hear. I slip off to my room, trying to brush away the awkwardness of the situation. Part of me wants to hide away in my room for the night, but something, maybe Francesca's promise from earlier, draws me to go. After a quick nap, I shower then dress with no expectations for the evening, other than a delicious meal.

Lights from the restaurant and sounds of traditional Italian music guide me across the stone bridge. The restaurant is warm and loud, and it smells amazing. I close my eyes for a moment and take in the scent of roasting garlic and baking bread and picture myself back in Franklin, in my grandmother's kitchen.

Amplified voices boom as the microphone comes alive, startling me. Drums and bells clang as the musicians and singers go up and down, serenading patrons on both levels of the restaurant.

"*Salute.*"

Silverware clinks on glasses. Cheers and laughter are everywhere. Boisterous conversations dominate the room between sets. Italians are loud. When the entertainment reappears, they sing, clap, and strong-arm guests to join in. After some time, I oblige. Wine and limoncello flows. The evening meal is like lunch with a party.

Laughing women are pulled from their seats, handed tiny tambourines, and dragged to the front of the room. Cheering crowds make it impossible to refuse. Despite my embarrassing lack of rhythm, I dance like no one is watching—and feel like a living cliché. Patrons swirl napkins in the air. Mama and Papa appear from the kitchen, and everyone cheers. The euphoria is infectious, and when I sit back down, I realize I'm grateful I came.

Daniel is there, alone, dressed in a dark-gray tee and jeans. He's leaning against a wall beside the door. His arms are crossed, and his expression is somewhere between tired and annoyed. Tipsy women approach him one by one. First, a smiling blonde, who doesn't look Italian at all, comes up, whispers in his ear, then reaches to put her hands through the back of his hair. He snatches her wrist then, with a softer expression, seems to apologize. She wobbles away, wearing a humiliated expression. Other women who look to be Italian approach. His half-smile and conversation show more patience. His arms, though, remain crossed. His disinterest is clear. As the last song plays, he scans the room, and his eyes stop on me. He lifts his hand in a brief wave, causing a flurry of butterflies to stir in my gut. The crowds thin, and when I look again, Daniel is gone. Feelings of disappointment surprise me. *Stop it, Abigail! You are a mess. Your life is a disaster!*

With the evening ending and my face sore from smiling, I slip out. Walking across the tiny stone bridge to my room, I see him standing alone beside the cliff. He's staring out at the sea, his face and eyes illuminated by the moon. He's relaxed and unguarded, apparently deep in thought. The lines around his eyes are softer, making him seem vulnerable somehow. His face is beautiful and sad, and I'm perplexed at being drawn to a man who's never spoken a word to me. It's obvious I'm drunk. I try to sneak by, but the grounds are empty and the night is silent enough to make my footsteps audible. He turns around, startling me. The clunky antique room key slips from my hand and makes a loud ping against the sidewalk. Daniel swipes at his eyes.

"*Mi dispiache,*" I mutter with a wave. "Umm, *mi camera.*" I point to my room beyond him, sidestepping across the path like an imbecile. "*Buona notte... ciao,*" I squeak out while opening the gate, embarrassed to have caught him having a personal moment.

He steps closer and talks to me for the first time. "I speak English," he says without even a trace of an Italian accent.

Confusion and hurt springs to the surface. "Why didn't you say anything when we met?" And it hits me. "You pretended not to speak English because you didn't want to talk to me." The thought is sobering.

He flashes a sad smile. "It's not that." He brushes his hands through his hair. "It's just my family, and those people in there." He points. "They're so loud. No one appreciates silence anymore, you know?" He turns back toward the water.

Still feeling embarrassed, I say good night and continue down the path to my room.

"Hey, wait. Abby, right?" His voice is closer. "I'm sorry. I should have said something earlier. I can be an asshole sometimes."

"It's okay. Have a good night." I close the gate to my patio, glancing over at the restaurant, which is still aglow. Cleanup clatter and voices drift from the kitchen in the rear. Out front, departing guests begin gathering on the lawn, their voices and laughter carrying.

He puts his hands in his rear jeans pockets. "Listen, you probably won't be getting much sleep until everyone clears out of here. So if you wanna hang out and talk, I'm good with that."

His American accent tempts me. I wouldn't have to strain to listen or apologize for my poor Italian. But I shouldn't.

"I had a great time. I didn't understand a word of anything, but it was fun. But I had so much limoncello, I'll probably have no trouble falling asleep."

As if on cue, Stefano's loud laughter echoes through the yard. He stumbles by the garden, flanked by two women wobbling in extraordinary high heels. I can't tell who's helping whom. With their faces upturned toward the full moon, Stefano and the women take turns howling.

Daniel snorts and turns to me. "Ah. Shit for brains. I think my uncle dropped him on his head when he was a baby. You still sure about that sleep?"

Drunken laughter echoes.

"No, I guess I'm not so sure."

He turns to walk away. "I'll go tell them to knock it off."

"No, wait. It's okay. He's just having a good time. It's been a while since I've seen anyone have that much fun."

"He's a good guy, and he means well, but he's like an aged-out frat boy."

"I can see that."

Stefano howls again.

Daniel looks over my shoulder then points to the sky. "Moon's full tonight, so he's an even bigger pain in the ass."

Oh, what the hell? I open the gate and invite him onto the porch to sit.

The moon is magical, especially over the sea. It casts a soft glow over the stacked houses, accentuating the beauty while hiding the flaws. Moonrise is underappreciated. Sunrises and sunsets get all the glory while the moon does the same amount of work without praise. Beams of moonlight shine down on the beach, dividing the sea in two before fading into the horizon. Mesmerized, I search for words, then he breaks the silence.

"So, why you here?"

I explain the relationship between our grandmothers and tell him how I came to meet his.

His eyes narrow. "Yeah. I heard about that. I'm just surprised you came all this way just to meet your grandmother's old friend."

"I know it seems crazy, but my grandmother and I were close. I lived with her all through high school." The real reason I left is not something he or anyone needs to know. "I hoped coming here might help me. I guess I've been a little lost since she died."

"I'm sorry. I get that."

Without talking, we sit back in our chairs for a time. He's right—silence can be nice. I sneak glances at him and notice for the first time that his eyes are deep blue like the Mediterranean in the midday sun. The silhouette of his face shows sharp angles and a strong jaw covered in week-old beard. I catch him looking at me.

He shifts in his chair to lean closer, clasps his hands together, and rests his chin on them. "So, Abby, what's your real story?"

I don't know whether to be offended that he doesn't believe me or fascinated that he knows there's more. Like always, alcohol loosens my tongue. "My story is long and boring, and trust me, you don't want to hear it."

His face softens, and his eyes brighten with curiosity. He tugs at his ear. "I think I do."

I work on deflecting, a trick I learned from Alex long ago. "Funny, I was thinking the same about you." I smile to lighten the conversation. "Why are *you* here? I mean out here, all alone."

"Ahh, trying to switch tactics, hmm. Clever." He grins as if he's impressed. "I was just about to take off for home."

I assumed he lived here with the family. "Oh? And where *is* home?"

He shrugs and looks down at his shoes, taking his time to answer. "It's complicated. I have a little place just outside Sorrento. But I haven't been there in a while. I've just been staying here. It's just easier sometimes."

"So why are you leaving tonight?"

He hesitates then smiles. "They gave you my room."

I'm so embarrassed and don't know what to say. "Why would they do that?"

Before he answers, I realize it was Stefano's doing. That must have been what he and Luciana were arguing about. "I feel awful."

"Don't. It's fine. I should get back to my place anyway."

"I understand not wanting to leave. I think they'd have to give my room away too."

"It's not really like that. They just want what's best for me, even Dumb-Dumb."

"Does he try to fix you up with every strange girl that visits?"

"Sadly, yeah. He's convinced because I don't get shit-faced and sleep with every girl that comes my way, that I'm missing out."

A slight pang of jealousy surprises me. "I saw those women tonight throwing themselves at you."

He shakes his head. "I'm not interested. I'd rather be alone."

My head is pleasantly woozy, and I want to ask if he's been married, but I lose my nerve. Looking out at the moon's reflection on the sea reminds me of my bayfront home in St. Augustine. I would sit out on the dock and stare up at the moon, hoping my life would get better. The first few years I lived there, I never imagined wanting to be anywhere else. But that changed. "This really is such a beautiful place."

"And we have the best damn limoncello on the planet, don't we?" He smiles.

"Oh my gosh, yes. I tried some today in town, but it was bitter. The stuff here is good, and sweet, without the bite."

"We make it here from our very own fruit. Those trees"—he points—"have been around since I was a kid. Dumb-Dumb and I used to catch hell for climbing them and stealing."

"Stealing? The lemons?"

He looks at me with confusion. "Lemons? Those were cannonballs." He sits up in his chair with an obvious boost of excitement. "We did what every bored farm boy did around here. Filled our sacks full, then dragged them down the mountain to the edge of the grove. We'd stake out the best spot and wait."

"For what?"

"The fishermen. The old men would unload their catches and be down there hosing off their boats and singing. They didn't have a care in the world. Didn't suspect a damn thing. Then out of nowhere—pow, pow. We'd pummel the hell out of their boats." He laughs at the memory; his wide smile reveals perfect white teeth. "My aim sucked, so I mostly missed, but Stefano, oh, he was good." Daniel rubs his hands together. "They'd cuss like hell and threaten to beat our asses. It was great. We'd run like we were on fire and swear to never do it again. Till next time. We were bad boys."

"Little boys are rotten."

He turns his face away in silence, making me wonder what I said wrong.

"They can be," he says.

He's quiet again, and I fill the void with alcohol-fueled words that have no business leaving my lips.

"You have ridiculously pretty eyes," I blurt out. I've been staring at them since he sat down. His lashes are so long, and they curl at the tips. I would kill for those.

He smiles, accepting my compliment. "So do you."

"No, I don't. They're dirt brown and ugly. My brother got the pretty eyes. They were like gemstones all melded together. I got shafted. Life isn't fair sometimes."

"No, life isn't fair at all." He's quiet then asks, "You talk about your brother in the past tense. Did he pass?"

Because the limoncello has loosened my lips, I tell him about Tommy and how when I was in seventh grade, he was killed by a suicide bomber in Kabul just before finishing his tour.

Daniel blinks slowly, sucks in a breath, stares at me for a moment, then looks away. "I'm sorry."

My body tenses as I remember my brother. "Well, the good old US Army delivered him back home to Tennessee as promised. Except in a flag-draped box." I let the memory play. "The last picture I have of Tommy is from Afghanistan. He was up in the mountains, wearing his old army backpack that I still use."

Daniel puts his hand on mine and gives it a squeeze. "I bet he'd like that."

Our conversation flows for hours. My armor, built up after years of choosing my words and preparing to be picked apart, chips away bit by bit. I learn that Daniel enlisted in the military and that he lost many friends. We talk about my waylaid dreams of becoming a doctor and how I dropped out of med school after the first year. He tells me how he left the army as soon as his twenty years were up and his benefits kicked in. The awkwardness and uncertainty evaporates as my attraction for him grows. I'm normally guarded and have never been so comfortable with anyone so quickly, not even girlfriends in college. I tell him about Ruby and how her eyes are the same as Tommy's. Then I ask if he has kids. He hasn't mentioned any.

His shoulders bow, and he looks away. Then he sits up straighter and changes the subject. "Hey, Doc, you said you needed saving earlier. What from?"

Not wanting to take a chance of uncovering something that will change the way I'm feeling, I decide not to ask any more questions for now. Instead, I smile at the nickname he's given me and continue unloading. "My family kinda fell apart when my brother died."

I think about the dark times when my mother refused to come out of her bedroom for days at a time. "My mom became a drunk. She eventually quit, but once she sobered up, she just up and left my dad and me on our farm in Tennessee."

"Ah. So that's where you're from." He rubs his hands on his inner thighs, contemplating. "Maybe she had reasons you couldn't see."

His words sting and make mine come out harsher than necessary. "Are you defending her? I can't think of a single good reason to leave your kid."

"I'm just saying maybe she didn't feel like she had a choice. It's not like you were on your own. She left you with people who loved you and probably thought they'd do better by you than she could."

"Yeah. I know she had her own demons. I guess once she stopped numbing herself with liquor, she couldn't bear what was left over." Being a mother to me wasn't enough for her to stick around. "Maybe you're right, and she truly believed I was better off without her in my life."

Daniel doesn't say anything.

"I was only thirteen. She came into my room one night, said, 'Pack a suitcase for Nonna's.' She dropped me off and never returned. We were poor, but I lived on a farm. I had chickens. I had to leave it all behind and go live in a small house with a postage-stamp-sized yard."

He rubs my arm. "I'm sorry. For all of it." He shifts in his chair and squeezes his eyes closed like he's holding back from saying something he'll regret. "You know none of that was your fault, right?"

"Of course," I lie.

"Is she still alive?"

"Yeah. She's some kind of hippie nomad. She lives off the land out West and travels around to different communes." My father filed a missing persons report on her a couple of weeks after she left. When the cops found her, she told them that she no longer had a family. But I won't say any of that to Daniel. I don't want him to know my dad didn't really want me either. He only ever tried half-heartedly to get me to come back to live with him. I do believe he knew I was better off with my mother's mother. Raising her estranged daughter's estranged daughter gave her purpose and brought life back to her.

Nonna dedicated her golden years to me. She made sure I was well-fed, loved, and heard. My voice mattered, and she taught me to be strong and argue when I knew I was right. I never came home to an empty house. Never went to bed with a growling stomach. Never went to school with pants that were too short or holes in my shoes, like I had before. I'm glad she isn't here to see what's become of my life. Bringing up the past I buried long ago makes me uncomfortable.

"Hey," I say. "Can we talk about something else?"

Daniel presses his palm to his forehead then shakes his head slowly. "So, how long you been married?" He nods toward my left hand.

His question catches me off guard. *Damn. My rings.* They've been there so long, I didn't think to take them off. *How do I tell him I wasn't enough for my husband either? Or that the charming, possessive man I married wishes I'd just offed myself, or that I almost did?* I shouldn't care how I look. Daniel's a stranger. But I cannot stand being on the receiving end of pity eyes. My whole life, with my brother's passing, my mother's leaving, and girlfriends who knew the problems Alex and I had, I've been the pathetic girl. I don't want to be her anymore.

Daniel looks away then shifts like he's about to get up, and I don't want him to go.

"It's a long story, but I'm not married anymore."

He leans forward in his seat, narrows his blue eyes, and studies my face like he senses a lie.

"I mean I'm not divorced yet, but the marriage is over."

"Are you sure?"

"One hundred percent."

"Okay then."

In a surprising move, he leans my way and touches his head to mine, long enough for me to catch the clean woodsy scent of his skin and make me realize just how lonely I am.

He sits back up, stiffens. "I'm sorry. I don't know what came over me."

His touch stirred an unrecognizable feeling in my core. The way his skin felt against mine, the way he smells, the way he blinks slowly when he looks at me. Something is happening inside, and it's scaring the hell out of me. I want to pull him back to me, but I'm afraid, so I pass it off as a joke.

"Hey, what's in that limoncello anyway? Is it like some kind of magical potion?"

"Something like that."

With a smile, he heats up my insides. "You can't blame everything on the limoncello."

"So what do you do with yourself these days? Besides, of course, keeping those liquor bottles straight?" I nod in the direction of the bar.

"That may or may not have been a little nervous energy." He smiles. "I help out here when I'm not traveling."

"Traveling. For work or pleasure?"

"Work," he says without offering more.

"What kind of work?"

"I'm a photographer." He tells me he used to shoot in the army, but now he mostly does freelance.

"You famous?"

"Nah. Nothing like that. I just shoot for a few magazines."

"Seriously? Which ones?"

"A little here and there for *T&L* and *Nat Geo*. And I've done a couple shoots for *Time*."

There's no arrogance to him at all. After spending my life with Alex, who never missed an opportunity to brag about his position at the hospital or a seat on a board, I find the modesty endearing.

He smiles. "It's been an adventure."

Talking about photography and travel loosens him up, and he goes on without prompts, telling me about last year's trips to Tanzania, Cambodia, and Chiang Mai. I soak up every word, every description. I'm in awe of his carefree life, his blue eyes, and his freedom to visit exotic places. Words flow then slow as the sky lightens. He's slouched in his chair at ease, or maybe just exhausted. The slight pink hue on the horizon means dawn is near, and I know the time has come for goodbyes.

I lean forward, preparing to stand. "It's pretty late. We should go to bed."

When his eyes widen, I realize how what I said sounded. He nods, grasps my hand, and doesn't let go. His eyes are on me. His voice is gruff. "Stay. Watch the sunrise with me first."

The warmth of his hand on mine sends a charge through me. His touch nearly undoes me. Being beside him tonight has made me forget. Even though I should say goodnight and get the hell away from him, my eyes hold his gaze.

I desperately want him to kiss me. Whatever this feeling is cannot happen right now. My life is a train wreck. But with his eyes on me, I can't look away.

We hold our gazes long enough for him to read my thoughts. He whispers, "Abby, no."

I should pretend to be confused, but my face burns with humiliation. "Good night, Daniel." I jump to my feet and rush to my room and press my back to the closed door. Without words, I just made a pass at a guy and got rejected. I plop down on the bed and try not to cry.

I figure he's long gone, but then there's a knock. "Abby, open the door, please."

I do. He steps inside and embraces me. Every inch of his body presses into mine, and my embarrassment evaporates.

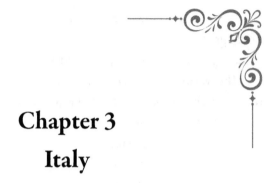

Chapter 3
Italy

Inside my rented room at La Trattoria, Daniel and I cling to one another. With my face pressed against the hard curvature of his chest, I inhale the scents of sweetgrass and sandalwood. Is it soap or maybe pheromones seeping from his pores? It makes little sense, but being in his arms feels safe and familiar.

He loosens his grip, and his voice is husky. "I should go." His eyes say otherwise.

I can't think. "Stay with me."

He takes a step back and tilts my chin upward. "Are you sure?"

I want to tell him just how messed up I've been and that for the first time in a very long while, I feel alive. It's because of him. "Please. I just—"

He hushes me with his finger to my lips and squeezes me against him.

Holding my cheeks in his palms, he stares into my eyes. "I don't know what this is, but I don't think either of us is ready for it." He blows out a breath. "I'll stay if you want me to, but nothing can happen until I know you're ready." He strokes my cheek with the back of his hand, and I will him to kiss me.

"How will you know?"

"Intuition." He rests his lips on top of my head then whispers, "We should try to catch a couple hours of shut-eye before this place gets crazy."

Knowing my normal bedtime attire would be dangerous, I go into the bathroom and slip out of my clothes and into gym shorts and a T-shirt. When I come out, he's already in bed, shirtless, but thankfully, his jeans are still on. His eyes are closed. I turn off the lights and climb into bed beside him, trying not to wake him. Morning light is making its way through the glass doors as I study the dark stubble on his angular jaw for a moment before turning my back to him. Within minutes, he envelops me with his body, wrapping his arms and legs around mine. He's out cold, and I'm wide awake, my body sizzling with desire as I lie beside a man, for the first time in nearly two decades, who is not my husband. With his heat and firmness pressed against me, sleep for me is inconceivable. His breathing is soft and slow, and his breath is humid against my neck. I lie motionless. My mind spirals with unfulfilled hunger.

My breathing syncs with the rhythm of his as my mind calms and drifts away to another place and time, to an island not far from here, where we lie tangled together on a deserted beach beneath the stars, listening to the waves lapping the shore.

I'm not sure how long we slept, but when my eyes open to the blazing sunlight, Daniel is gone. No goodbye. No note. Did he wake with a clear mind and realize being with me was a mistake? Thoughts of waking to a squinting Alex hovering inches from my face fill my head.

"Sweetheart, do you want me to get you an appointment for some Botox and maybe some fillers? You know the longer you leave those lines, the more permanent they'll become."

Was Daniel put off by seeing me in the morning light?

For an eternity, I am still. I lie in the fetal position against the cool cotton sheets that smell of my almost lover. The past twenty-four hours seem unreal. Breathing slowly, I allow the emptiness to ebb and flow through me. I never even got the chance to taste him on my lips. I feel exposed and alive with currents of fire and unspent energy still sizzling within. The intensity of our connection, the way our bodies fit together, the way our breathing synced in unison, burns. Why would he leave me so raw and unfinished?

The thought of leaving here without ever seeing him again sinks my heart into my stomach. And I remember for the first time that Daniel is the grandson of Francesca, my nonna's best friend. *Was it a coincidence that brought me here? Is he the happiness she promised I'd find?*

Another man wanted me, even if only for a moment.

After little sleep, my eyes burn, but it's time to go. I pull back the covers and climb out of bed feeling sad, but very much alive. Our brief encounter lit an ember and shined a light in a place I only ever expected darkness. For that, I am grateful.

I shower, change, then step out onto my balcony as Mama delivers the most delicious breakfast of my life—more baba au rhum, along with fresh grapes and strawberries. I devour every bite, washing it down with back-to-back cappuccinos. I wish I could at least say goodbye to Daniel.

As I'm finishing the last of my cappuccino, Mama walks over and stands beside my table, her hands rubbing at her apron. With uncertainty, she says, "Daniel go back."

Does she mean he will be back or that he's gone—forever? When I ask, she shakes her head, letting me know she doesn't understand, and utters the phrase, "*Non capisco.*"

So I say goodbye to Mama, roll and stuff my belongings into my backpack, and strap it on to leave. Outside of La Trattoria, I sit on the bench and wait for the bus to take me to a place I've yet to discover.

Luciana joins me. "I hope you enjoyed your stay."

My thoughts turn to Daniel, and I fight the urge to ask about him. "I did. Thank you for your hospitality and for allowing me to talk to your nonna." I remember the letters in my pack. "Is there any way you could translate one of the letters between our grandmothers? I know it's a lot to ask, but I could use a mood lift." I smile, hoping she'll agree.

"It is no problem."

I hand her the stack, and she chooses the most recent one.

"Dearest Francesca, I am writing you from Amalfi, where we wait for the ferry to take us to Naples then America. I am sad to leave you and our beautiful country, but I know we must go. Mama says I should spend the day in Ravello, rather than staring at her with my long face. Are you aware a Hollywood movie was recently filmed there? Humphrey Bogart is the leading star. I believe it is called *Beat the Devil*. I cannot wait to see the picture someday. I will continue this letter from above. *Ciao,* for now.

"Ciao again, Francesca. Please, pack a bag and make your way to Ravello. You will go mad with love for this town. The views are spectacular. It is charming and leaves me wondering no longer why American pictures are being made here. Soon everyone will flock to Italy to stroll the paths here. I am having lunch and watching the pignoli gatherers nearby. I will write from America. All my love, Rubina."

I vaguely recall watching the Humphrey Bogart movie with Nonna as a child. I remember the way she smiled through her tears while we sat together on her old plaid sofa, snuggled beneath her mother's wool afghan.

I thank Luciana and board the bus, knowing just where I'll go. On the way to Amalfi, I sit on the right side of the bus, closer to the edge, with an unobstructed view of the sea. Passengers trickle on and off during our windy ride while my mind imagines Nonna roaming around Ravello, about to leave the only place she's ever known.

"*Ultima fermata.*" The driver interrupts my thoughts.

We've arrived at the last stop, Amalfi. I step off the bus to be engulfed by a sea of people. I push through the crowds and make my way up the hill. *Gelaterias* and charmless souvenir shops line the streets.

Desperate to get away from the congestion, I keep walking until I spot a cathedral in the distance. I climb the sixty-two stairs and slip inside the Duomo di Amalfi behind a tour group. The rich, smoky smell of incense fills my nose, invoking a sense of familiarity. I stroll through the thousand-year-old church at my own pace, sneaking a listen from the guide every now and then.

According to the tour guide, Saint Andrew, brother of Saint Peter and patron saint of Amalfi, is buried in a crypt beneath us. I am drawn to the rack of half-burned candles. I light one and drop to my knees to say yet another prayer, this time beneath a thirteenth-century crucifix. I thank God for my life and for bringing me to Italy. I feel strange doing it, but I also thank him for bringing Daniel to me, even if only for a moment. Two churches and two prayers in two days lessens my shame and helps me feel more spiritually connected than I have in years. There's something about these old cathedrals.

Outside, I board a small local bus heading up the mountain to the town of Ravello, the town my grandmother was enamored by. Her last glimpse of Italy. Ravello is as she described, more peaceful and picturesque than Amalfi, but not quite as beautiful as Positano. The weather is mild and perfect, with a slight breeze. I spend the next few hours wandering the narrow stone-walled pedestrian streets, passing few people. My stomach growls, reminding me I haven't eaten since breakfast. At an open-air café with a postcard-worthy view of mountains and tree-filled valleys, I take a seat and watch men climb tall ladders leaning against trees. I ask my waiter what the men are doing.

"Collecting pignoli," he says.

The men, he explains, are performing the tedious task of collecting pine cones for the few small pine nuts inside. This is what my grandmother was talking about in her letter! I had no idea pine nuts were gathered this way.

I sit for a while, sipping Chianti while savoring every bite of my late lunch—smoked provolone and roasted vegetables. I watch as couples pass by, arm in arm. My feelings of enlightenment and gratefulness from this morning evolve into unworthiness. *Didn't I even deserve a goodbye?* I look into the faces of passing strangers. Once, I'm so sure I see Daniel, I abandon my meal and rush to the street, only to be disappointed.

BACK DOWN IN AMALFI, I board the SITA. The route goes directly back to Positano then on to Sorrento, a much larger town with plentiful accommodations. On impulse, I disembark when the bus rolls to its first stop. Maybe my subconscious is at play, pathetically hoping for one last glimpse of Daniel. Both feet are barely on the ground when the bus rolls away, leaving me no time to change my mind. The afternoon heat has dissipated, and the sun is beginning to set as I walk along the beach, stopping in front of an old man at an easel. His swift strokes fill the canvas with bold colors as he recreates the pyramid of buildings in front of him. He captures the magic of this place and mesmerizes me with his talent. I would love to own this masterpiece, but like Daniel, I know it isn't mine to keep.

I look up and long to be at the top of the mountain behind me, back at La Trattoria for one more night, with him. But he made it clear he wanted to get away from me, so I have no choice but to move on.

In the darkness, I board the bus to Sorrento, knowing I'll spend the rest of my life longing for the feelings I had last night. For once, Alex wasn't in my thoughts at all. Despite him, I felt stronger and hopeful for a future on my own. It shouldn't matter if Daniel was only a once-in-a-lifetime encounter. Being beside him made me feel illustrious.

What's Thoreau's quote about not chasing happiness?

I step off the bus, breathing in honeysuckle-scented air as I glance around the deserted station. The bus pulls away, and he's there, seated on a wooden bench beneath the streetlight. Half a dozen empty coffee cups litter the ground by his feet. I exhale all at once, the lack of oxygen leaving me dizzy. I squeeze my eyes closed and open them again, to be sure he's real.

The voice inside whispers a warning. *He'll disappear again.* I hush it and compose myself, resisting the urge to run and jump into his arms.

When our eyes connect, he stands and ambles toward me. He's wearing blue jeans and another gray T-shirt, this time with an American flag emblem on the sleeve.

"Hey, Doc." His voice is sheepish, apologetic.

"Daniel." I project more of a squeak than the confident voice I aim for. "What are you doing here?"

He shrugs and offers a sad smile. "I was in the neighborhood."

"I don't understand. How'd you know I'd be here?"

"This route is the only way out, so I just hoped you didn't catch a ride or take a ferry."

I fold my arms protectively and ask how long he's been waiting.

"Not long," he lies. Ignoring my defensive posture, he wraps his arms around me and squeezes for a moment before pulling away to look into my eyes. "I'm sorry I left this morning." He clears his throat. "It was a dick move. I went out for a quick run and just kept going. I needed to get my head right." He looks at me for understanding then puts his hands on my shoulders. Shaking them gently, he groans. "You said your marriage is over, and I want to believe that.

You're thousands of miles from home, and it's easy to see you're hurting. I just don't want to add to that."

Wanting him to understand how certain I am, I say, "You're right—I'm a little lost, but I'm figuring it out. I'm just going to travel for a couple of weeks with no real plans. This trip has nothing to do with deciding whether or not to stay married. It's over. I've never been more sure of anything." Unsure of how he'll respond, I let him off the hook. "I don't have any sort of expectations, if that's what you're worried about."

He grins and looks at the ground then back at me. "Look, I'm just going to say this. It's been a really long time since I met someone I could talk to. Sleeping next to you last night was the hardest thing I've done in ages." He laughs then touches his fingertips to my cheek and exhales. "I'm happy I found you again before you took off." He pauses, shifting his feet. "I'd love to hang out for however long you're here, if you're cool with that?"

Jumbled feelings swirl through me like a West Texas tornado, and I resist the urge to pull him down to kiss me. I know my life is a mess and that I should be smart. I should wish him well, shake his hand, then walk away. I look up into his eyes, which are bluer than blue, and see my reflection and my smile staring back at me. My gut tells my head to shut it.

"I don't know."

He looks at the ground then back at me with a slight grin. "You're a little stubborn, aren't you?"

To hell with the timing. To hell with Alex. "I don't know if I can be with a man that only wears gray. Do you own any other colored shirts? Anything, pink or purple even?"

He laughs. "There's nothing wrong with gray."

Taking my hand, he guides me down Corso d' Italia, the busy main street leading from Sorrento to Sant'Agnello.

"Where are we going?"

"You'll see."

We walk until we reach an old towering oak, then he leads me between two crumbling buildings and onto a well-lit narrow concrete path. The path turns to dirt and darkness. A big dog growls and snarls as it pounces against a rusted metal fence, the only thing stopping it from attacking us.

I stumble backward, and Daniel reaches for me with a laugh. "He won't hurt you. He just likes to intimidate visitors."

"Well, he does a great job."

The remainder of the dirt path is lined with fragrant lemon trees. We walk up a set of stairs and across the dimly lit street above. Passing through heavy, rusted iron gates, we enter a yard overlooking hundreds of lighted buildings. The house is small, two levels of white stucco with a clay-tiled roof.

"I haven't had company in a long time, so it's not the cleanest." He fumbles for the keys, takes out a long slender brass one with a filigree top, and slides it into the lock. With two loud clicks, the door unlocks.

"I don't care about that," I say. "This is your house?"

"It's been in my family for a long time. It belonged to my mother." He shrugs. "Now I guess it belongs to me." He pushes the solid wooden door open with a creaky groan and presses his hand lightly on the small of my back to guide me inside.

Butterflies flutter in the pit of my stomach as I rub my hands along the rich cherry-wood walls of the foyer and living room. Brass sconces light the way and offer a glimpse of gilt-framed oil paintings and large antique furnishings. The house smells slightly of dust and old money.

Daniel switches on a lamp and drops my backpack in the foyer. He turns and looks at me. "You said you don't have any plans. So *mi casa es tu casa*. Stay as long as you like."

"Are you sure?"

He strokes my cheek with the back of his warm hand. "I'm happy for the company."

"Me too."

He escorts me up the marble stairs with his hand in mine, filling me with anticipation. With each step, I imagine him slipping off his gray shirt and pressing his bare chest to mine. Near the top, he glances my way and sucks in his bottom lip, leaving it wet. I can almost taste his kiss.

Inside the master bedroom, he flips on the bedside lamp. "You can have this room. It gets great morning light and has a sweet view of the sea."

"Where will you sleep?"

"I'll be across the hall if you need me."

I need him, all right, but I steady my expression to hide the disappointment. He steps around me and leans into the doorway. "I know we were up late, so if you want to catch some shut-eye, I can leave you to it."

I don't want to be alone. "I'm honestly not even tired."

On the backyard patio, we sit side by side on cast iron chaises that overlook the sea. Though the view is nothing like Positano, the full moon casts a serene light upon the water. Daniel brought out cushions and a silky cashmere throw for me, perfect for spring evenings. I'm wrapped up, sipping a warm cup of chamomile-and-honey tea and wondering about the woman who once wrapped herself in it. Daniel doesn't seem like the kind of guy to choose cashmere.

It's none of your business. I push the thought aside and slip easily into deep comfortable conversation with him, just as we had the night before.

"Where'd you grow up anyway? Your English is flawless, so it obviously wasn't Italy."

He rolls his eyes. "I don't know, Doc. I think you missed your calling as a detective."

"Very funny."

"Mostly Texas."

"But you don't have an accent."

He smiles, fiddling with his hands. "It slips out every once in a while. I've worked hard to lose it."

I automatically think of my dad and his Texan pride, the thick drawl he was proud of. "Where in Texas?"

"You wouldn't know it."

"Try me."

He smiles again. "North Texas. A little one-horse town."

"There're a million one-horse towns."

"It's called Nowhere."

A shiver jolts through me.

"You okay?"

Not really. A nervous laugh slips out. *Is he joking? But he can't know. How is it possible?* "My dad is from Nowhere too."

He sits up straighter, his eyes still on me. He must be thinking what I'm thinking. "No way."

"Way. Born and raised."

We go on talking about Nowhere. He tells me about being a kid in a town with only two diners, self-proclaimed to be *gour-met* since they put *sal-mon* on the menu. We talk about the old run-down middle-high school both he and my dad attended. I only visited once, but the place left an impression on me. And not in a good way. I tried to see the charm my dad saw, but I was a kid dragged off a farm to a dusty triple-digit town in the dead of summer.

"I still can't believe your dad is from my shitty little hometown."

"Me neither. He used to complain about it in one breath, then in the next, say he'd move back someday."

"Nowhere does that to ya. Makes ya love it and hate it all at once. But you couldn't pay me to live there again."

It doesn't take long before the conversation leads to my marriage. Like a Rocky Mountain avalanche, the long story of my years with Alex tumbles out.

Daniel rubs his eyes. "I'm sorry to say, but he sounds like a sociopath."

Alex may be a lot of things, but I don't think he's anything more than a narcissist. And that's not uncommon among other male medical professionals of his stature. Or maybe it's just our circle of friends. It's been so long since I've had more than a passing conversation with a man who wasn't a physician.

"It's weird," I tell Daniel. "Before I found out about the affair, I never realized how unhappy I'd been all those years." Finding out about Jack put me in a tailspin and made me think everything that had happened was my fault. With the truth about what I almost did on my lips, I pause.

"What is it? You okay?"

I look up to keep the tears from spilling over. "Not too long ago, I was in a pretty dark place."

He leans over and studies my face. "Me too."

I've been afraid to ask for fear of knowing the reason behind the aura of sadness that surrounds him, but I can't help myself. "Were you married?"

He holds my gaze then lowers his eyes, letting his dark lashes rest on his cheekbones for a moment. The serious expression that rarely changes darkens.

"I was. Once." He doesn't elaborate, and the emptiness behind his eyes keeps me from pressing.

I want to see his smile again. The connection between us may simply be two lonely souls, but it feels like something more. I look at his sultry mouth and resist the temptation to ask him to go to bed with me again.

My cheeks grow hot. "I'm sorry. I've never talked this much in my life."

"Don't be. I like talking to you. But you know, this time you can't blame the limoncello."

In the doorway to the master bedroom, he reaches for me at last and pulls me to his chest. I pull back to look up at him, hoping he'll finally kiss me. Instead, he runs his fingers through my hair and sighs. "I don't trust myself to come in there with you."

"Why?"

"I think you and I both know what'll happen if I do."

I know he's right, but it doesn't stop me from wanting him.

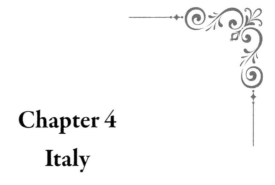

Chapter 4
Italy

Iwake to the smell of strong coffee. I haven't slept this well since before Ruby was born. According to the clock, it's almost eleven. As I lazily pull back the covers, Daniel comes in, wearing athletic shorts and no shirt.

"No. No. Back in that bed." He sets a tray of croissants, two tiny espresso cups, and a cappuccino on the bed. "Your choice." He raises his brow. "Or you could drink them both."

"Look at you. Breakfast and coffee in bed. I could get used to this." I stretch my arms and reach for the tray.

With the late-morning sun casting its light upon him, Daniel seems different, lighter, younger, and even more beautiful. The crease between his brows is gone, and through his thick lashes, his eyes appear even bluer than before, with tiny flecks of gold I didn't notice before.

"What are you thinking?" he asks with a smile. "You have a mischievous grin, and your eyes are barely open."

"Nothing really." In the light of day, I've become shy. "I'm happy to be here with you."

He sits down on the edge of the bed and rubs his palm across my cheek. "I'm happy to have you. You're so pretty, especially in this light, without makeup. I'd love to grab my camera and take a few shots of you."

My face burns with embarrassment. "No way." I cover my eyes with a pillow, imagining the smattering of freckles across my cheeks and nose.

He pulls the pillow away. "I won't. I promise. Try this." He touches a still-warm chocolate croissant to my lips.

I take an enthusiastic bite. "Mmm. Oh my gosh, that tastes like heaven."

He laughs. "It does, doesn't it? Hey, I'm gonna head out and run some errands. You okay here for a bit?"

"I have coffee and pastry. Absolutely. See you when you get back."

"I have some stuff planned for us, if you're okay with that?"

"I'm open to anything."

"Be ready in about an hour." He smiles at me like an adolescent schoolboy.

Once he's out the door, I dash around madly to make myself presentable. I wish I had nice clothes with me. I opt for a sundress and sandals and toss a bikini into my small tote bag in case a beach is involved. Looking for a ponytail holder, I unzip one of the small compartments in my pack and spot my birth control pills, which I keep forgetting to take. At home, I was religious about it, but since being away, I keep forgetting. I pop two in my mouth, look in the mirror, and pull my auburn hair back into a high ponytail. I twist the rings from the ring finger of my left hand and hold them to the light. European cut, the diamond is almost three carats. It's been passed down for four generations, beginning with Alex's great-great-grandmother and ending with me. They're tainted now. I could pass them down to Ruby, but I worry they're cursed. My mind drifts to the day Alex proposed.

No, I won't go there. No negative thoughts today. I tuck the rings away in my toiletry bag, knowing there's a chance I might need to sell them to survive if our divorce doesn't go as planned.

Daniel appears in the doorway, wearing black shorts, hiking sandals, and another gray T-shirt. "Hey, Doc. You ready to go?"

I size him up, debating whether or not to tease him about his drab-colored clothes. "I am."

"Well, then, let's go."

"Where we going anyway?"

"It's a surprise."

I try to hide my nervousness.

"If it's okay with you, I was thinking we'd go out on the boat with a few of my old friends? If you'd rather not, it's no problem. We can just hang out here."

If I stay in the house with him all day, I know what will happen, and that's not at all a bad thing. But he told me it's been a while since he's felt like socializing, and I can tell he wants to go.

"Sure, I'd love to go out on the boat." Despite feeling anxious, I force a smile. I worry about so many things—meeting his friends, my awful Italian, and wearing a bathing suit in the bright sunlight. At least I thought to pack one.

We drive to the dock at the base of the mountain, where the ferries and cruise ships unload passengers.

"I didn't know what you liked, so I picked up one of everything from the market." He displays his bounty of snacks. "Don't worry. There'll be little scavengers on the boat to eat whatever we don't."

As we walk toward the dock, I peek through the bags, and I'm intrigued by the variety of Italian crackers and cookies. Hanging out with people I've never met, ones I can't communicate with, makes me uneasy. I barely know Daniel, and I could be his flavor of the week. What if picking up lonely tourist girls and showing them off to his buddies the next day is routine for him? I don't really believe that, but I could be wrong.

I suddenly feel like a fool and want to leave. He'll probably disappear from my life again in the next couple of days anyway. None of this should be happening right now. Anxiety begins in the pit of my stomach and spreads upward through my chest and throat. I should turn around to walk the other way, but before I have a chance, he stops and turns to me.

His eyes lock on mine with a look of concern. "You okay?"

"Yep, great."

"Are you sure? You don't look okay."

"I'm fine, really."

"When a woman says she's fine, she's usually lying."

I am. "I'm just a little nervous."

"Don't be. They're all going to love you. I promise."

He takes my clammy hand in his, and we make our way to a boat where two couples and two little girls are waiting. For some reason, I thought it was only going to be guy friends and their kids, but now there are women to judge me as well. Whoever sees my stomach will know I'm a mother. I can't take off my dress. A panic attack looms.

Breathe through it. You've got this. Five, four, three, two, one...

In front of me, I see five things—a boat, a pier, the sea, a tree, and a house in the distance. *Four.* Daniel's hand is touching mine, flip-flops are on my feet, my purse on my shoulder. Making a fist, I squeeze my fingernails to my palm. *Good, I feel that. Three.* I hear the rumbling of the boat's engine, sea spray crashes against the rocks, and gulls screech above. *Two.* The sea air smells of decaying fish and salt. I press my face into Daniel's sleeve, inhaling deeply. He smells of fabric softener and clean man. *One.* Mint from leftover toothpaste still flavors my tongue. In the minute the exercise took, I start to feel better. I step aboard the boat, anxiety attack averted.

Daniel introduces me to everyone, and to my relief, they all speak decent English. His friends work in the hospitality industry, so they have to be multilingual. They are postcard-perfect Italian families, each with a daughter. Pietro and Giulia are in their midtwenties, both with perfect trim, sun-kissed bodies. Their daughter, Valentina, recently turned five. Massimo and Sabina are in their late thirties, closer to my age. Sabina is expecting their second child, a boy, she tells me, to "complete their *famiglia*." Their daughter, Chiara, is eight and cannot wait to be a big sister. They'd been trying to conceive again since Valentina was a baby. "Lots and lots of practice," Sabina jokes. Everyone laughs. The guys cheer and slap Massimo on the back.

We spend the morning and part of the afternoon cruising along the coast before Daniel gets the idea to visit an island called Ischia. In rapid Italian, he and his friends debate whether to take me to Capri or Ischia. Daniel wins, and we breeze past Capri, a tourist island for the rich and famous and those pretending to be, he says.

"Ischia is the real deal, where Italians go to relax." He tells me how the mountainous island is actually an inactive volcano full of hot healing springs and thermal pools. His family and friends used to spend weekends there at the beach, digging holes and burying foil-wrapped meals of potatoes and chicken to cook in the hot sand.

The playful banter and laughter between these couples has me longing for what I never had during my marriage. Time spent with other couples would turn tense by the end of the night, and if I discussed anything without his involvement, Alex would feel left out and accuse me of flirting. I learned to be sure to include him and to not make eye contact with men. He still found fault, though.

It wasn't always like that, though. I had pleasant memories of the early years, when he still looked at me, before the light in his eyes went out. Living in the greatest place I could imagine, popping in and out of boutiques along the cobblestone streets of St. Augustine. Pushing Ruby in her stroller along the bayfront, where we would sit and watch the dolphins play. Riding our bikes to our favorite farm-to-table restaurants for lunch. Listening to live music along Saint George Street. But those days were short-lived and are long gone.

Being here with Daniel and his friends is different. It's easy and almost makes me forget I don't belong. He and I are just another couple in the group. I was being unreasonable earlier, worrying about women he's been with. It shouldn't matter if there have been a million before me and if they have all been out with his friends. I have no claim to him. I'm going to enjoy this time and pretend to be whole.

Giulia and Sabina serve us lunch on the boat. Trays of antipasti—prosciutto, salami, mortadella, and other cured meats I don't eat or recognize—are spread out with professional precision. The hard cheeses, I eat with gusto. Giant wedges of parmigiano and pecorino with a variety of olives, preserved peppers, artichokes, cipolline onions, and sun-dried tomatoes make the platter look like something out of *Bon Appetit* magazine.

"Abby, we like you," Giulia whispers to me. "He seems happy."

"But don't hurt him," Sabina adds. "He's been through hell, okay."

"We're just friends right now," I say, knowing that's not entirely true.

The women give each other a look. Giulia purses her lips. "Maybe that is what you tell yourself, but no." She leans closer. "We see the way he looks at you." They giggle.

After our food settles, we put on our snorkeling gear. Trying to breathe through my mouth makes me anxious and forgetful. The goggles fog instantly. Daniel shows me how to spit-clean them and how to float so my snorkel won't fill with water. It takes some time to get the technique, but it is so worth the effort. Yellow coral, red sea fans, and clusters of anemones line the shallow bottom. The experience is magical, like being inside an aquarium. An octopus slithers by. I cannot believe I live in Florida and have never snorkeled. Daniel points out a decent-sized barracuda. Its silvery skin shimmers in the sunlight. That's enough for me.

After we leave the water, he teases me relentlessly for both being afraid of a fish and for never having snorkeled. I don't mind.

The guys pull up the anchor and move the boat closer to the beach so the girls can play. Daniel and I leave them to visit the medieval Aragonese Castle, which is old news to his friends. We wade through the shallow water and across the causeway to the pre-seventeenth-century castle. The dark tunnel is creepy. It's cold and smells of wet earth. When I learn of its very own torture museum complete with head crushing and testicle-squashing trestles, I'm done. I pull Daniel out of there and back onto the grounds into the sunshine, all the while watching his amusement at my shock. Next, we make our way through the chapels. The first is consecrated to Saint John Joseph of the Cross[1], the patron saint of the island. In the light and the churches, with people nearby, I am much more at ease.

"Hey, I have an idea," Daniel says playfully. "Let's stay the night here."

The hairs on the back of my neck rise. "Inside this castle? You're kidding, right?"

"Why not? I've never done it. It'll be an adventure."

"I was almost eaten by a barracuda, so I think I've had my fill of adventure for the day. No way am I staying in this creepy castle."

He laughs, linking his arm through mine. "You're a stubborn one, Doc. What's the matter? You don't think I'm strong enough to protect you?"

"From ghosts and evil spirits? Umm, no."

"All right, we'll go someplace else if you want to, but let's stay on the island. We can catch a ride back tomorrow. You good with that?"

I give him the side eye. "Find us a place with no evil spirits?"

"Deal."

"You promise?"

He traces a cross over his chest.

---

1.   http://en.wikipedia.org/wiki/Saint_John_Joseph_of_the_Cross

Back across the old stone bridge, we gather our belongings from the boat and bid his friends *arrivederci*, air-kissing and thanking them. Then we make our way down a cobblestone street, much like St. Augustine's, and walk until we come to a small punch-colored hotel by the sea.

"Daniel, ahhh, Daniel." A tall, tanned Italian version of Salma Hayek with waves of hair cascading down her back steps from behind a desk. She embraces him long enough to make me uncomfortable, and she's dressed to kill with heels higher than I could manage. She speaks in Italian, the tones varying by octaves. I can't understand a single word. Daniel nods and smiles, letting her go on for a full minute or two before looking at me with raised eyebrows and a smile. I slink back, imagining how I must look after a day on the boat in my wrinkled sundress.

He pulls me closer and interrupts his boisterous friend to introduce me.

"Emanuela, meet Abby, my, umm, friend." He looks at me with uncertainty, and though it shouldn't, the word *friend* stings a little. "Abby's visiting from America. Abby, this is my friend, Emanuela."

Friend? Is she the same kind of *friend* as me? Does she spend the night at his house as well? I smile, pretending not to be jealous, and reach out my hand. Emanuela skips the handshake, grabs my shoulders, and air-kisses my cheeks. She seems genuinely excited to make my acquaintance.

"Very, very nice to meet you, Abby," she says warmly, taking my hand in hers.

Daniel says, "Emanuela is giving us her best room tonight."

Room? As in singular? "Thank you."

"It is my pleasure." Once again, she grabs Daniel and starts rambling in Italian.

"English, please," Daniel says, "for Abby. She's not yet fluent in Italian. Soon, she will be, though." He winks at me.

"*Mi dispiache*—ahh, I mean I am sorry, Abby." Emanuela smiles at me and slaps a key at Daniel's muscled chest, sparking another pang of jealousy in me.

Plush, gilded antique furniture adorns the room, and in the center is a single king-sized bed. I bite my lip, contemplating what this means for us.

"There's a pull-out right there for me," Daniel says, stepping closer. "If you'd rather I get a separate room, I will."

I protest. I'd rather he sleep next to me, but I'll keep that to myself for now.

Daniel pulls back the heavy drapes and opens the double balcony doors to reveal a sky in hues of pink and purple. "Look at this light. It's the golden hour. It doesn't get more perfect than this." We sit together on the balcony and watch as the sun sinks into the inky sea.

Salty air blends with the scents of him and relaxes me. Throughout the day, each touch, even accidental, sent my mind spiraling to deliciously dark places, but now that we're back in the room, I'm unusually calm. The attraction to Daniel is more than me wanting to fill an empty space. I'm reveling in emotions, confusing want with need. I've been sad or numb for so long, my thoughts are jumbled. Tears threaten to spill from my eyes, but for different reasons this time. Contentment worries me. It never lasts. The day has been soul refreshing and too good to be true. Even still, I don't want it to end. I've lived life with so little fun and adventure.

Daniel holds out his hand, and I grab it, knowing his scent will linger on me long after he lets go. "Whatcha thinking?"

"I had a really nice time today. Your friends are amazing."

"They are, aren't they? I knew you'd like them. And they loved you."

"Really?"

"Really. They're so happy to see me with someone."

"You mean you don't take all the girls you meet out with your friends?" I regret the words instantly.

He forces a smile and shakes his head. "You hungry?"

Despite eating pounds of almonds, biscotti, crackers, and cheeses today, I am. "I'm so hungry, I could eat your arm."

"*Andiamo a mangiare.*"

"Let's go eat?" I say with question.

"*Brava. Brava.*"

Outside the hotel, he takes my hand and leads me to a small restaurant a few blocks away. The owner, an older man, greets him with a smile and an embrace. Before he can introduce us, Salvatore is called into the kitchen.

"You know people everywhere, don't you?"

"Not everywhere." He winks.

When I see the rest of the restaurant's patrons, I realize how underdressed I am. Daniel insists I look beautiful, but I know my outfit screams "American tourist." We're seated at a table by a window overlooking the water, though it's too dark to see outside. The lamp hanging above our table casts a warm glow on Daniel's face and lights his eyes in a way I haven't seen. Light blue gives way to midnight with gold flecks like stars. Windows to the soul. I've seen sorrow, seriousness, and so much kindness today. For brief moments, I've seen lust. Now, though, they're harder to read.

He pours us a glass of house Chianti already on the table and raises his glass to me. "Here's to more days like today with beautiful weather and fine friends." He clinks his glass to mine. "*Salute.*"

"*Salute,*" I repeat.

We devour the special—house-made fettuccini with lobster tail drizzled in a lemon cream sauce, followed by tiramisu and, of course, limoncello shots.

"Not bad, huh?" He raises his shot glass and takes a sip.

"No. Actually, this one is very good." I take another sip. "Wow, I don't want to hurt your feelings, but it's just as good as your family's."

He clutches his hand to his chest, flashing me a wounded look.

"Sorry, I'm just being honest."

He smiles. "I'm messing with you. It is ours. We make it for them."

"Trying to make me feel bad?" I ask.

"You're a straight shooter, aren't you?"

I'm not really. Not anymore. I was before I met Alex. I used to be too loud and excitable, especially if alcohol was involved. I would throw my opinion into conversations just to get playful debates going. I enjoyed the banter and stimulation. But I had no filter and often made a fool of myself. Being married to Alex definitely refined and toned me down. Over the years, I lost the ability to participate in meaningful conversations. I don't know if I got dumber or he got smarter and outgrew me intellectually, but whenever we debated anything medical related, I ended up being wrong. Discussions with friends about any type of political or world events usually ended in arguments later. I either embarrassed him or ended up letting his colleagues flirt with me. It was easier just to let Alex lead conversations and keep my opinions to myself.

Away from him, I don't want to do that anymore. Instead, I'll keep the vow I made to myself and speak the truth. "Yep. I just say whatever's on my mind."

"I love it." He raises his hand, and our waiter comes and refills our limoncello shots.

Daniel raises his glass to meet mine. "*L'onestà è la migliore politica*. To the truth. *Salute*."

"*Salute*."

We down our shots, then he looks at my left hand, takes it in his, and smiles. "You took your rings off."

"I should have done it a long time ago."

He gives me the look again that I can't read, then he presses my hand to his lips and kisses the spot where my rings rested. A shock jolts through me. He closes his eyes, smiles a weak smile, and gazes at me, making my heart stutter. Removing the napkin from his lap, he signals for a check. "Ready to go back, or you want to walk around a bit?"

Anticipation fills me with the memory of his body pressed to mine that first night. I imagine his fingers against my bare skin. "I think I'd rather have you to myself for tonight."

He smiles but doesn't respond. As we stand, my knees wobble. *Was I too forward? Is he going to reject me again?*

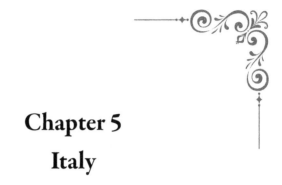

Chapter 5

Italy

On the walk back, he's quiet. As we round the bend to the hotel, he steps across the street to stand closer to the water. "I used to come here a lot. I stopped appreciating it." He looks at me with eyes full of memories. "Like a lot of other things."

Boats and houses light the coast. In the distance, the sounds of restaurant patrons echo along the water. He bites his lip then lifts my chin to study me.

"Are you gonna kiss me or what?" I ask.

He wets his bottom lip then leans down, putting the back of my head in his hands to pull me closer. His kiss is gentle at first, tasting of Chianti and limoncello. I try not to faint. He pulls back for a moment, seeks approval, then continues. His tongue sweeps mine. Our teeth bump as we find our groove. My hands are around his neck, holding him in place.

Please don't stop. Ever. I want to drag him to our room and tear the shirt off his body. I run my hands across his muscled chest and imagine unbuttoning his jeans right there in the street for all the world to see. My insides liquefy.

He breaks the kiss and takes a step back, rubbing his fingers across his wet lips. His eyes reveal a new look I haven't seen. Desperation. I know he feels it as much as I do.

"Ready to go back to the room?"

My knees shake. I nod.

Inside the hotel room, Daniel pulls me toward the bed, and I practically knock him over. I have never wanted someone this badly. He lifts me on top of him, and I match my body to his, settling in all the right places. My legs straddle him, and the thin dress I'm wearing rides high on my thighs as I will his hands to move lower. He obeys. A deep groan slips out as he arches up and presses against me, blurring my thoughts and stealing my breath until I nearly lose consciousness. Without warning, Daniel stiffens and stills. Before I can open my mouth to speak, he slips out from under me and off the bed.

He rakes his hands across his face and through his hair then blows out a breath. "I'm sorry, Abby. I can't."

What just happened? He was all in. "Did I do something wrong?"

He sits down on the edge of the bed. "It's not you. I swear."

"Then what is it? I don't understand."

He leans in and brushes my cheek with his palms. "I don't know. I'm just not sure you're ready."

I want to shake him and scream about how ready I am. The self-conscious part of me worries I did something that made him change his mind. The other part of me, the one that's convinced she'll die of unfulfilled hunger, wants to pull him back against my skin and show him what he's missing. But I am a coward. I do nothing.

"Let's get some sleep." He kisses me on the forehead then makes his way to the pull-out, twenty feet away, while I close my eyes and lie heavy with a twisted knot of longing.

IN THE MORNING, WITH bleary eyes after little sleep, we catch a ferry back to Sorrento and make our way to Daniel's house. He's looking at me and touching me with adoration, but I need more. It's been an eternity since I've felt desirable and even longer since I've wanted anyone this way. Why can't I bring myself to ask him why he stopped?

Once we step into the foyer, he pulls me to him. "Hey, Doc, why don't you go upstairs and get some rest while I run to the restaurant. They need help with inventory."

Too tired to protest, I agree.

"I'll be back in a couple of hours." He kisses the top of my head then is gone.

In the bedroom, I slip beneath the cool crisp sheets and drift off. When I wake, Daniel is still gone.

I clutch the cold sculpted wrought-iron railing and walk down the marble stairs into the foyer. Sun beams through the windows, casting light on the gilded living room furniture covered in burgundy and cream fabrics. The selection and arrangement of furniture looks as if a high-end decorator chose it. Oil paintings in thick gold frames hanging throughout remind me of a set from an old mafia movie. The kitchen is bright and inviting with countertops and flooring of typical Italian Carrera marble. The white cabinets are the only modern thing in the whole house.

A weathered pine farm table, similar to the one Nonna had, sitting in the center takes me back. I have so many memories of sitting at the table with her, laughing and looking through college brochures, reading off recipes to her once her eyesight faded. That kitchen was always filled with the scent of her baking and cooking—amaretti and pignoli cookies, lasagna with fresh-made noodles, and garlicky *fagioli* soups.

She always quadrupled the amount of garlic in a recipe. "To make it *delizioso* and to keepa you healthy," she would say in her heavily accented English, before kissing her closed hand then opening it slowly like a flower greeting the sun. I always wondered if the garlic was more to keep the boys away from me.

My grandfather, her husband, had died before I was born. I knew having me there was good for her and worried what would become of her once I left for college.

Running my fingers over Daniel's table, I trace its ancient cracks as I study the tidy kitchen. Despite the beauty of this old house, a sadness lingers here. None of it suits Daniel or any other person in our age group. It's preserved as if someone's ancestors died here and no one ever bothered to change anything.

If only these walls could talk.

Wandering back through the living room, I stop to study a vibrant oil rendering of Sorrento. I cannot imagine being gifted enough to paint a scene this realistic. A young girl wears a flowing white gauze dress and struggles to carry a wicker basket of lemons down a path similar to the one we walked last night. The buildings aren't crumbling, though. They're bright white, beautiful with colorful flower boxes and yards filled with lemon and olive trees. The gardens are bursting with bright-red tomatoes, eggplants, and green peppers. At the bottom of the hill, the sea continues forever. To the right is Mount Vesuvius, the one that destroyed the city of Pompeii and killed thousands of residents. How could something so beautiful, so innocuous looking become such a destructive force?

The bodies of residents were preserved, frozen in the position they had died, some on their knees, praying fruitlessly. Did they have faith in God, or were they merely desperate at the end of their rope, knowing they were about to die? I imagine their lives at the moments leading up to the eruption, a destructive force looming on the horizon. There have been times in my life when I've felt that exact way—like the end was coming. I never even bothered to pray, though.

My former therapist, Alex's colleague, assured me I was going through a melodramatic phase. He told me to be more grateful for the wonderful life I had. I believed him. After finding out about the affair, I wonder if his *truths* weren't meant to keep me with a man I should have left years earlier.

I take a seat on the cream settee to wait for Daniel. But boredom and curiosity strike. A grand wooden desk with lion's paws and brass keyholes beckons. I try to brush the temptation away but fail. I open the middle drawer for a quick peek and find envelopes with the name Daniel Quinn. I whisper his name aloud, relishing the sound as it rolls off my tongue.

A gleaming brass key shimmers in the sunlight. I love old keys. The shapes, their etchings, the weight in my hands. The secrets and untold stories they keep protected. My grandmother used to collect them. I turn the key in my hand, knowing it will fit the locked side drawers. Before I come to my senses, I slide it into one tiny lock and feel a tiny thrill as it clicks and turns without hesitation.

Inside the first drawer, I find matchbox cars, a handful of plastic army men, and a navy-blue Gameboy. *Why are these toys locked away in here?* My mind races. My hands rummage deeper, coming upon a silver picture frame. The smiling face of a young boy maybe five or six years old looks up at me. His wide eyes are bright and blue with flecks of gold. Like Daniel's. My stomach lurches.

Thoughts of Alex's secret son flood my brain and paralyze me. Rattling keys and footsteps approach the front door. My heart pounds as I toss the key back where I found it and slam the drawer closed. Daniel opens the front door, and from across the room, his eyes lock on mine.

In front of Daniel's living room desk, my feet are stone. I don't know what to say or do, so I'm silent and still. With an unreadable expression, he places the paper grocery bag he's carrying on the coffee table, steps closer, and embraces me. I bury my face in his neck, knowing if I look up, my eyes will give me away. Embarrassment burns my cheeks, confusion my brain. I have no idea what that little boy means or how to react. If he has a son, why would he hide it?

There's no sign of children, and he's made no mention of a son these past few days. Surely he would have told me if he was a father. With my sympathetic nervous system in overdrive, I want to flee, but I made a promise to myself to speak my mind.

Daniel kisses the top of my head and pulls back to look at me. "You okay?"

He knows.

"I'm fine," I lie, stretching my arms and escaping to the kitchen. I take a deep breath to steady my voice and speak as casually as possible. "Just woke up from the longest nap ever." There's no way I can ask about the boy. Not yet.

Daniel follows me, sets the bag on the kitchen table, then removes groceries.

"I brought us some dinner. Figured you might be okay with staying in for a quiet night."

"Sounds great." The truth is I don't know how I'm going to pretend everything is normal. I know he knows.

Together, we prepare dinner—a flaky whitefish he bought from the docks, organic homegrown asparagus, and tomatoes from the La Trattoria gardens. We broil the vegetables with a little garlic and olive oil and sauté the fish in lemon, butter, and capers. Everything is fresh and delicious. Throughout dinner, Daniel is cordial and polite. My guilt hangs heavily between us. I can't take another second.

"Listen, I need to ask you..."

He puts his hand up, still chewing his food. His eyes are wide and solemn.

"Whatever it is, don't. Not yet. Please." He shakes his head. "These past few days have been... I just don't want them to end. If that means putting off reality a little longer, I'm good with that. Please."

I know I should grab him by the arms and make him tell me about the boy, but the word slips out before I can protest. "Okay." I don't understand, but maybe there's a logical explanation. The son of an old girlfriend, perhaps.

Daniel squeezes my hand and forces a smile. "Listen, a photography assignment just opened up in Paris. I haven't accepted it yet, but if you want, we could hop over for a few days and hang out."

"Yes," I say without hesitation. I've always wanted to see the most romantic city in the world, and I know once I go back home to Florida, I won't have an opportunity to travel for a very long time. Life without Alex's financial support will be tough. All those years of volunteering should have been spent preparing for the possibility that I would need to support myself. I pray he'll give me enough money in our divorce settlement to buy a small place of my own. I'm a med school dropout living in a tourist town with limited job opportunities. I'm going to be broke. But I'm not going to dwell. Instead, I'll forget my problems and go to Paris, where I can sit at roadside cafés, sipping cappuccinos and scarfing down flaky croissants. I would also like to escape this old house of secrets.

"There's a flight out in the morning."

"Then let's go."

Journal Entry
April 15th, 2008

Dear Me,

Something strange happened tonight after our monthly dinner with Alex's parents at Collage. Excellent food, painful company, as usual. On our walk home, we took the Bayfront instead of the usual shortcut down Saint George Street, and as we got closer to O.C. Whites, I saw Allyson and Sophia sitting under the jasmine canopy, sharing drinks and laughs. I crossed over to say hi, with Alex right behind me. They were deep in conversation and didn't see me coming.

I heard Allyson say, "She's obviously a smart woman. She got into medical school. How can she be so stupid?"

Sophia laughed and said, "Well, she did drop out."

"Not because she couldn't handle it. He made her quit."

"I don't know. Maybe she just doesn't want to know. I don't know if I would."

I interrupted and startled the hell out of them. Allyson jumped up, with a deer-in-the-headlights look, and I knew they'd been talking about me. She hugged me and started chattering nonsense like she does when she gets nervous. Sophia just sat there in awkward silence, fiddling with her hands, not looking at me. It felt like a sucker-punch in the face, but I held back my tears and left with Alex.

On the walk home, he reminded me that they've never been more than friends of convenience because he's friends with their husbands. I didn't believe it before, but he's right. I've been so stupid.

The last couple of times I've invited Allyson for coffee, she's made excuses. Too busy with fundraisers, doctors' appointments, kids—you name it. Last Thursday, while Alex was working late, I asked Sophia to come by for a glass of wine (an offer she never refuses), and she made up something about wanting to spend time with the kids. Her kids! The nonstop fighting kids she can't wait to get the hell away from.

These women have been my so-called friends for over a decade. I know their secrets, and they know mine. I've always stepped up and stepped in when they needed me. All along, I've been the outsider and never knew it. Our arguments have always been about Alex. They can't understand having a husband who loves them the way he loves me. He says they're just jealous because we share everything. Once, Allyson didn't speak to me for a week after finding out her texts and emails were copied to Alex's iPad. Alex and I both tried to fix the problem, but it kept recurring, so we gave up. I should have told her, but I didn't want to hear Sophia's digs again about Stockholm syndrome, which is ridiculous. Not wanting to go barhopping or having a separate bank account is normal. Alex earns the money, so there's no reason for separate accounts, and I'd rather have them over for wine than go out any day. It has nothing to do with Alex not letting me. He goes out of his way for us to get together with a standing order to deliver wine and apps on the third Thursday of the month. They used to appreciate that about him, and I'm sure he'd let me go out if I wanted to, which I don't.

I'm lucky to have such a great guy. How many husbands let their wives stay home and just volunteer? It definitely helps fill the void for not practicing medicine. Maybe I shouldn't have given up trying to convince him to let me go back to med school, but I hate upsetting him. Maybe once Ruby is gone, I'll try again, but for now, the looks on kids' faces when I've taught them to tie their shoes or draw a perfect live oak makes my heart swell. And the gratitude of the Meals on Wheels customers when I deliver their food and sit down to chat with them is humbling. Most days, I'm their only visitor, so I make sure to spend time talking with them. Talking to the women from the Betty Griffin domestic abuse program makes me feel like what I have to say matters. I know what it feels like to be invisible, because sometimes Alex spends so much time at the hospital, he doesn't really have time for me. I don't know what it feels like to be abused, but we connect in so many ways, like kindred spirits, and I truly believe I'm making a difference in their lives. I just wish I could do more. When Ruby's not at b-ball practice or art class, she joins me. Giving back to our community has always been a priority for me, and I'm so happy she enjoys helping others. I wish Alex had made more of an effort, but he helps in his own way by allowing me to donate my time. Most men would insist a stay-at-home wife spend every second on our home and family. I really am the luckiest girl in the world.

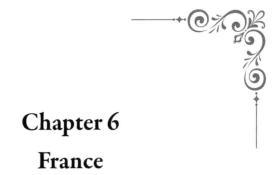

Chapter 6
France

In the morning, I find myself sitting beside Daniel with a belly full of butterflies on a last-minute Air France flight bound for Paris. By afternoon, we step out of the airport and into a taxi. The spring skies are bright blue. Daniel's friend Peter is traveling, so he's offered us use of his tiny Parisian apartment. It's tucked away in a quiet alley beside the magnificent Notre Dame Cathedral.

I wait outside in the warm breeze while Daniel retrieves the key from a wine shop across the street. I want to stay out here on the streets and soak in the sights and sounds forever. A saxophonist along with other street musicians play in the distance. The delicious sounds fill my ears. Impeccably dressed couples pass by, hand in hand. Across the street on a wall beside the river, a young couple makes out, oblivious to the world around them. I want days filled with love like that. I never dreamed I would see Paris. Daniel reappears, bringing me back down to earth. He takes my hand and places it to his lips without a word, sending shivers down my spine.

The one-room apartment is on the fourth floor, with twenty-foot ceilings, a king-sized bed in the center, and a tiny kitchenette tucked into a closet-sized corner. Weathered beams line the ceiling, and a life-sized portrait of a not-so-beautiful woman, with eyes that seem to follow us, hangs beside the bed. Across the room, there's a fireplace large enough to stand in. Parisians must be masters of tight spaces.

In the afternoon, piano melodies fill the building. We prop open the door and dance together in the cozy space. I can tell by the tender way he touches me and the way his gaze lingers that tonight is going to be the night we're together.

In the tiny kitchen, we create a small and simple meal with fresh ingredients from the market. Daniel tries to nudge me out so he can do the cooking.

"Stop being so stubborn, woman. Go relax."

"Fine," I tell him. I pour the wine, a nice burgundy he brought back from the shop. I'm so used to doing everything at home, it's hard to let someone else take over, especially when it comes to cooking.

Daniel really does have culinary skills, and it's sweet watching him beam with pride each time I take a bite and moan.

As the evening winds down, the butterflies in my stomach come alive. Other than in the tiny kitchen, the bed is the only place to sit. I can't tell if it's nervousness or uncertainty, but Daniel is spending an exorbitant amount of time tidying up. It's like he's going for the world's record for cleanest dishes.

I move behind him, putting my arms around his waist. "Come to bed."

He turns off the faucet and faces me. Then he dries his hand on a dishtowel and wraps me in his arms. "Are you sure *you're* ready?"

I think of the last two times we came so close, and he hit the brakes. "Are you?"

He half smiles, leans down, and kisses me slowly at first, then with urgency. His eyes move slowly from my neck to my breasts, then farther down as he undresses me slowly and deliberately. "I am. Very much so."

I slide out of my panties and let them drop to the floor as I melt into him. It hasn't yet been a full week, but it feels like I've waited for an eternity. He pulls his shirt over his head, and even though I've seen him shirtless before, my breath catches. I run my hands along his chest and abs made of granite. He presses his lips to my breasts then my stomach, and back up to my neck and mouth again. He bites my bottom lip and sucks it into his mouth, making me lose my mind. I reach for the zipper of his jeans, but he takes both of my wrists in his hand and gently tugs me to the bathroom. His jeans and black boxer briefs drop to the floor, and I couldn't look away if there was a gun to my temple.

Inside the shower, I turn away, feeling self-conscious in the light, until he turns me around and pulls my hands away from my body to have a look.

"You are perfect." His big hands are lathered with soap. He slowly glides them all over me, cleansing me of my old life. I run my wet, soapy fingers along the sculpted curves of his body, tracing his shoulders, biceps, and pecs. I've never felt a masterpiece quite like this. He turns off the shower, dries me like a china doll, then finally takes me to bed.

His gaze fixes on mine. "Don't let me go, Abby." He pulls me in, squeezing me so tightly, I need oxygen.

"I couldn't if I wanted to," I manage.

And with that, he slips on a condom and is inside me, moving with precision, as smoothly and slowly as a sax player in a smoky basement lounge.

WE SLEEP AND WAKE IN a tangle of sweat and tears, making love between the hours, clinging to each other as if our lives depend on it. Morning light creeps through the glass doors of the bedroom as Daniel rolls onto his stomach, exhausted. I can barely move. I've never believed in fairytales, but if they were real, it would be like this. Maybe all the bad days of my life have led me here, to him.

With my hands beneath the sheet, I slide them along the smooth skin of his muscled back. His breathing is soft and even. He's out cold. Between his shoulder blades, my fingers connect with jagged raised lines and stop cold. Was he wounded in combat? Did he even see a war? I lean over for a closer look, and my heart sinks. They don't look like blast or gunshot wounds, but they're certainly not precision cuts made by a professional. Whoever took care of his injuries didn't know what they were doing. I should be able to identify the cause of scars. It was the last unit I studied before withdrawing from med school.

I put my lips to the marks and whisper a question I know he won't answer. "Who hurt you?"

I've been so concerned about his reaction to the faint lines on my abdomen that I never considered how inconsequential they might be. My scars are proof of life. His are a reminder of something grim, and I don't even know what it is. As I begin to drift off with my arms protectively around Daniel, I realize that for the first time in almost twenty years, another man was inside me. I never imagined being so connected to anyone. I thought I was too broken to feel like this.

In the blissful fog of half-awake, half-asleep, Alex intrudes my head. His fingers are on my stomach, tracing the stretch marks. Like so many times before, I try to cover them up, but he stops me. *Don't worry, sweetheart. Your scars are beautiful to me. They're meant to show the world what you and I made together.*

In the morning, I wake to the sight of Daniel's wide blue eyes staring at me. He smiles and touches the back of his hand to my cheek. "Good morning, beautiful."

After planting a peck on his lips, I turn to face away then slide back to nestle against him until every inch of us reconnects. I can't imagine what I must look like after last night. I'm fully content, and to be honest, a little sore. He presses into me, making it clear he's ready for round four. *Or is it five?*

"Easy, cowboy. I think I need a shower and maybe an ice pack."

After a deep groan and stretch, he stands. "Lucky for you, I can help with both."

We have breakfast at an outdoor café table across the street. Between nibbles of almond croissant, I ask the question it took all morning to gather the nerve for.

"What happened to your back?"

He gives me a puzzled look like he doesn't understand the question.

"The scars. Are they from combat?"

He puts an elbow on the table and rests his chin in his palm. The lines around his eyes that had softened days earlier reappear. "I care so much about you, but I'm not ready to talk about that. I hope you understand." And just like that, he's a thousand miles away, and I feel like a jerk for sending him there.

I change the subject to try to bring him back around. "You can only eat one thing for the rest of your life. What's it gonna be?"

"That's easy. A big fat New York strip, medium rare."

"Ugh. I'd eat leaves and grass before I'd eat a dead cow."

"If you're gonna keep up with me, you're gonna need to up your protein." He winks.

"Okay. Your turn. Ask me anything."

"So, this is what we're playing," he says.

I nod.

"Okay, favorite music."

"That's easy. I like all music."

"Impossible. No one likes all music," he says.

"I do. Well, except for maybe rap and heavy metal."

"Which bands?" he asks.

"Lifehouse. Mumford, Maroon Five, Lumineers—oh, and Bob Marley."

"We're good so far. I like all of those," he says.

"Whenever Ruby or I get stressed, we sing the lyrics to 'Three Little Birds.' I started it when she was little, and she picked right up on the words. It was so cute how smart she was—still is." The memory of her as a toddler makes me smile, and I turn on my phone to find a photo of her at age four to show Daniel, then another more recent one with me.

"She was a beautiful little girl," he says with a sad smile. "And she grew up to be a beautiful woman, just like her mother." Daniel looks away then back at me with a heavy sigh.

"How about classics?" He obviously doesn't want to talk about Ruby, and I try not to be hurt. Maybe he's trying not to picture me back at home with my family, especially since we haven't really discussed when I'll be leaving. The truth is, I'm not ready to think about leaving him.

"I used to love Pink Floyd, Eagles, Def Leppard, and definitely Loverboy."

He pretends to choke on his latte. "Loverboy?"

"Yes. Loverboy. *Lovin' Every Minute of It.* I had cases of cassettes. I'd walk around town with my Walkman, singing my heart out. My grandmother couldn't stand anything playing in the house other than really old stuff like Frank Sinatra or Bing Crosby." I smile at the memory of her singing in the kitchen while stirring an enormous pot of bubbling marinara.

"Frank's the man."

I laugh. "You're kidding. You like Frank Sinatra? Okay, then, you can't make fun of me for this one. My all-time favorite singer is George Jones."

"Country!" He squints his eyes closed, shakes his head, and stands. "I think we're done here. I can't be associated with you."

"You like Frank! How can you make fun of George?"

"Because George was a drunk Texan who couldn't carry a tune. Ol' Blue Eyes, on the other hand, was a class act. Plus"—he clutches his hand to his heart—"he's Italian."

"But. What about 'He Stopped Loving Her Today'? You can't say that wasn't a beautiful song."

He sits back down. "If you wanna sit around and wallow in sadness without doing anything, sure."

He might be onto something. I've always been drawn to songs, movies, and books that make me cry. Maybe it's because they're familiar and I'm comfortable with the darkness, or maybe it's because I've been too afraid of change. "I just can't believe you don't like country music."

"And I can't believe you do."

"I'm from Tennessee."

"I'm from Texas, and you couldn't pay me to listen to a bunch of pitiful people singing about their broken pickups and dead dogs and women who ran off with some other cowboy."

"Not all country music is like that. You have no taste. Okay, let's talk about favorite movies, then. Hopefully, you can redeem yourself here."

"That's easy." He looks up in thought. "*Ace Ventura, Caddyshack, Airplane!*. But the best movie of all time is definitely *Me, Myself, and Irene*."

I can barely speak. "Please, for the love of God, tell me you're teasing."

His face is expressionless. "Why?"

"Okay, I'm just pulling your leg," he finally says.

"My father used to say that all the time. My grandmother never got the translation quite right. She'd say, 'No *pulla* my *feets*,' when I'd tell her I got an A on a test."

"She sounds like she was a lot of fun."

"She was the sweetest. I still can't believe our grandmothers were best friends growing up."

"I know. What are the odds? Think about this. What if they'd stayed close and we'd met years ago? As kids even. You and I might have ended up together years before we ever met other people."

I think about the concept of having married someone like Daniel instead of Alex. What would my life have been like as a military wife instead of a doctor's? Would I have finished medical school? Or would we have moved around too much to have made it work? Life is really strange.

"Okay, back to the movies. I want to know your real favorites," I say.

"Let's see. I liked *Shawshank Redemption*, and definitely *Die Hard*, especially during Christmas."

"*Die Hard* is not a Christmas movie. You've lost your mind."

"It absolutely is!"

He laughs then stands, tugging me out of the chair for a hug.

"I don't know about you, Doc..." He side-eyes me.

I lightly punch his tricep. "I don't know about you either."

Bubbly with contentment, I slide my arm through his. We make our way down the street.

"So what's *your* favorite movie?"

"No question. *Sweet Home Alabama*."

"Of course it is. Country girl."

"What's that supposed to mean? You're a Texan who doesn't like George Jones. You should be ashamed."

"I am, deeply," he teases.

"So what was your life like growing up? I mean, how often did you go back and forth between Italy and the States? What were your parents like?"

"You sure do ask a lot of questions." He taps me on the nose playfully.

"I want to know everything about you."

"But I like you and don't wanna scare you off just yet."

I squeeze his arm to my side. "Tell me your secrets, and I'll tell you mine."

He laughs. "I think you already spilled them all, Doc."

"I told you it was the limoncello."

"Oh, here we go again."

"I have plenty of secrets I haven't told you."

Chapter 7

France

Daniel and I begin and end our days with lovemaking, drifting off and waking tangled in each other's arms. During daylight hours, thoughts of Alex don't exist. But there's something about the night. The happier I become, the more I sense his presence. Some nights when we return, I swear I smell the slightest hint of vanilla and tobacco from his Cohibas. I know it's impossible, but when I take a deep breath, my nostrils fill with the smell of his eight-hundred-dollar Clive Christian cologne. Notes of bergamot are embedded so deeply in my brain that I'm able to conjure up smells that aren't even there. Forty-five hundred miles separate us.

The more connected Daniel and I are, the more restless the nights are for him too. It's as if an invisible force is keeping us apart, like poles of magnets. Daniel has begun thrashing in his sleep. I rub his back and whisper him back to sleep, the way I did for Ruby when she had nightmares as a child. In the morning, when I try to talk to him, he's embarrassed and apologetic. When I ask what haunts his dreams, he says he doesn't remember.

We stroll sidewalks and browse shops along the Avenue des Champs Élyseés, Paris's most famous street. Daniel takes me to a lesser-known shopping area—Avenue des Ternes in the 17th arrondissement, where I purchase a tall red Eiffel Tower mug, something to remember my time here, with him.

The Batobus takes us all along the Seine River to one of Paris's famous outdoor markets, the focus of Daniel's next assignment. I watch as he studies stacks and quarter wheels of cheese then snaps shots from various angles.

"This light is too harsh for good shots. Ideally, you want a nice cloudy day."

"Why?" I ask, wanting to learn everything I can. I've always been interested but lacked the patience to learn much more than how to take a picture using the auto setting.

"Because the clouds act as a diffuser to the sun. Tomorrow's supposed to be sunny, so I'll have to come back early, before the midday sun."

I'm impressed to learn that my new lover is multilingual and speaks fluent French.

"My French is actually atrocious, but I keep trying anyway. For work."

The cheese vendor offers us a sample of an artisanal cheese made from raw milk rather than pasteurized, the only way it's legally made in the US. The Reblochon is creamy, delicious, and bursting with flavor.

On the Pont des Arts bridge, Daniel removes an ancient-looking silver padlock with a coat of arms inscription from his pocket and hands it to me.

"Just a warning," he says. "I'm about to do something cheesy." He pulls a marker from his pocket, takes the lock, and turns it over to write on it. Daniel + Abby 2019. He attaches it to the bridge, tosses the tiny filigree key into the water, and kisses my forehead.

"Now you might really be stuck with me."

"Oh no," I tease, wishing it were true. I've read about the lock-covered bridges, but seeing forty-five tons of locks in real life is unbelievable.

"The Italians started this, of course. You know how we are about love." He winks.

"Of course they did, and yes, I do know a thing or two about Italian love." The words burn my cheeks.

Daniel squeezes me.

I ask a question that pops into my mind. "The night we met, what made you like me anyway? All those women were throwing themselves at you. Why me?"

He looks surprised and hesitates long enough to make me nervous.

"What? Tell me."

He stifles a laugh and licks his lips. "It was your dancing."

"My dancing?"

"Yeah, where'd you learn those moves?" He gives me a gentle elbow to the ribs. "Let me guess... Jazzercise or..." He doubles over in laughter. "Some seventy-year-old white guy teach you?"

I punch his arm, feeling embarrassed, then hold my head high, pretending to be proud of myself. "I know I have no rhythm. Something came over me that night, and I didn't care."

He turns serious. "And that's exactly what drew me to you. You didn't care who was watching. You were so into it."

"Smooth. Way to backpedal."

I FALL IN LOVE WITH the Louvre. Da Vinci's *Mona Lisa* has a Times-Square-sized-crowd gathered nearby, so we squeeze through and gawk instead at Veronese's life-size *Wedding at Cana*.

"Ruby would go crazy for this place. She has such a talent for art. She could draw before she could write." I snap pictures of the paintings and sculptures with my phone, making sure it's on airplane mode.

He smiles. "I think every teenage girl falls for Paris. I blame Net-flix."

"Ruby's not like a typical teenager. She doesn't romanticize any-thing. She's very pragmatic and stubborn. So, so stubborn."

"Huh, wonder where she got that from?"

"I wonder."

"I hope I get to meet her someday."

"You'd really like her."

He squeezes my hand. "If she's anything like her mother, I know I will."

"She's so much like me, only a thousand times more confident."

"I'm sure that's because you were a great mother."

"I was. I am." I may not have confidence in many areas of my life, but he's right. She's always been the center of my world. I made sure she grew up never feeling unloved like I did. One day, when our lives are settled, maybe I'll get her to fly from Boston and meet me here.

The Eiffel Tower is a photogenic metal monstrosity that turns out to be much prettier in pictures. Machine-gun-toting soldiers sur-round it and cause my chest to tighten. Daniel says because of all the terrorist threats, this is Paris's new normal. On the first level of the tower, we're crowded by people. I try to release the stress and appreci-ate the views. Happy couples and families below form single-file lines for tickets. Then I think I see him.

My heart thuds in my chest, and I slip behind Daniel to get a bet-ter look. The tall man with dark hair has a familiar gait and a crisp white button-up with rolled sleeves. He's overdressed, especially for the heat. It must be eighty degrees. I lean over the railing for a bet-ter look as he disappears into the crowd. I didn't see his face, but in-stinct rattles me. Crowds around me scurry, and people are shouting in French. I don't know what's happening. I've lost Daniel and can't understand a word.

Daniel appears and grabs me. "We have to go. There's a bomb threat."

Five, four, three, two, one...

Daniel tries to pull me, but I cannot move. I struggle to get air into my lungs. He holds my face in his hands and promises we'll be okay. Then he rubs my back and gently pushes me through the crowd. My mind races. Could that have been Alex? Could he have called in a bomb threat?

"It's all right, Doc. This happens a lot." Daniel escorts me down the stairs and away from the metal monster.

"You're shaking," he says, pulling me close. "It's okay. We're out of blast range."

He's shaking too. I hold him tightly, trying to ground myself. I take deep breaths and pray Alex isn't watching. My fingers reach for the spots between Daniel's shoulder blades. Beneath his shirt is physical proof of the much larger battles he's endured.

We're both on edge for the rest of the afternoon and evening. Daniel feeds off my tension, or maybe it's just his own. I'm more rattled from thinking I saw Alex than from the bomb scare. Daniel hasn't relaxed since either. I've read about veterans and know it's hard for them to talk about combat, especially if they were wounded, but I wish he would open up to me.

In bed beside him, I try again. "What hurt you? Please tell me."

"How much longer before you go home?" he asks softly, but there's an edge to his voice.

"I'm not sure, but what does that have to do with my question?"

He shuts his eyes and turns away from me. "I'm sorry, but I'm too tired to talk about this right now." For the first time since we've been in Paris, he doesn't try to make love to me.

In the morning, I wake irritated in an empty bed. Daniel is out for a run, his note says. Ruby and I have exchanged emails a few times. Hers seem short and make me worry her father has said unkind things about me. They have a special bond that I've never tried to interfere with.

She says she's having a blast and that they're heading to the mountains and won't have a signal again until they reach Lima next week. The distance and time between us has me feeling out of sorts. We've never been apart this long before, and knowing she's off in another country has been on my mind today more than ever. This is how my anxiety works. Once one incident sets it off, it grows into unrealistic worries. I know she's in good hands, but everything is out of my control. Before I can turn off the phone, an email dings and pops open to fill my screen:

Sweetheart,

I'm lost without you. I need you! The sooner you come back, the sooner we can get this whole thing sorted out. I'm sorry you're hurting, but I am too and your little vacation is only making matters worse.

First off, I won't apologize for my son. He's remarkable, and once you get to know him, you'll see that. I realize I should have told you about him sooner. Understand I tried many times, but the longer I waited, the harder it became, and the easier it was not to tell you. I suspected you'd figure it out so I could stop keeping my boy hidden away like some hideous monster. I'm relieved you finally know the truth. Perhaps, if you weren't always so preoccupied, you would have picked up on the hints sooner. Maybe if you devoted more time to our family, to me, you would have seen the signs. You should have noticed how unhappy I was! I was literally living in hell keeping this secret, Abby, and you didn't even see it. I'm not blaming you. Please understand that. It's just that I planned for you to be smarter, and if you had, life would be vastly different now.

To keep you apprised, I've starting custody proceedings, and Jack's birth mother will be out of the picture for good. She's taking a job in Paris, so he'll be living with us. Knowing Ruby is heading off to college has had you unbalanced for some time, and I know you're out there try-

ing to figure out what the future holds. When you get back, you're going to fall in love with Jack. Being a mother has always been your calling, and Jack will definitely occupy your time and heart. We'll raise him together in a stable home with two loving parents, the same way we raised our girl.

Anyway, enjoy your alone time, but don't get too used to it. We'll be here waiting for you when you return.

Always, Alex

Chapter 8

France

Weeks ago, I might have convinced myself I could somehow find a way to forgive Alex, but since being away from him, I've grown. His affair isn't my fault, and how dare he assume I'll raise his son. How ironic his lover is taking a job in this very city I'm in with my own lover.

I toss back the covers and shower, feeling the ever-changing metamorphosis inside me. It's not just Alex that has me riled. I'm annoyed with Daniel. He's being evasive, making me feel like he doesn't trust me. I know very little about his family and his past. Our conversations flow until I get too close. If I ask questions, he freezes up, and it's not fair to me. Talking about my parents hasn't been easy, yet I've shared so much with him, especially about my struggles to forgive my father.

Daniel's parents died in a fire while he was stationed in the Middle East, and that's all I know. He changes the subject when I ask about his marriage. And I haven't forgotten the little boy in the desk drawer. I think of him every single day but can't bring myself to straight up ask about him. When I talk about children, Daniel drifts away, and I don't understand any of it.

Sitting on the lawn of the Louvre, with tomato-mozzarella sandwiches from the Paul's Bakery truck, I clear my throat and speak the sentence I rehearsed earlier in the shower. "Are you ever going to open up to me? We've gotten so close, and you have this wall. I've told you everything about me."

He shifts his position on the ground and looks away. I'm not letting him off the hook this time. I want the truth.

"I'm trying to be patient, but you avoid my questions, and I'm starting to wonder why you're keeping secrets from me." I open my mouth to demand he tell me about the boy in the desk, but the words catch in my throat.

He stops chewing, swallows, and looks down at his lap. Then he looks away long enough that I know I'm not going to get answers. The voice of a stranger, low and foreign, responds. "Listen, I don't want to ruin what little time we have left rehashing my past." He pats my leg like I'm a puppy, nods, then looks at me as if it's settled. "There's nothing to worry about."

Fighting back tears of frustration, I turn away.

"Look, what's the point? For all I know, when we leave here, you'll go back to that asshole of yours. I don't harass you about the past... or the future. We're living in the now and taking things as they come, and I thought that's what you wanted."

This is going to be it—our first, and maybe last, fight. I try to stay calm. But I'm determined not to let him off the hook.

I swallow against the lump in my throat. "I don't need to know everything about us or our future, but I do need to know what I'm getting into with you. You've told me nothing about past relationships or your marriage. I don't even know if you're actually single. And what about the scars? What are you hiding?" I fumble with my hands, nervously waiting for answers. This time, I'm not moving without them.

Instead of the understanding I expect, rage flashes in his eyes. He stands and throws his lunch in the trash bin with such force, the glass bottle shatters. Then he walks away, leaving me alone on the lawn. People around me whisper. I cry like a weak heap of disappointment.

I tell myself he'll turn around, but he doesn't. He gets smaller and smaller then vanishes altogether. I remain there, choking back sobs, ignoring the stares, until my tears run dry.

As always with me, fury builds slowly and steadily. My frustration becomes sadness then anger. Daniel showed me who he is twice now. He's a man who walks away when things get uncomfortable. I should run too. *What the hell am I doing anyway? I'm supposed to be taking time for myself, learning to be on my own.*

Despite him, I decide after a few hours to continue my journey and maybe visit one more country before going home to dissolve my marriage. With a plan in place and fire in my soul, I get up and walk the streets alone before boarding the Batobus. I get off on the third stop. If Daniel is at the apartment when I return, I'll leave first thing in the morning. If he's gone, I'll stay another day until I figure out my next move. I'm thankful to have the spare key.

The Latin Quarter swarms with life. In a different mindset, I would love this area. Shop and restaurant owners stand in doorways beneath neon lights, calling out to patrons, inviting them inside. Eloquently decorated signs and chalkboards advertise daily specials. Meats in every shape and size spin on spits and create a confusing menagerie of aromas. The sights and smells overload my senses. Quartier Latin is livelier and more unique than any other place in Paris.

Down a less-crowded side street away from the chaos, I come to a narrow building, seemingly too narrow for a restaurant. I sit at one of the three empty outside tables and order a glass of Bordeaux and some pissaladières, tiny onion and anchovy tarts, I barely touch. I stall to give Daniel more time to gather his things and leave. I can't be there to watch him go. I won't be able to hold back, and I don't want my anger to be his last memory of me. Of us. *Let him remember leaving me crying in Paris on the lawn at the Louvre. He deserves that memory.*

Once the sun sets, I leave. With my head lighter and my heart heavier, I stroll back in the direction that seems right, getting slightly lost anyway. Everyone knows where Notre Dame is, so asking for directions is easy.

The closer I get to the apartment, the darker my mood becomes. I'm certain the apartment will be empty without so much as a good-bye note. Daniel has no way to find me. He doesn't even have my phone number. This time, we'll be lost to each other for good. Things happen for a reason. To keep my heart from splitting, I think of a dozen different mantras. Better now than later. As much as this separation will hurt once it truly hits me, I know that the longer he stayed, the worse it would be when he eventually left. If not now, a month, a year, maybe ten years from now. Even if he didn't have his own demons to deal with, once we were back in the States, Alex would drive him away. I say all the right things to my head, but this illogical heart of mine isn't listening.

I punch in the code and enter the courtyard then the main corridor, walking as slowly as possible up the stairs. The piano melodies drift through the stairwell, bringing me to a pause. I sear the sensation of this moment in my brain—the taste of wine on my lips, the empty pit in my stomach, and the sadness and anger still stirring through me. This is one of those pivotal moments in life, and once I open that apartment door, no matter what the outcome, my glass heart will shatter. Either he'll be gone, or his words will break me.

With a few steady breaths to prepare myself, I put the key in the lock, turn the handle, and slowly push open the door.

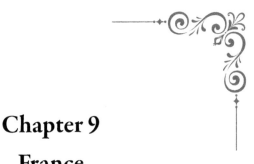

Chapter 9

France

Inside the apartment, Daniel's leather travel bag is on the bed, filled but not yet zipped. He's leaving, but not yet gone. He's sitting at the tiny table by the window, with bloodshot eyes and a half-empty bottle of Beaujolais in front of him. The air is stale and hot, filled with despair. Seeing him vulnerable like this makes me want to step in, wrap my arms around his body, and tell him I don't care about his past and that he can keep all the secrets he wants. All I want is for him to take me in his arms. But I've come a long way in a short time. And I deserve truth.

I cross my arms. "Hey, thought you'd be gone by now."

His voice is low and gravelly. "Sit down, Abby."

I step closer but remain standing.

"You still want to know about me? About my wife?" He looks up at me. Anger flashes through his eyes.

His *wife*? He didn't use the word *ex*.

I wait.

"I'll tell you everything then go." He stares at me, his jaw tight. "I didn't get a divorce." He shakes his head, making a gruff nasally sound.

My body stiffens.

"How about the kid in the drawer?" He waits for a response that doesn't come. "I know you saw him. His little toys too. Go ahead, ask me."

All this time, he did know. "Is he your son?"

"Yes. Crosby." He says it again, slowly, letting the name linger on his tongue. "Crosby... He was five."

Was. My stomach twists, and I swallow hard to fight rising vomit.

"He's dead. They're all dead." He raises his brows. "My parents. My wife. My kid. I never got to say goodbye to any of them." He looks away, pressing a closed fist to his lips.

I hold my jaws together to keep my teeth from chattering.

"My wife and son are dead because of me." He lets out a high-pitched, manic laugh. "And there it is. That's my past. That's what you wanted to know. Does it make you feel better?" He laughs again, his voice hoarse and cracked, on the verge of hysteria. His legs shake beneath the table. "That's my big secret. I have no one in this world. I'm not meant to be happy."

I'm going to be sick. That beautiful blue-eyed boy in his desk is his dead son. I step past him into the kitchen, grab hold of the chair to avoid collapsing, and empty my stomach into the trash bin.

When I finish heaving, I look up. Daniel's clenched fists tremble. His face twists in agony as his eyes flash with emotion. He lets out a few ragged breaths.

"I don't know what to say."

"You say goodbye. This is where it ends. You let me walk away so you can move on with your life. Forget about me." He steps around me and picks up his bag.

"No. I won't. Not until I know everything." My voice is strong and loud. "I know you."

"You don't know me. You're a sad girl, Doc. You see what you want to see." His words cut deep. "Look us up. The last name's Quinn. Daniel, Georgia, and Crosby Quinn. It's why I left the

States." He laughs then steps forward. "To get away from the reporters and the police and the fucking neighbors with their tuna noodle casseroles." A sob slips out.

I reach for him, grab his shaky hands, slow my breathing, and try to clear my head. "Daniel, what happened?"

He collapses into a seated position on the bed then drops his head into his hands, weeping. Then he takes a steadying breath, and barely above a whisper, he says, "I was drinking." He pauses, stares out the window, then looks at me.

I search his eyes, waiting for him to continue.

He stands and paces the room. Then just as I expect him to walk out the door, he sits back down. "We were all at a party by our house. We got into an argument. I'd been away working so much and just wanted to unwind a little." He swallows. "I had a couple of drinks, thinking we'd be there for hours. But then Crosby wasn't feeling well." He squeezes his eyes closed for a moment. "I should have called an Uber. If I had, they'd still be alive. God." He clutches a fistful of his own hair. "Don't you see, Abby? I killed them. Me. I gave my boy life then yanked it away, like it meant nothing. He was in kindergarten, for Christ's sake." He puts his head in his hands, and his shoulders shake as he sobs.

I drop to my knees, wrap my arms around him, and whisper, "It's okay. Everything is going to be okay."

He pulls back, shaking his head in fury. "No. It'll never be okay. My parents burned to death while I was in Baghdad. I should have been there." He sobs.

I know I should stop, but I have to know the whole story. If I don't press him, he'll never tell me. "Daniel, tell me about the accident," I say gently and sit back down. "Please."

Listening to the sound of his shaky breathing, I wait.

He drags air, holds it for a long while, then exhales loudly. "We ran to the car. It was dark and pissing rain." He shakes his head. "Our relationship wasn't in the best place, but I loved her and just wasn't there for her. My job consumed me. We thought things would be different once I retired from the army, but they weren't. She got used to living without me while I was deployed, and when I came home, it was like I was an outsider interrupting her life. We were trying, though." He wipes his nose with the back of his hand.

"Crosby was asleep in the back. I told her I had to leave on assignment in a couple days, and she started crying. She said that maybe I should just stay gone this time. Tears and makeup were running down her face, and it killed me. The rain was coming down in sheets, and I was having trouble seeing."

He pauses and looks out the kitchen window. "The road was deserted, so I pulled off to the shoulder to sit a minute and try to calm her. I didn't want her to wake Crosby." He blows out a breath. "As soon as the car stopped, she jumped out. It was fucking freezing, and she was just standing there, looking out in the valley." He shivers. "I got out too. I wanted her to get back in the car so we could go home and talk." He groans. "I called her name, but she wouldn't budge. By the time I made it around to the front of the car—" He swallows hard and chokes. "These bright lights blinded me." He holds his hand up and squints.

"I stepped out of the road onto the shoulder to let the truck pass. He had room to go by." Daniel squeezes his eyes shut. "It happened so fucking fast. The truck swerved and slammed right into the car. My boy was strapped in his booster seat, asleep." He shudders, looking at me wide-eyed. "The impact was so loud. The truck pushed the car right into Georgia, right down into the ravine below. I dove for the back door as it went over, but there was nothing I could do. My shirt, my stupid fucking shirt, saved me. It got tangled part of the way down, on some half-dead tree sticking out from the cliff. I just hung there. Tried to throw myself off but couldn't even fucking get that right. I just hung there and watched everything burn at the bottom."

Daniel groans. "That was it. They were gone, both scorched. Ashes to ashes, dust to dust, just like my mom and dad."

The scars on his back aren't from combat. He lives each day branded with a constant reminder of the accident that killed his wife and son.

When I think he has nothing left, he continues. "The truck backed up and took off, and I couldn't give any worthwhile description. When I woke, rescue workers had rappelled down and were pulling me up. I fought them and tried to kick off. But they wouldn't let me go. I just wanted to be dead."

He lowers his voice, fumbling with the hem of his T-shirt. "If I hadn't been drinking, I wouldn't have pulled over." He shakes his head like he's pushing the memories back into place. "Next thing I know, I'm awake in the hospital, stitched up and in a fucking psych ward." He looks at me briefly and stands, picking up his bag again. "So that's that. That's my story."

"Don't go," I beg. "This wasn't your fault."

He hangs his head. I know shock when I see it. There's no way I'm letting him leave here. My medical training takes over, and I take the bag from him and place it on the floor. I steer him onto the bed and wrap myself around him.

"It's okay now," I whisper, rubbing my hands through his hair. "You have me, and I'm not letting you go." I hold him until his breath steadies into the rhythm of sleep. Then I lie beside him, stroking his back. His reasons for withholding the truth are clear now.

As I drift off, my last thoughts are of regret—how I've spent so much time self-absorbed with pettiness in the grand scheme of things. I want to take it all back. I shouldn't have pressured him. I caused him to relive this nightmare until he split into a million tiny pieces.

IN THE MORNING, WE wake lazily with our legs tangled beneath the sheets. Daniel's blue eyes are bright again and miraculously show no signs of last night's horror. My eyes burn, and my body aches with the exhaustion only a mental toll can cause. He kisses my neck, his scratchy scruff abrasive against my skin. He pulls me to him, enveloping me. My body is a perfect fit to his, my back to his chest, my rear to his groin. Low groans escape him as he presses against me, his hands exploring. With his eagerness apparent, he parts my legs and enters me swiftly, urgently, leaving me breathless. When we finish, he turns me to face him, pulls my face to his chest, and rubs my head.

"We need to talk."

"I know we do." He pulls back to look at my face. "I'm so sorry for last night. I should have told you everything before. I just didn't know how. It's been almost five years since they died, and I've just never been able to talk about it or about them. I try to make myself forget. It's just easier that way."

"That's not healthy."

"You're probably right. I'm fine most of the time, but sometimes at night, I have these vivid nightmares about the accident. Then I'm off for a couple of days." He pulls me to him. "I know I can be such a mess, and I'm sorry."

I debate whether or not to recommend counseling, but I'm sure he's heard it a million times before. Besides, I'm in no position to judge anyone.

"Hey, Doc, I've got another assignment. If you want me to take it, we'll go. It's just a quick train ride away, in Amsterdam."

I still have so many questions. How long ago did his parents die in the blaze? Did they catch the driver who killed his wife and son? I push the thoughts away, though, and agree to walk blindly with him. "*Andiamo.*"

I roll my clothes and toiletries back into my pack. Unzipping the side pocket, I gently caress the bundle of letters from Francesca and look at her grandson across the room, imagining the delight our grandmothers would share if they could see us now.

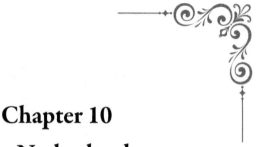

Chapter 10
The Netherlands

Plush seats and complimentary meals come standard with the first-class tickets Daniel insisted on purchasing for the French Thalys railway. We sip a pale burgundy and nibble cheese from trays. Daniel tries to convince me to try a sliver of fuzzy gray cheese.

"Come on, stubborn girl. Just take a little bite."

The smell is pungent, like blue cheese on a corpse. The texture in my mouth causes me to gag, and I spit it discreetly into my napkin.

Daniel tries to control his laughter. "Not for you, huh?"

I'm trying—and failing—to become an adventurous eater. French food, mostly rich and heavy with cream and meat, doesn't appeal to me. The way the French eat animal parts that Americans discard is admirable. Tongues, brains, and stomachs of cows and various parts of chickens, including the rooster's red crowns, are not only used in French cuisine but considered delicacies. Because the only meat I eat is fish, if it were not for Daniel's cooking, boulangeries, and the open-air markets overflowing with cheese and colorful produce, I would have starved.

While Daniel is off taking a call from his editor, I decide to check my email, hoping for news from my girl. Instead, I find a message from Alex. The subject says, "Please read." Against my better judgment, I open it.

Abby,

I get your message loud and clear. I screwed up, and I'm sorry. I wish I could go back and change the past. Just tell me what to do, and I'll do it. How do I make this right? I will do anything you say if you'll just come home.

I admit I'm nothing without you. I would never have finished medical school and certainly never become the medical director of a hospital. That was all you supporting me the way I needed. It's ridiculous when you think about it, isn't it? I'm in charge of all those departments; those people listen to me. They respect me, Abby, but the thing of it is, none of that matters without you by my side.

Without you, I'd still be tossing women aside like garbage when I was done with them. You changed me. I knew the first moment I saw you. I've never had to work so long and hard to convince a girl to have a cup of coffee. You made me realize in order to get something worth having, I had to work for it. You taught me that! Why do you think I worked so hard all these years? I wanted you to be proud of me. I wanted you to love me again the way you did in the beginning. I made a mistake, Abby, one tiny mistake nine years ago, and it has changed everything—our future, our marriage, our family. Before you left, you asked for the whole story. I wanted to tell you, but I was afraid you'd leave. You accused me of bringing home drugs, hoping you'd kill yourself? If you really believe that, you need more extensive treatment than I thought. When you come home, we will get you taken care of. Really, that's all I've ever wanted was to take care of you. You are my wife. I tried to give you the life that you never had. I made sure you never wanted for a thing. Your leaving doesn't seem fair.

To get it all out in the open, I will tell you what you need to know:

Jack's mother was a patient of mine. Her name's Lauren Cordova. She reminded me a lot of you when we met. At first, there was nothing personal about our relationship, strictly doctor-patient stuff. But then I let my guard down, and it progressed from there. Things weren't great between you and me, and I hate to admit it, but I enjoyed her attention.

It began the night of Ruby's dance recital. I called you on my way back to the hospital. Do you remember our conversation? I asked if we were okay and if you were still in love with me. Do you know what you said, Abby? You told me you didn't know. You broke my heart. I was hurting, so I texted her just for an ego boost. I shouldn't have done that. But that's how it started.

Afterward, I immediately thought of you. I was sick. I hated myself for a long time after.

By morning, everything was clear. I'd get us back on the right track—you and me, no matter how hard. I don't know where our marriage went wrong, but I'd turn it around. I came home with an enormous bouquet of red roses for you. Do you remember? When you saw them, you immediately asked me what I'd done. That's how you treated me. You were so cynical. It was like you knew.

For the next few months, I agonized over what happened. Not only did she cause me to break my marital vow, but she made me violate the physician's code of ethics. I worried she'd report me to the board and possibly say the sex wasn't consensual. The stress finally started to fade until months later, I saw her name on my books. I wanted to have the office cancel, but I didn't. My mind raced all day. I told myself I'd be nice to her and falsely accept the blame for what happened with us.

But then I opened the door. Lauren was sitting on the table with her hands folded over her swollen abdomen. My heart sank. Abby, you can't imagine what that moment felt like for me.

She made it clear she wasn't having an abortion. The thought of killing her right there in the office crossed my mind. My hands around her throat. I wanted to make it all go away. I didn't care about her at all. I didn't know what to do. She told me she didn't want my money and didn't want to wreck my life. She thought I should know about the baby and that it was a boy. The son that should have been yours and mine. That was it, Abby. She was gone.

I could've left it like that. Sometimes I wonder if I should have. I had to be sure the baby was mine. She told me if I wanted proof, I'd have to wait until he was born. So I wanted to be there in the room. I wanted to make sure the test was done immediately after birth. No way was I having her leave the hospital without the test. She agreed to let me be in the delivery room, and Mark agreed to go in to assist even though he wasn't her OB. I knew Mark would make sure the test was done quickly and confidentially.

Once the baby was born and Lauren was asleep, I took him out of his plastic bassinet and sat holding him in a chair by the window so I could look at him. His wide eyes studied me as if he was trying to take me in all at once. It was like he knew I was leaving him. None of this was his fault. He was here. He was real. I couldn't abandon him, Abby. I wanted to be a part of his life. I told his mother I would take care of him always if he was indeed mine. The tests came back. I had a son.

The last eight years have been tough. I saw him a couple of times a week, but he wanted to be with me more. I had so much guilt not being able to share him with you and Ruby. That's it—the whole story.

There is something to be said about the truth setting you free. I do feel better. I hope now that you know everything, you do too. Once you come home, we can sit down and really talk. No more secrets. No more lies. We can begin the healing process together.

Come home, please.

Always,

A

My God. What does he expect me to do with this? Details of his infidelity and twisted truths fix nothing. For years, I tried to talk to him about our problems. I delete the words and furiously bite the skin around my fingernails—a long-ago-abandoned habit. Alex will not ruin my time away. I practice meditation breathing and do my best to allow feelings of anger and unworthiness to flow through and evaporate, a technique I learned that works much better than resisting. I hope to eventually be able to teach Daniel. By the time he returns, I'm back, living in the present, calm again.

During the remaining three-hour ride to Amsterdam, I rest my head on his shoulder and admire the French countryside. We roll past lavender fields and old stone villages with scenery vastly different from the graffiti- and trash-covered cities along Italy's tracks. France is more beautiful than I imagined, and I haven't yet seen the coast. But the language is difficult, and trying to pronounce French words phonetically is impossible. Daniel tried to teach me, but I gave up quickly. It hits me—I have no idea how to speak even a word of Dutch.

"You'll be fine," Daniel assures me. "They speak fluent English in the Netherlands."

"That's a relief. As exciting as it's been being surrounded by all these different customs and foreign languages, it'll be nice to understand what people are saying."

"Don't get too excited there, American girl." He squeezes my thigh. "They still speak to each other in Dutch, so you probably won't get too much."

"So let me get this straight—they'll understand every word I say, but I won't understand them unless they want me to."

He smiles. "Yep, you got it."

I feel like an idiot and wish I'd taken the time to learn a second or third language.

"Don't tell me you speak Dutch too?"

"A handful of words. The language is as hard as hell. It's taken me years to not get laughed at when I tried."

Not only is he incredibly hot, he's also smart. "How many languages do you speak?"

"Just Italian, obviously, and a little French."

"What about Dutch? You just said—"

"Seriously, Doc, a handful of words at most. Well, and a little Spanish, because it's similar to Italian."

I squeeze his arm to me. "I'm impressed."

"You're easily impressed then." He leans down and kisses my forehead.

"What other secrets are you keeping from me, Daniel Quinn?"

He smiles. "Guess you'll have to stick around to find out."

AT AMSTERDAM'S APTLY named Grand Central Station, Daniel leads me through the tangle of trams and people.

"I'm guessing you know where you're going."

"Maybe." He winks, pulling me onto Tram 19, where he buys a book of tickets for the next few days.

The tram stops in Jordaan, and we step off and stroll the streets, hand in hand. Wind howls in from the North Sea, and I press into Daniel for added warmth. With the weather so cold, it's hard to believe summer is near. We cross flower-lined canal-street bridges, pass dozens of docked houseboats, then turn down a quiet road to a neighborhood bar-restaurant, Café Pret, which looks more like a house. Three tiny café tables sit out front, chair legs resting on the narrow street edge. As we step into the restaurant, I rub my arms vigorously, trying to warm up. Antique portraits hang on rich wood-paneled walls. Wide oak-planked floors and large bouquets of wild-flowers on the wooden bar top create a homey vibe.

"Wait here a sec."

Daniel heads toward the bar, and I watch curiously as the tall, well-built bartender turns to face Daniel. His face lights up with instant recognition. With a wild smile, he walks briskly from behind the bar to embrace Daniel. I study the barkeep's perfect nose, bright-green eyes, and expression, which is full of genuine happiness. A long narrow scar runs along the left side of his cheek, vanishes beneath his chin, then reappears along his neck, marring his otherwise-perfect chiseled face. His cropped hair, muscled physique, and body language are similar to Daniel's and make me think he must be former military. I try not to stare, but from the corner of my eye, I notice him looking from Daniel to me. The barkeep pats Daniel on the back as they head toward me.

Daniel says, "Abby, this is Michael. Michael, Abby."

I offer my hand, but Michael embraces me like a long-lost sister. "Have a seat, you two. How about some hot tea... or maybe something a little stronger?"

I study him. "Tea would be great."

Daniel adds, "Same."

Michael leaves then reappears carrying two clear glass mugs overflowing with waterlogged weeds. "It's fresh mint." He smiles at my bewildered expression. "I take it you're used to those dried tea bags, Abby."

"The only time I've had mint like this has been with rum and lime," I say with a smile.

He laughs. "Ahh, well, I could arrange that if you'd like?"

"No, thanks. It's a little early for me."

"Try it with some honey."

I pour, stir, and swallow, allowing the sweet liquid to warm my core.

Michael returns with two big bowls of steaming asparagus soup and warm bread, which hits the spot. He takes a seat at our table.

"How do you two know each other?" I look to Michael, who looks to Daniel.

"We served together," Daniel says.

I'm curious to know what happened to his face.

"Our boy here saved my life." Michael pats Daniel's back as Daniel shakes his head.

"It's nothing you wouldn't have done for me or anyone out there."

"What happened?"

The guys exchange a look.

"Ah..." Michael shakes his head. "I'm afraid that's a conversation for another time."

"Definitely one with drinks," Daniel adds.

I apologize. Apparently, I learned nothing about asking people to relive traumatic experiences. I can be such an idiot. We finish our soup and tea while Michael splits his time between us and the customers. Daniel tells him of his latest assignment, the red-light district.

"You're in for a real treat, Abby," Michael says.

I'm not sure if he's teasing. "Am I really?"

He laughs. "No! An eye-opener yes, but definitely not a treat."

Daniel shakes his head then lays a twenty-euro bill on the bar. "Well, I guess we'll be heading out. It was good to see you, man. Let's do a better job keeping in touch."

Michael turns away, reaches up between the liquor bottles, and pulls out a large antique key. He lays it on top of the bill with a clunk and slides it across the bar to Daniel. "Take this and stay at the apartment. No one stays there anymore. Really, take it. And don't insult me with your money." They stare at each other for an eternity, communicating something I don't quite understand.

"Okay. Thanks. Love you, brother." He picks up the key and the twenty.

Outside of the restaurant, I comment, "He seemed really happy to see you."

"He's just happy to see me with you."

I'm touched.

"He's a good guy, and he knows how hard these past few years have been on me." He reaches for my hand. "You're the first girl I've brought around to any of my friends."

"How long's it been since you've dated?"

"I haven't. I mean, not since my wife."

"You haven't been with anyone in five years?"

He goes quiet, and I realize what I just asked.

"Never mind. That's none of my business."

"No it's fine. I want to be completely honest with you moving forward, even when it's uncomfortable. I get lonely sometimes, and occasionally I find myself with someone, just not anything serious."

I hate that I'm jealous and don't know what to say. He's a hot single guy—of course he's having sex.

"Look, if it makes you feel any better, I haven't slept in bed beside another woman since I was married. You're the first."

And I'd like to be the last.

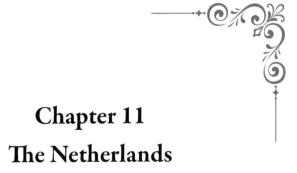

Chapter 11
The Netherlands

Cycling is the preferred mode of transportation here for everyone. Toddlers, school-aged kids, smartly dressed business people, mothers with babies, and even the elderly whiz by. Some bikes have wooden wheelbarrows or trailers attached. Others have child seats in both the front and back.

We pass boutiques, cheese shops, and both coffee and tea houses. In front of Albert Heijn, a small supermarket, an unattended bicycle cart with a little boy, who is maybe five, leans against the brick building. I can't help but think of Daniel's son. Seeing other children must remind him of Crosby, because his smile doesn't quite reach the eyes. The more we walk, the more unaccompanied children I notice. Daniel says it's not uncommon.

"Europeans think Americans are backward the way they shelter their children from experiences that help them grow then turn around and buy them video games so they can spend all their free time sitting in basements, stealing cars and blasting each other with machine guns. Kids here are more mature and responsible because of the way they're raised. America needs to change."

"I agree, but I don't see it happening. I still don't like Ruby to be away from me, and she's grown."

"Sometimes it doesn't matter how hard you try to protect them."

Sometimes I speak without thinking, forgetting that he's lost a child.

When we reach the house containing our apartment, Daniel pauses at the front door. "Have you heard of Dutch stairs?"

"No. Why?"

A giant grin spreads across his face. "Prepare yourself."

When he opens the door, a wide fixed wooden ladder is before me. No actual stairs in sight. And our apartment is on the second floor, which by American standards, is on the third level of the house. These so-called stairs are already dangerous, with rungs barely deep enough for toes. Stacks of letters and packages scattered on every few stairs make them even more treacherous. In disbelief, I pull myself up one by one, barely able to contain my laughter. Daniel tries to help me, but I push him away like an independent toddler, insisting he let me experience my maiden Dutch-stair climb on my own.

He stands ahead, or more like atop of me, shaking his head and laughing. "Come on, stubborn girl. You've got this."

The massive building was once a single-family home. A rope attached to the front door goes all the way to the top floor, so when guests ring the buzzer, rather than going down to let them in, residents pull the rope to unlock the door. The apartment is cozy, with a bedroom so small, the bed takes up the entire space. A church bell chimes so loudly, it startles me, which makes Daniel laugh.

"It's the old Westerkerk Church around the corner. Better get used to it. It goes off every fifteen minutes."

Dear God, I'll never sleep.

We drop our belongings and head out. Amsterdam is different than its reputation for wildness, prostitution, and pot. Despite the gray skies and bitter coldness, I'm at ease.

Daniel steers us clear of the infamous red-light district, promising to take me later. At the market, we grab enough items for the next few days—coffee, fruit, wine, bread, and cheese. They have so many different types of cheese—young, old, and ancient Goudas, Edams, and Parmesans, all inexpensive compared to the States. I'm anxious to try them all. We pass by a four-foot-high stack of unrefrigerated eggs.

Daniel laughs at my shock. "The law back in the States requires that eggs be washed, which takes away their natural protective coating. Most places in the world, except maybe Australia, the US, and I think Japan, leave their eggs unwashed and unrefrigerated."

On the walk back, I peer into the windows of the tall Dutch townhomes. Some are four or five levels tall, with windows as wide as the houses. At the top of each house is a large hook for hoisting furniture.

In Amsterdam, many of the Dutch appear to be a curtainless culture, at least on the ground level. The uncovered windows allow a glimpse inside their lives. It's like looking into living dollhouses. Families gather around the tables, chatting and sharing meals. Kids run around playing, all within full view of the world. I love watching the families going on about their lives, not caring who sees. Still, I worry the sight is painful for Daniel, so I don't mention it.

"Every new place we go, you light up like a kid in a candy shop," he teases.

With the exception of a handful of all-inclusive Bahamian resort trips with Alex, I haven't traveled. Alex has little interest in any culture besides his own. The only reason Ruby and I got him to go to Keeper's Cay was because one of his board members owns the island. Being pampered and waited on for a few days was nice, but Ruby and I never felt right about all the attention. We wanted to leave the grounds and mingle with locals in the markets and shops, but Alex wouldn't have it. He said it was unclean and unsafe. So we stayed and had mani-pedis and sipped virgin piña coladas by the pool. Alex was never keen on me drinking in public. It makes me giggly and loud. Daniel hasn't yet noticed, thankfully. I try not to worry about him seeing the real me and having a change of heart. We're so comfortable and fit so well together, but maybe that happens in a lot of new relationships. I don't have enough experience dating as a thirtysomething woman.

The most exciting thing about traveling to a new place is learning the culture. The local food, and the way they dress, talk, and eat—I find it all so fascinating. I could really get used to a life of travel, especially with this man beside me. I thread my arm through his. "I love seeing all of this for the first time with you."

"I'm happy to be your travel guide. And just a reminder—I do work for tips." He winks.

At nightfall, I convince Daniel to take me through the red-light district. He'll have to go back later to shoot, but he agrees to take me along to scout out the scene. It's worse than I imagined. The canal-lined streets are mobbed with people of different nationalities, ages, and all walks of life. Neon lights and signs shock my senses. Live sex, peepshows, and erotic museums are plentiful. Neon-lit windowless canal houses showcase nearly naked women. Watching the bikini-clad girls both mesmerizes and sickens me. Men come and go in the tiny rooms we pass.

A young girl around Ruby's age sits on the side of the pedestrian roadway, a puddle of vomit on the ground in front of her. Her friends are crouched beside her. Daniel stops to ask if she's okay.

"She just had too much to drink," one friend says.

"It's not safe for you girls to be out here at night. Where are your parents?"

"At the hotel," the vomiting girl says. She looks at her watch. "Oh shit. We're late. My dad's going to kill us." She tries to stand but stumbles.

Daniel catches her. "Come on, let's go. We'll make sure you get back safely." He looks over at me. "You okay with that, Abby?"

I think of Ruby and how grateful I would be for someone to help her in this situation. "Absolutely." I help hold the girl up while the five of us make our way down the crowded streets.

Thirty minutes later, we deposit the trio in the lobby of the Hilton.

"So what'd ya think?"

"I didn't expect it to be so seedy."

He squeezes my hand. "I know. The story I'm shooting for is about the girls and how they end up here."

The image of him in those tiny rooms with half-naked girls rattles me. I didn't used to be like this, but Alex has opened my eyes—or maybe he's rubbed off on me. "So you have to come back and photograph the prostitutes?"

He side-eyes me then shoots me a cocky half-smile. "Ahh. Is someone a little jealous?" He pulls me against him. "I promise you I have no interest in what they're offering."

We push our way through the stumbling drunks to escape the chaos. Back at the apartment, Daniel loads up his gear and kisses me goodbye. While he's gone, I immerse myself in late-night American television. There are only a handful of channels, but they're all in English. Having heard so little, the words are music to my ears. I settle in to *Gilmore Girls* reruns and think of Ruby. We've watched all seven seasons three times. We identify with Lorelei and Rory so much. Though she won't admit it, I swear Ruby chose Harvard because it was Rory's first choice. I'm so excited for her future—and for mine. I never imagined getting divorced at my age, but I know it's for the best. Though I'm terrified, being independent again thrills me just a little.

"*Gilmore Girls*?" Daniel laughs at the sight of me curled up on the couch, halfway through the third episode.

"How was your evening with the hookers?"

Giving me a look, he drops his gear bag and tries to hug me. "That's not nice."

I know he's right. They're just trying to make a living like everyone else. I put my arm out to stop him. "Not a chance until you shower."

After he showers, he takes me to bed, and I forget all about my little jealous pang.

THE FOLLOWING DAYS, we wander the streets and the museums, drinking dozens of hot teas and coffees to stay warm. We rent a boat and tour the canals, which offer such a different view from below the streets. I watch in awe as groups of teenagers cruise by in their sloops, with radios blaring and beers in hand. I guess this is Amsterdam's version of teenaged joyriding. We ride bikes all over. It took some convincing to get me on one, but I finally agreed to be brave and go for it. The bike traffic is intimidating, with hundreds zooming by every minute.

I'm proud of my new adventurous self. I've done more this past week than in my entire life and have been terrified every step of the way. But I'm not sad, and I'm not numb. I feel every prickly feeling.

We pull over to take a break in front of the Anne Frank museum, park our bikes, then sit on a bench. Daniel leans over and slips a small antique gold key on a chain around my neck. He leans in, latches it, and smiles.

"I keep this in my gear bag for luck, but I see the way you marvel at all the old hotel keys, so I want you to have it."

I picture it around the neck of his wife.

He looks into my eyes. "I've never given it to anyone, in case you're wondering."

"It looks like a real key."

"It is."

"What's it go to?"

"I can't give up all my secrets at once." He winks. "You'll have no reason to keep me around." He smiles like he can't tell a lie. "Okay, look, my mom had this little old antique chest about yea big." He holds his hands about a foot apart. "I grew up wondering what the hell she kept in there, because no one was allowed near that damn box." He tilts his head to the side. "After she died, I discovered her secret."

The look on his face makes me nervous. "Well, what was it?"

"Chocolate. Freakin' chocolate. About ten pounds of it. She'd kept a stash of Belgian chocolate locked up so her husband and kid couldn't get to it. How crazy is that?"

"Can I ask you about the fire, or is it too much?"

He pulls me closer and kisses the top of my head. "They were on vacation in Phuket, this insane party island in Thailand. It was an electrical fire started in the bar below the room where they were staying. They never should have been there, but my mom had this insane idea that she wanted to visit every country in the world." He smiles a sad smile. "She was adventurous as hell but was the worst trip planner. She'd see a handful of pictures on Instagram and immediately buy plane tickets without knowing a thing." A memory makes him laugh. "They once ended up in Cancun on spring break. Mom saw an ad for seniors and got confused, thinking the resort catered to old people. She still had a great time, but my dad was pissed."

"I think I would have loved your mother."

"And she would have loved you."

The key around my neck reminds me of one Nonna kept tucked away in her sock drawer. Whenever I needed cash for a new dress or shoes for a school dance, she would dig through the drawer, unrolling and re-rolling socks until finding the hidden key. Then she unlocked the old wooden jewelry box, a handmade gift from her father. I argued with her and refused the money, but I quickly learned how stubborn an old Italian woman could be. I sat on her bed and fiddled with the key, running my fingers around the filigree and etchings while listening to stories about her mama.

Outside of the apartment, we sit on a bench in silence, knowing our time together in Amsterdam is coming to a close. I have so much to deal with back home. But the longer I'm away, the easier my problems are to put off.

Reading my thoughts, Daniel takes my hand and says, "Look, as much as I don't want you to go, I think you need to head back to Florida and deal with your shit. You need to set things right, for everyone's sake. I can hook you up with a good attorney so you can divorce that SOB if that's still what you want." He looks at me with questions in his eyes. "It's time to stop burying your head in the sand. It's been weeks."

"I know you're right, and yes, of course it's what I want. I want to be with you." I hesitate. "If you're sure it's what you want."

"This thing with us has moved so fast. I know we said we'd take it one day at a time. I just don't want you to have regrets later, and I sure as hell don't want to be the reason you break up your family, so if there's any doubt you could work things out with..." He hesitates and looks as if he tasted something foul. "Him. I just don't want you to roll over one day in bed, look at me, and be sorry."

I ease into my words. "My marriage is finished. I knew it before I met you. I left St. Augustine to gain clarity and, like I said, to find a way to be closer to my grandmother. I'm so thankful to have met yours." I smile at the memory. "I hoped time away would give me the strength I needed. And it has. Meeting you was unexpected but has nothing to do with dissolving my marriage. I do want to be with you. I've never wanted anything more."

His smile reaches his eyes. "I still can't wrap my head around all of this. You and me. What are the odds?"

"I still blame the limoncello," I tease.

He laughs. "Of course you do."

I wish I could just meet Ruby at her new dorm in Boston to help her settle then fly back to Italy without ever having to go home again. I would leave everything behind if it meant not facing Alex. I don't suggest that, though, because I worry Daniel will concur. I need to be responsible and go home to face the music. I'm so afraid if I let go of this happiness, even for a moment, it'll slip away for good.

After Tommy died, I wished for a knight to show up and save me. When my parents disappeared from my life one at a time, I convinced myself I was better off without them. When Alex came along, showering me with attention, I figured he was as close as I would get. He may have been controlling and not always so nice, but he swore he would never leave me. Looking back, I see my friends were right. I was living in a fantasy bubble. I gave up my job then my dreams of medical school for him, and it still wasn't enough. I wasn't enough.

Once my fire burned out, he may not have left, but he no longer wanted me. Alex is manipulative and will probably blame me when I tell him I'm leaving. But it won't matter. I'm still moving on. For the first time in my life, I feel lucky—like the stars aligned to give me what I needed. Maybe it was fate. Maybe I had a little help from my grandmother. All I know is I plan to follow my heart and see where things lead.

Back at the apartment, I watch and learn as Daniel edits then turns in his photos. I stare into the blank faces of Amsterdam sex workers while he adjusts the angles and crops the images best suited for the article.

"I know this is crazy after me telling you it was time to go home, but any chance you want to make one more stop with me? I need to do some location scouting for a shoot. It won't take long."

The thought of avoiding the reality that awaits me for one more day has magnificent appeal. And Ruby is still away. "Yes, anywhere but St. Augustine sounds good to me."

Journal Entry
December 8th, 1999

Dear Me,

I know I haven't written in ages. I seem to only make time when I can't get out of my hole. This time, I've been there awhile. Alex keeps bringing home different antidepressants for me to try. I haven't taken anything since Ruby was a baby because they either make me throw up or make me feel like a zombie. I was doing so well without anything, then I did something to snap me back into reality. The only thing I'll ever be is a wife and mother. I will never be a doctor. Why isn't that enough?

It's almost Christmas, and I'm going to focus on the positive. My little lovie is almost six. She's the light of my life! She's reading third-grade books, and between Dora the Explorer and me, we've taught her to speak a ton of basic Spanish. She's definitely more advanced than the other kindergartners at her school! Watching her grow and seeing the world through her eyes is the most amazing gift.

When I sing "You Are My Sunshine" to her, she freezes in place and belts out the lyrics as loud as she can. It's the cutest thing.

She had a rough start at the beginning of the school year and came down with something the first week. Alex thought it was nothing, but I was completely freaked out. After a high fever and seizure, we ended up in the ER, where they did a bunch of tests that all came back normal. I actually prayed. And who knows? Maybe God actually answered me. A few days later, she was completely back to her normal bubbly self.

A couple of weeks later, I accepted my position at the University of Florida's medical school. Most of my classes would be held in Jacksonville, and I'd only need to travel to the Gainesville campus once a week for labs. I had everything planned out to make sure nothing at home changed for anyone but me. The problem was I snuck around to make it happen and even made up a half-truth to go back home to Tennessee to get my records. I told Alex I needed to clear up some financial paperwork for my father, which was true, but I could have done it via mail. I was scared, but proud to accomplish what I did without him knowing. Each day, I drove myself nuts, sneaking to the mailbox to check for an acceptance letter. Alex likes to be the one to get the mail. I prayed he wouldn't check our security cameras from the hospital and catch me. When the letter finally came, I was so excited I cranked up my iTunes and had a dance party in the kitchen with Ruby by my side, jumping around and squealing with no clue why. I know now I shouldn't have snuck around and lied; I was just worried he'd be angry and do something to stop me and hoped telling him after the fact would help him accept it. He says we're a team and should do everything together. I was wrong. And I know being a wife and mom should be enough for me. I hate that I'm selfish and want more.

The night I told him I put Ruby to bed early, made us a nice dinner, lit candles, and poured his favorite pricey pinot, praying he'd see how happy I was and say I could go. It didn't go that way. I pleaded and promised to make sure nothing would change at home. I'd pre-prep meals on weekends and make sure I was always here when Ruby was home. I would only study when he was gone and she was in bed, but he was pissed like I've never seen. Alex tore my acceptance letter to pieces and threw it in the trash while I stood there, bawling like a baby. Then he called his mother to rant and so she could tell me I belonged at home, not out in a field full of men, trying to prove my self-worth.

I bring everything on myself. I should never have done what I did. Alex even said if I'd done things like a normal person and talked to him before applying, things might have turned out differently. I was so angry at myself, but now I'm just blah. What the hell is wrong with me?

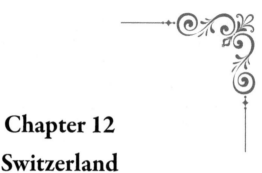

Chapter 12
Switzerland

Daniel's pre-dawn terrors wake me. This nightmare is worse than the previous ones. The continuous chiming of the Westerkerk's bell has made sleep difficult already. Daniel's head thrashes from side to side.

"Shhh," I whisper in his ear to settle him. "You're okay."

He quiets without waking, and I drift back into a light slumber.

In the morning light, I'm half-dreaming, half-awake with him behind me, against me. His mouth moves along my neck and shoulder then nuzzles my ear. His hands caress me. I reach behind and guide him inside, forgetting about the condom.

"I'm not wearing anything. Are you sure?" he whispers.

"I'm on the pill. We're fine."

His arms embrace me and hold on for life. Caught between this world and another, we move together in rhythm; the friction and slickness push me to the edge. I gasp. He turns me over, pulls my face toward him and presses me into the softness of the pillow, entering me again. Our breaths sync, peak, and stop, until we can hardly breathe. I roll away to rejoin the world and promise myself to take the pill when I get up.

AFTER A QUICK FLIGHT and short train ride, Daniel and I arrive in Interlaken, Switzerland, where the skies are clear, sunny, and surprisingly warm, compared to Amsterdam. The people in town are mostly non-natives, Indians and Asians. The tall shops, hotels, and restaurants are lackluster and without charm. We pass a Swiss clock shop with a window display of cuckoo clocks on our way to a nearby park. Beyond the flowers and trees, snow-capped mountains sit in the distance. Their peaks ascend through the clouds.

Because it's been on my mind for some time, I ask, "Can we talk about the nightmares?"

"Did I wake you? I'm sorry."

"Have you tried talking to someone about them?"

"You mean a shrink? Hell, no."

"I think it might help."

"I don't even remember the dreams. Besides, shrinks are bad news. They get you kicked out of the military. The government can't be on the hook for putting traumatized men on tour. We learn early to bottle our shit up. No talking to shrinks, no matter how bad it gets."

"That's ridiculous and unhealthy, and you're retired, remember?"

"You're right, Doc." He kisses my hand. "Maybe one day I'll do it for you."

"You know I'll never be a doctor, right? That ship has sailed. I'm too old."

"Never say never. You don't know what the future holds. Three more years is nothing."

He's right, but the reality is going to be more like me working one or two low-level jobs to get by. There'll be no time for school, especially not med school.

"So, what are your plans when you get back?"

His question surprises me. It's the first time he's come out and asked a direct question about my future. I've already thought everything through. I just wasn't sure how much to share with him.

"Well, I've been looking at short-term rentals online and have a couple of appointments next week. I plan to go home for a few days, pack my personal belongings and move into a new place before Ruby gets home from Peru."

"Think he'll give you a hard time?"

I think he'll do whatever he can to make my leaving difficult. In his twisted brain, he probably thinks my ignoring his emails is a good thing. "I'm not sure. I haven't spoken to him, and considering the way we left things, my message was loud and clear. I'll be fine."

Now that I'm more self-confident, the thought of starting over isn't so bleak. Ruby will only have a couple of weeks at home before she leaves for Boston. If for some reason Alex and I can come to an agreement, I may stay until we take her to Boston, but I don't want to bring that up.

"Once your girl is at Harvard, think you might wanna come stay at my place for a while?" He adds with a grin, "Or forever? We can make that our home base and travel the world if you want."

"I would love nothing more. I'm just not sure how divorce proceedings work. Do I need to stay in the States until they're finalized?"

"I don't think so. A couple of my buddies went through it while we were on tour."

We stroll around the park, hand in hand, watching paragliders land in an open field. Daniel pulls out a tiny moleskin and takes notes on the sun, weather conditions, and time. Either he'll come back, or another photographer will to take shots for a story for *National Geographic.*

"You realize your phone has a notepad built in, don't you?"

"I'd rather use pen and paper. I'm old-school, baby."

"Any desire to try that?" I ask, pointing at the multi-colored in-flatable wings in the sky.

"It's not as fun as it looks. Besides, our feet are on the ground for a reason."

"You've done it before?"

"Not by choice."

"No, no. Arms in, legs down, ahhh." Daniel cringes. "That's gonna hurt. He locked his knees. You never lock your knees."

I'm intrigued. "What a thrill I bet that is. In my new life, I'm go-ing to try everything."

He winks. "I hope I'm there every step of the way."

"I hope so too."

"Oh shit." Daniel points to the guy coming down fast with an expression of terror on his face. He hits the ground with a thud, and people quickly crowd around to make sure he's all right. He gets up, waves, and limps away.

Daniel puts his arm around me. "Stick with me, Doc. We'll do lots of exciting things, without breaking our legs." He kisses the top of my head, and we walk on.

I keep looking around, waiting for an old friend of Daniel's to pop out from behind a tree or get up from a park bench, maybe with an apartment to offer. "So, no friends here?"

He laughs. "No. Too cold for my friends."

"You mean we actually have to pay for a hotel?" I exaggerate my tone. "My God, and I thought I had a guy with connections."

With a sheepish smile, he says, "Well, I do get reimbursed. But we need to go a couple of miles from here to Wilderswil. It's quieter and cooler anyway. We can grab the local train or take a bus."

"Sounds good to me. Whatever you want."

"Ahhh," he moans. "I see something I want right now."

Flattered, I smile. But he steps around me and grabs my hand to pull me across the street. "Chocolate."

We head into the Grand Café at Restaurant Schuh, which happens to be an elaborate *chocolateria*. I order tea.

Daniel orders a hot chocolate. "This place has the best hot chocolate in the world."

With the paragliders still in full view from our seats inside the restaurant, I think of how evasive Daniel has been about his time in the military. I haven't pressed him because I didn't want to dredge up old feelings about my brother, but I'm stronger now, so I ask him to tell me one of his favorite memories.

"When I first got there, straight out of basic training, there was this big guy. I mean linebacker big." He gestures with his hands. "I was just a skinny kid. Anyway, this guy had thick blond hair he was always combing like there was enough there to comb. We all had buzz cuts. He was a complete asshole. Nobody liked him. He started on me the day I showed up, calling me 'pretty boy' and jacking up my bed after I'd make it for inspection. He rode my ass every day, and there was nothing I could do because he was three times my size."

He smiles at the memory. "Anyway, the other guys weren't going to stick up for me, so I had to do something. A few weeks in, we had some bigwigs coming to tour the base." Daniel chuckles. "That big asshole comes out of the showers, screaming how he'd kill us all. He was dripping wet, with bald patches on his head. Apparently, someone added Nair to his shampoo."

"You did that."

Daniel puts his fist to his lips, stifling laughter. "He never messed with me again. The guys knew what happened too, so I earned myself a whole lot of respect that day."

"I can't believe you. Remind me never to get on your bad side."

He reaches for my hand and kisses my palm. "You could never."

I think of my brother and his shaggy blond hair and crazy eyes, and I wonder what he would look like today if he were alive. The weight of losing him feels a lot like carrying stones in my soul.

"Tommy struggled in the beginning too," I tell Daniel. "I didn't know it until my dad told me later. It broke my heart. He'd send me letters from the Middle East, but I was a kid. They were always upbeat and made it seem like he was having a blast traveling."

"Yeah, when you're away, the last thing you want to do is upset the people back home who care about you."

"Tommy was always in trouble for playing tricks on my father. He'd put bugs—and not the plastic kind—in our ice cube trays. Once, he squeezed out all my dad's toothpaste and replaced it with hemorrhoid cream. I thought my father would kill him." Alex never liked when I talked about Tommy. He said rehashing my past life was unhealthy. At the time, I thought he was right, but now, telling stories to Daniel makes me feel closer to Tommy.

"I wish he was still here. I miss him."

Daniel's smile fades. "I know what you mean."

"I know you do."

He looks at me with his sad blue eyes. "The past is the past. Nothing we can do but move forward and honor the memories."

We finish our desserts and head back to the center of town. Along the way to the bus and train station, we pass more Chinese and Indian restaurants than Swiss, which surprises me.

The local train to Wilderswil looks as if it's been plucked straight from a Hallmark Christmas special. Traditional Swiss Tudor-style houses line the streets of the village. When I imagined Switzerland, this authenticity is what I pictured. Other than the solitary grocery store, the few businesses are converted houses. The Grizzly Inn is charming, with a giant carved wooden bear mascot and a cozy restaurant serving traditional Swiss food.

The gray-haired man at the front desk looks up through his wire-rimmed spectacles when we walk in. He checks us in and hands us brochures. "You must take the train to Jungfrau. It is eleven thousand feet and is the tallest mountain in all of Europe."

Daniel looks at me, clearly amused by the man's enthusiasm.

"The train leaves in the mornings and afternoons, but I recommend the afternoon so the clouds have a chance to burn off."

"Well, I guess I know where we're going tomorrow?"

"Sounds good to me."

Twin beds pushed together and stacked high with fluffy down comforters and pillows swallow us when we lie down. The TV in the corner is a heavy relic like the one my grandmother had in the eighties. An old sink with a rusty faucet and a continuous drip sits in the corner. The Grizzly is quaint if nothing else.

Once Daniel is asleep, I lie quietly in the fluffy bed and think of home. I've never been away so long. I don't want to, but I miss St. Augustine. The entire city is walkable, and the beaches are only a short bike ride away. Growing up far from the water in Franklin, I longed to live by the water.

When Alex and I married, his parents surprised us with a newly renovated historic Victorian on Marine Street. I wanted to refuse their gift and be proud enough to continue our plan to move outside of town, to a place within our budget, until we earned enough on our own to afford something better. But Alex convinced me that refusing would crush his mom and dad. Back then, they were kinder and spun the house as an investment for our future children, saying, "You'll pass it down to your children, and them to theirs."

Later, Alex told me that neither he nor his parents could stand the thought of us living in a seedy rental. The Marine Street house will always be special to me. Ruby took her first steps in that living room. After her first heartbreak, we sat out on our dock, and she laid her head in my lap and cried. I'll miss our home, the town, and all the eccentric people I've come to call friends. It's all I've known for most of my adult life.

Ruby and I walked those old brick streets thousands of times, heading to her school on Saint George almost every day since kindergarten. I'll miss the clip-clop of the horse-drawn carriages, and even being stuck behind them when I'm in a hurry. I'll miss the city hall meetings with speakers dressed as pirates and presenters singing songs to make a point. I'll miss Friday night Art Walks, Sunday bike rides on the beach, and the monotony of my days spent waiting for Ruby to get home to tell me about hers. I have so many sweet memories in St. Augustine. There's no place I would rather live.

I also remember the things I won't miss... I won't miss Alex being away at conferences for days, not answering his phone, leaving me thinking the worst, his belittling moods, or the times he would come home smelling of bourbon, his beloved Cohiba cigars, and perfume, which I chose to ignore. I won't forget his gentle reminders of how I married up and how I should be thankful he chose me. I won't miss the times he refused to sleep with me, telling me he just wasn't in the mood, then surprising me with Nutrisystem subscriptions and workout videos to do at home. And when I told him I wanted to reapply to med school, he convinced me I had too much on my plate. When I reapplied anyway, he said I was selfish. I will carry the scars from him making me feel like he was the only person who could ever love me, and that the only place for me in this world was at home as his wife.

No matter how bad things were, though, Alex never laid a hand on me. How could a man have been so unkind to his wife, yet so loving and supportive of his daughter? I should have seen all before. If he had been anything but wonderful to Ruby, I would have left years ago. Watching him with her made me believe he was good and that maybe I *was* to blame. I thought if I could do better—be better—then he would treat me the way he treated her.

Even though I'm comfortable with Daniel peacefully sleeping beside me, I'm restless and unable to relax. The faucet drips steadily in the pitch darkness as my mind conjures up the smell of Cohibas. With each plop, the past and future converge in my brain and remind me what I'm about to return to. Bringing Daniel into this messy life of mine might be a mistake. I don't know how Alex is going to react to my leaving. Had it not been for the Montgomery money and connections, I tell myself I would have left years ago. According to *Forbes Magazine,* the Montgomerys are one of the top one hundred wealthiest families in the South. I always feared if I left I would lose Ruby to be raised by them. Alex casually mentioned through the years that he and his daughter were a package. He would say it in a passive-aggressive way that could be construed as a joke to those who didn't know him like I did. I'm grateful that she will be living in the Northeast, far away from any drama.

I lie awake, motionless on my side of the bed, buried beneath a sea of fluff, until the sky shows its first twinge of light. When I finally get up, I press my fingertips to the chilled window. Heavy clouds hang low, making it quite dark for seven o'clock. At home, this would be a day Ruby and I would curl up on the couch under piles of blankets and watch Lifetime movies or more *Gilmore Girls.*

Daniel stirs and says in his deep, sleepy voice, "Why are you up?"

"Believe it or not, it's seven already. It's just foggy and dark."

"It'll burn off. Come here." He beckons. "Let me hold you."

I crawl beneath the comforter next to his heated body and try to relax. Though I'm anxious and restless, I realize it's been quite a while since I've felt a panic attack threatening me. For that, I am grateful.

"All right, Doc, it's obvious I can't fix you. Let's go get you some grub."

Despite being early, the kitchen and dining room are already filled with tourists. I nibble on a single slice of toast and tease Daniel about his plate overflowing with bacon, eggs, sausage, and pancakes.

"All right, spill it," he says. "What's got you so antsy?"

Going home and dealing with Alex. But I won't say that. "I'm just not ready to leave you."

"Look, I know the feeling. I'm not ready either, but once you do what you need to do, you'll feel better." He reaches for my hand. "You and I will be back together at my place in what? A month, tops?"

I know he's right, but a sick feeling fills my stomach. I try to tell myself it's just the anxiety, but I know it's more. "A month is a long time."

"You'll be busy getting your girl ready for college. It'll go by so fast."

Thinking of shopping for dorm stuff and packing everything up is exciting. I know how much she's been looking forward to it. "You're right."

He smiles. "So, you ready to plant your feet on Europe's highest mountain?"

I'm thankful we purchased warmer clothes. He leaves me in the lobby to go grab his camera bag from the room. As I sit in a chair by the window, a smell fills my nostrils, and my stomach sinks. In the ashtray on the table beside me is a stub of a cigar with the unmistakable gold-foiled Cohiba wrapper. My heart stops, and panic blooms.

Five, four, three, two, one... The smell hasn't been in my head. *Is he here?* His cigars aren't that uncommon. *Are they? Get a grip, Abby!*

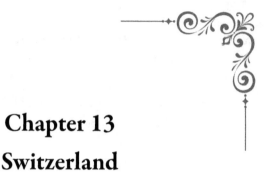

Chapter 13
Switzerland

At the train station, the clerk hands us a brochure with photos of couples and children playing in the snow. "It's a wonderfully clear day to go up to hike or tube. You will not be disappointed."

The train operates on a cog-and-wheel system similar to theme-park roller coasters and makes me a little uneasy each time it connects at the base of an incline. We pass farms with sheep grazing alongside weathered old barns and fields of vibrant yellow wildflowers in full bloom. As we climb farther, the scenery changes to snow and ice, and the temperature drops. Blue skies give way to dense fog until we can no longer see outside the windows. Daniel shifts in his seat, growing visibly uncomfortable. His hand stiffens in mine.

"What's wrong?"

At first, he's reluctant to share and claims it's nothing.

"Remember when you asked what happened to Michael?"

I nod.

"About halfway through our first tour, we were up in the mountains in Northern Afghanistan on a day that looked a whole lot like this. It was supposed to be a simple mission. We were just there gathering intel." He looks out the window and pauses. "The Chinook dropped us about a hundred klicks away on the west side of this bitch of a mountain. The terrain was rough, steep, and slick with loose rocks. It took a few days of hiking, and we were dressed in full battle

120

rattle, about an extra fifty pounds on us. None of us had slept, and we were tired as hell. We just wanted to get the assignment over with."

He blows out a breath, and I squeeze his hand.

"We were closing in, and Michael stops dead in his tracks and says, 'Brother, I got a bad feeling.' Michael always got bad feelings. He was right about half the time. The other half, we just busted his balls about. I figured this was one of those times. I wanted to get done and out." He looks at me and rubs his lips. "He was right about this one. The bastards knew we were coming."

"So what happened?"

He hesitates long enough that I'm not sure he'll answer. "We were the only two that made it out. I walked away without a scratch. But Michael's branded for life. Every time he looks in the fucking mirror, he's reminded of that day I blew him off." He shakes his head. "Sometimes, the nightmares, they take me right back. I have so much freaking guilt."

Knowing how hard it must be for him to tell me this story, I'm gentle with my words. "He said you saved his life. Is there really anything you could have done differently?"

"I might have saved Michael, but I didn't do anything for my other three guys. I was responsible for everyone. I walked away, and they didn't."

"I'm so sorry you went through that." I lean into him. "Thank you for opening up to me. I know how hard it has been for you to talk about your past."

He rubs his eyes with his palms. "I'm just a mess all around. You sure you want to be with me?"

His vulnerability makes me feel even closer to him. "I'm sure."

An hour later, we pull into the fog-shrouded station at eleven thousand feet and disembark. Daniel's still sullen. "Well, looks like the weather's not going to change. Don't think I'll be scouting much in this."

My head started hurting the last thirty minutes of the ride and has begun splitting. I didn't want to say anything during the ride, but I'm suddenly dizzy. Daniel guides me through the crowd to a restaurant called Bollywood and buys me an eight-dollar bottled water. We sit on a bench beneath a window with snow piled maybe eight or nine feet high while I wait for my symptoms to ease.

"I know all about it but have never experienced altitude sickness before."

"It happens to a lot of people up here. We're pretty high up, and we haven't had much time to acclimate. That's my fault. I should have known better."

"*You* should have? I'm the one with medical training. Then again, I did drop out."

He pulls me to him for a side hug. "Oh, stop."

I try to laugh. "We're just a mess today, aren't we?"

"We should have stayed in bed."

Once I start to feel better, we try to go outside, but a large man stops us at the door. "No one is allowed outside. There's an avalanche risk."

We're both disappointed, but we manage to pass an hour looking at ice sculptures before heading back to the train.

As I settle in for the ride back down, Daniel puts his arm around me and pulls me to him.

"I'm sorry we didn't get to see anything and that I felt like crap."

He kisses the top of my head. "Don't apologize. It's not your fault."

"I'm still happy to have this time with you."

"That makes two of us, Doc."

I stare out the window and focus on the breathtaking scenery as it turns from uninhabitable mountains to rolling hills with bits of green grass peeking through.

Midway down the mountains, the train rolls into the village of Harder Kulm. There's still plenty of snow on the ground, but the skies are blue, and the sun is bright and warm. A dozen or so people sit around at the wooden picnic tables, eating and drinking.

"Let's get off and grab a beer or some hot cider," Daniel says.

We order cider and an apple streusel to share and sit at an empty picnic table overlooking the mountains. The weather is chilly but crisp, and because we're bundled, it's nearly perfect. With both hands, I reach for Daniel's.

"I should go home tomorrow. I've been thinking about it and think it'd be best to go get stuff settled before Ruby gets home." I have a bad feeling that I can't place. I keep thinking about how oblivious Alex has been in the emails. What if my news catches him completely off guard? I need to make things right before Ruby is there. "I don't want to leave you, but—"

"You don't need to explain. I get it." He squeezes my hands. "I'm grateful to have had you this long." He forces a smile that doesn't reach his eyes.

"You're making it sound like I'm not coming back."

He doesn't answer right away. "I'm just being realistic. Look, Doc, you know where I was a few weeks ago when we met." He shakes his head, remembering. "I've come so far since then. And I told myself that I'd be happy with whatever time we had. I may or not have even told the big guy up there." He nods to the sky.

I giggle, remembering our first encounter. "When we first met, you looked like you hated me."

He smiles a genuine smile. "You scared me. The way you carried yourself. Fucking gorgeous, with no clue. Right away, I knew if I talked to you, I'd be done for, and sure enough"—he snaps his fingers—"that's just what happened."

"Maybe I cast a magic spell on you," I tease. "Or..."

"Don't even say it." He shakes his head again. "It wasn't the limoncello anyway. Remember it was your hot dance moves."

I take a swing at him.

"Seriously, Doc, I'm more grateful than you can know. That first night that we sat out on the patio and talked... It was the first time I'd felt a connection with anyone. You opened right up and let me see into you. You trusted me. That's so rare and special." He reaches up and strokes my cheek. The way the sunlight reflects from the snow and brightens his blue eyes melts me.

"Tell me I won't lose you. Tell me you won't change your mind. Tell me you won't go back to him. No matter what happens. Promise me."

"I promise."

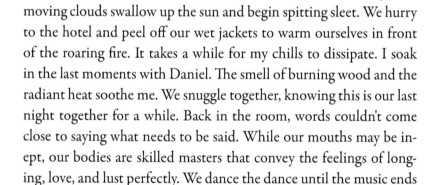

BACK IN TOWN, AS WE make our way to the hotel, heavy, fast-moving clouds swallow up the sun and begin spitting sleet. We hurry to the hotel and peel off our wet jackets to warm ourselves in front of the roaring fire. It takes a while for my chills to dissipate. I soak in the last moments with Daniel. The smell of burning wood and the radiant heat soothe me. We snuggle together, knowing this is our last night together for a while. Back in the room, words couldn't come close to saying what needs to be said. While our mouths may be inept, our bodies are skilled masters that convey the feelings of longing, love, and lust perfectly. We dance the dance until the music ends and exhaustion takes hold, disjoining our sticky, spent bodies long enough to cool. We come together again, and I drift off in his arms, complete.

Low, guttural moans wake me. I blink my eyes into focus and see Daniel's comforter in a heap on the floor. The sheets from his side of the bed are pulled off.

His face is pained. His head thrashes from side to side. "No. No. No."

This is the worst I've seen. I reach for him to calm the nightmare. "It's okay. You're okay."

When that doesn't work, I shake him gently and say his name louder. "Daniel!"

His eyes spring open. He grabs my wrist so hard, it feels like it might snap. I scream in pain. He drops my arm and jolts upright. Looking around wildly, he pants and struggles to catch his breath. He hurt me. The thought wounds me more than the physical pain.

I've read about PTSD and witnessed his nightmares, but none have been like this. Never physical. Seconds pass before he realizes what he's done.

"Did I hurt you?" His eyes are wide.

"No," I lie.

"Are you sure?" He reaches for my throbbing arm.

I pull away and wrap my arms around him so he can't see what he's done. "I'm positive. You were having night terrors. I shouldn't have touched you."

He squeezes me tightly. "I'm so very sorry. I haven't had a nightmare like that in years."

"What was it?"

"The accident. The medics pulling me up and me fighting them to let me go." His body trembles against mine.

"Daniel, you need to see someone."

"I will. I promise you. As soon as I get back to Italy, I'll make an appointment." He rubs my cheeks with his hands. "Are you sure I didn't hurt you?"

Feeling the bruise form on my wrist, I promise he didn't. The bruise will heal. I'm not sure he would.

AT THE AIRPORT, MY heart pounding, I stand with Daniel in front of the Delta counter. Surrounded by departing tourists, we cling to each other. I hold him with all I have, fighting that nagging feeling that if I let go, it'll be forever. Last night, we had it all figured out and everything seemed right, but now, I'm not so sure. Moments pass, then Daniel inhales sharply, releases me, turns, and walks away.

He doesn't look back. I'm left standing, motionless in the crowd, shivering. I watch him become a tiny speck before disappearing into the distance. I board my first flight to JFK. The flight will be long, so I order a beer then another—anything to help me forget, to numb my mind from what I'm leaving behind and to what waits ahead.

I drift off. Vivid dreams haunt my sleep. It's dark and cold. I'm alone in the woods, running for my life. My long white cotton dress catches on a branch then tears away. I'm nearly naked and barefoot. Branches and rocks tear the undersides of my feet, leaving a trail of blood behind me. There's no escaping. I will never get away. I'm shaken and unsure what the dream means, if anything. Is it an omen or just anxiety? I keep thinking I'm going to breeze in and out of St. Augustine, but will Alex let me go that easily?

After the first flight, I make my way through customs in just under two hours, and I'm at the next gate with time to spare. I email Ruby to let her know I'll be home soon and see an unread email from Alex:

Abby,

I'm trying my best with you, but my patience is wearing thin. How could you completely ignore the fact that your daughter was coming home and not be here to greet her? I left you several voice mails letting you know she was coming home early. I take it you never bothered to listen to them. This isn't like you, and I'm not sure what has happened to your mothering instincts. Ruby was brokenhearted that you didn't care enough about her—about our family—to be at the airport to pick her up. Don't worry. I covered for you. Our family needs to come before our own desires. You used to know this.

Jack was here with my mother, waiting to meet Ruby when we got home. So yes, she knows about him and already loves having a little brother. I probably should have waited for you to return from your vacation, but I wasn't sure when that would be. I explained the circumstances to Ruby, and she was extremely open-minded and understanding.

The children and I are very much looking forward to your return. I hope it will be soon. Since you've been gone, I had movers come relocate some things so Jack could have a bedroom of his own. I've converted your office to his room since it's the biggest and has the best light. Your belongings are back in our bedroom, where they should be anyway. I love watching you and the way the sunlight comes through the window and makes your hair glow like fire. You're beautiful, and I miss you. Please get home.

All my heart,

Alex.

Reading his words infuriates me. Ruby wasn't supposed to be home until the weekend. I have no idea why her plans changed. She never mentioned anything in our email exchanges. And I can't believe he told her about Jack! She must be so upset. With seething anger and shaking hands, I scan my boarding pass and step into the jetbridge to board.

PART 2

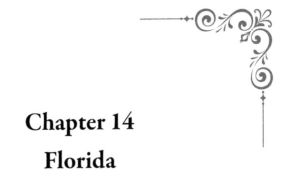

Chapter 14
Florida

The plane touches down a little after dark, jolting me awake. Outside of security, from fifty feet away, I spot my golden-haired girl wearing yoga pants, an oversized sweatshirt, and a wide smile that doesn't quite reach her eyes. Alex and his son are there too, beside her, talking. They haven't noticed me yet. I planned to Uber home, so I'm shocked to see them.

When Ruby spots me, she comes running and nearly knocks me over with her embrace. I scan her face for signs of trouble. Dark circles line her eyes, and they look a little bloodshot. I place the back of my hand on her forehead. "You feeling okay?"

"I'm just tired."

The way she clings to me leaves me skeptical, but she left on a summer trip and came home to a surprise brother. She knows me well enough to know my leaving had more to do with just needing to get away. "Why are you back early?"

"I just missed home. And you, of course," she adds with a half-smile. "I wanted to be here when you got back." She twirls her hair. "Since I'm leaving for school soon."

"We all missed you, sweetheart." Alex pulls Ruby from me and takes her place. "Now it's my turn to hug my wife."

He embraces me as if nothing were wrong between us. His voice, his touch, and the familiar smell of Cohibas make me recoil. My body stiffens, my hands barely making contact with Alex. *Get a grip!*

"Hi, sweetheart," he says. "We're so happy to see you. Aren't we, kids?"

Ruby rolls her eyes.

Alex's son looks up, forcing a smile. "Hello." He reaches for my hand. "I'm Jack Alexander Montgomery," he says slowly, enunciating his full name.

With an opportunity to pull away from Alex, I bend down to his level and shake his hand. "Nice to meet you, Jack."

"It is nice to meet you as well." His adult-like introduction complete, he looks to his father for approval.

"Why don't you give her a hug?"

Jack leans in, embracing me awkwardly before taking Alex's hand.

"Good boy," Alex says, as if addressing an obedient dog.

"Wait, let me take that." Alex reaches behind me, removes my backpack with a look of disdain, and places it on his shoulder. He's always hated the pack and any reminder of my life before him. He's thrown it away a few times, but I've always managed to rescue it before the trash men hauled it away.

Ruby grabs my hand as we walk toward the parking garage. For her sake, I'm going to try to pretend that all of this is normal.

"So tell me everything about your trip. How's Jess? Was she sad you left early?"

"You know how dramatic she can be. She'll get over it."

"Did something happen between you two?"

"Not really."

Her voice is flat with uncertainty, and I wish I could just turn around and walk her back into the airport so the two of us could fly away from here. I have no idea what Alex has put in her head. She has to be in shock.

She tells me about meeting interesting tribes and trying both guinea pig and alpaca. "The guinea pig was greasy like duck or dark-meat chicken."

My stomach flips at the thought.

Outside of the airport, Florida's familiar evening warmth cloaks itself around me. Alex places his arm around my opposite shoulder, walking with a bounce in his step and a smile on his face. He looks happier than I've seen him in years, as if now that I'm home, the world is right again. I can't understand him. The anxiety I feared is absent. Instead, I'm once again comfortably numb. I look at this man, my partner of nearly two decades—my keeper—and feel nothing but indifference.

This man who made me feel small all these years is not an emperor. He's just a man. In life's grand scheme, he is small; our problems are even smaller.

We take the stairs to the second floor of the lighted garage and continue walking. The purposeful sound of Alex's shoes echo against the concrete walls. He stops at a black Range Rover.

"Surprise." He looks to me for a response as the kids climb into the backseat. "Figured we needed something roomier with Jack." He smiles, opening my door like a true gentleman. As we're pulling out, Alex asks, "Who wants ice cream?"

There's no response until Ruby says flatly, "I'm not really feeling it, Dad."

"And I'm lactose intolerant, remember?" Jack adds in a small voice.

"Well, we could get you some sorbet then. How does that sound, buddy?"

Jack shrugs, disinterested.

"Come on, family," Alex says with an unfamiliar chipperness.

"I'm sorry," I say. "But I'm exhausted. It's been a long flight, and it's late. Can we do it another time?"

"I'm tired too," Ruby says.

"Boo," Alex teases. "Of course, we'll go another time." He pats my hand. "Let's get you both home and tucked into bed."

The car ride is long, and I fill the silence by asking Ruby questions about Peru and about college, anything to keep the topic light. She's quiet, and I know she's probably barely holding herself together.

I tell them about my bad experience visiting Jungfrau.

Through the dashboard lights, Alex eyes me with suspicion, his brows furrow. "Did you read any of the emails I sent you?"

"Can we talk later?"

"Of course we can, sweetheart. I'm so happy you're home." He pats my hand again.

I cringe and face the window, closing my eyes.

Back home, Ruby goes to the shower, and I survey the rooms. Nothing has changed except my office is now Jack's bedroom, fully furnished and decorated like he's always been here.

"Where's my stuff?"

Alex is giddy. "Wait until you see what I've done for you, sweetheart. Follow me." He takes my hand and leads me to the master suite. At first, I don't see anything different. Then I realize the closet is now twice as wide. He gently pushes me toward the closet extension and stops me at the doors.

"You ready?" He's wide-eyed and smiling. "Close your eyes... Okay, okay. Open them."

The doors are open, revealing an ultra-modern white laminate built-in desk with lighted shelves on both sides and cork covering the back wall. Two chromed glass pendants hang above the desk.

"Wow. It's very nice... and so modern," I say, both trying not to hurt his feelings and sorry he has gone through all the trouble when

I won't be staying. I open and close the drawers and spend a moment looking at the desk as I struggle for kind words.

"Listen, sweetheart, I know it's not your style, but I figured once you used it a few times, you'd warm up, so I took a chance and had this all custom made, to surprise you."

Panic sets in as I think about my most cherished piece of furniture, an antique writing desk from my grandmother. "Where is my desk?"

"I thought you could use something new."

"Is it in the garage? Where is it, Alex?"

When he looks down at the floor, I realize it's gone.

"Don't be mad, but I donated it to the Betty Griffin Center."

Rage surges through me. This is low, even for him. "When? I have to buy it back."

"I'm sure it's found a new home by now. They picked it up last week. I'm sorry, I thought you'd appreciate what I did for you. I guess I was wrong, as usual." He sits down on the bed, his shoulders slumped, but this time, I don't feel the slightest bit sorry for him. This is typical Alex, trying to erase who I was before him. It's only ironic he donated my grandmother's heirloom desk to the battered women's charity I volunteer with. I'm speechless, yet I know I've created this monster. I fed it, nurtured it, and allowed it to grow, always hoping it would change, but doing nothing to stop it. Now it's too big.

"Listen, Abigail, I'm trying to help you to stop living in the past. Being so attached to material things isn't healthy. It's a piece of furniture, for Christ's sake."

"Says the man who just bought a new Range Rover." I hold my tongue and instead take in a long breath, trying to swallow my anger. I have a great deal to say, but I won't waste my strength. It's pointless. He'll either pretend he doesn't get it, or he truly won't. I am exhausted and need to talk to Ruby.

"I need some sleep."

"Well, come on. I'll get you tucked in and make sure the kids stay quiet."

"I'm staying in the guest room."

He looks up at me, his sullen eyes narrowing. "You know, I expected after all this time away from the kids and me, that you'd want to be with us. I also expected you'd want to sleep next to your husband." He shakes his head. "I try so hard to please you, Abigail, but nothing seems to work. Good night." He vanishes into the bathroom, closing the door harder than necessary.

He must be delusional right now to think I would crawl into bed beside him. I can't even bring myself to feel sorry for him. I head upstairs to Ruby's room and find her sitting cross-legged on her bed, propped up by her fluffy fuchsia and aqua pillows. The sight of her unaware of my presence, wearing bulky headphones, with her eyes buried in a book on her lap, warms me. Her expressions change from melancholy to anger. How she can listen to music and be so deeply engrossed in a book is beyond me.

She finds good in everyone. Despite my issues, I managed to raise her to be empathetic toward others, to ensure she understood that us humans are multi-faceted complicated creatures. I prayed she would have a giant heart full of love and kindness for everyone, including those who don't always deserve it, and she does. When I look at her, I'm proud to have sacrificed whatever it took to give her the stability of a two-parent home. She couldn't be more level-headed and well-adjusted. And now that she's practically an adult, I'm going to turn her life upside down.

I crawl into her soft bed beside her.

Startled, she speaks too loudly. "Sorry, I didn't hear you come in." She turns off her music, moves the book to her nightstand, and slides down to face me.

I put my arm around her and kiss her on the cheek. "I've missed you like crazy."

"Me too," she says, nuzzling into me like a little girl. "I've been so worried about you. Things sure got weird while we were gone, huh?"

"I'd say."

She nods. "It's because of him, isn't it? The reason you took off?"

I look into her bright eyes and gather my thoughts. Tonight, her irises are more blue than green, but the flecks of gold are as bright as ever.

"Dad told me everything." She rolls her eyes and smiles a nervous smile. "Or at least his version of it."

"What did he say?"

"That you were on the verge of getting divorced when he met Jack's mom, but he decided he loved you way too much to split up."

Alex would never tarnish his image with his daughter by telling her the whole truth. We weren't in a great place, but divorce was never discussed.

I'm mentally drained but need to know why she's not more upset about having an unexpected brother. "How long have you known about Jack?"

"Dad told me last week."

"That's why you changed your flight, isn't it?"

She nods, her eyes full of pity. "We talked, and he sent me a few really long emails. He asked me not to say anything to you and said you went away to mentally prepare yourself for being a mom again." She squeezes me. "That's why I've been kinda avoiding you. I'm sorry. Honestly, I know how bad he screwed up. I've been worried about how you'd do with me gone. Jack seems like a neat kid. I think it'll be good for you both to have him here." She smiles as if it's been settled. "I'm really happy you two are going to work it out." She looks at me with her puppy eyes.

I'm tempted to lay out the whole truth, but we're both tired, and she deserves a night of thinking her world is safe with me home. "Lovie, there's a lot we need to discuss and some things I need to talk to your dad about tomorrow. Plus, I'm exhausted."

"Wait." She places her headphones on my ears and presses play on her phone. Bob Marley's "Three Little Birds," our stress song, fills my ears and brings a smile to my face.

I remove the headphones and pull her in for a hug, taking in the comforting and familiar smell of her coconut shampoo.

"Let's get a good night's sleep and talk tomorrow. We can spend all day in our pj's, catching up. I can't wait to hear more about Peru."

When I let go, she shudders and lets out a small moan.

"What is it?"

"Just cramps."

That's not right. Our cycles are synced. "It's that time again?"

"I don't know, maybe. Or it could be all the weird food."

I think of the guinea pig and alpaca and scan my brain for symptoms of intestinal parasites. "Any diarrhea or vomiting? Nausea? You didn't drink the water over there, did you? What about ice?"

She dismisses me in typical teenage fashion. "No and no. Stop worrying, woman. I'm fine. Go get some rest."

More than likely, it's nerves. The news about Jack has rocked her world. Even though Alex has told her everything is fine between us, I'm sure she senses it's not. I kiss her on the forehead and tiptoe to the guestroom next door, hoping Alex won't hear my footsteps. The fluffy down comforter, similar to the Swiss ones, swallows me. My mind begins to drift, but I won't go there, not until things are in order here. Instead, I lie in the darkness, worrying about my girl. I tend to overreact when it comes to her health. I should have returned sooner. I should have insisted she talk to me more while she was away. I would have known she already knew about Jack.

Not that I'm making excuses for him, but Alex didn't have it easy growing up. His multi-generational-blue-blooded father neglected both him and his mother. I'm pretty sure Richard Montgomery, a charismatic man with just enough gray at the temples to make him distinguished, had several mistresses as well. Alex alluded to it a few times without fully admitting it, and I wouldn't be surprised if he still carries on with other women. Back then, Margeaux spent more time with her plastic surgeon and charity committees than with her son, and she hasn't changed.

Perception and perfection are everything to both of them. Alex said that even as a child, he never saw her unless she was perfectly coiffed, as she was each morning for breakfast. He was rarely allowed in her bedroom, which was separate from her husband's. Nannies raised him, and because Margeaux preferred things done a certain way, including child-rearing, when a nanny didn't meet Margeaux's expectations or got "soft," she was immediately replaced. Once he became a teen, Alex learned to manipulate the nannies into getting whatever he wanted, including alcohol and pot, by threatening to have them fired. With parents like his, it's a wonder he's successful and not living in the streets, addicted to heroin.

During our early years, family friends would comment on how lucky I was to have a man so committed and handsome. I'd heard stories and seen the faces of women who tried to bed him when I wasn't around. When they noticed me coming, they would throw in some sticky-sweet compliments about me. I saw right through them. So did Alex. He knew women wanted him because he was a Montgomery. Alex has always been a charmer. He relished the attention he received, but I never imagined our lives would turn out this way.

I can't understand why he wouldn't come clean about Jack. Maybe if he'd told me about his affair in the beginning, things might have turned out differently. But all the years of unhappiness and all the dishonesty, all the years of believing everything was my fault made forgiveness impossible. I should have left long before now.

Tonight, I'll sleep. Tomorrow, I'll start the process of letting go.

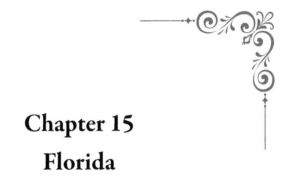

Chapter 15
Florida

Sounds of clattering dishes and smells of bacon rouse me from deep, disorienting sleep. Alex has always enjoyed getting up early on Sundays to make breakfast while I sleep in. Waking to the noises and smells of food being prepared takes me back to Franklin, to my little bedroom off the kitchen of my grandmother's house. She, too, let me sleep in on Sundays. She took pride in making sure I woke up to a huge breakfast before church. Some Sundays, my father would come by to see me.

Florida sunbeams peer through the parted sheers, bathing the room in morning light. God, how I miss my grandmother, and how I'll miss this house. Downstairs, Alex speaks softly to Jack. His words emanate patience and love. If things were different, I would be honored to eavesdrop.

Still wearing last night's clothes, I sneak down the stairs, past the kitchen, to the master bath to shower. The bright white bathroom is nearly large enough to be a bedroom. Stepping onto the cold tile transports me back to a month earlier—to the hopeless place I was in when I first learned of Jack's existence. I step into the oversized shower, turn on the jets, close my eyes, and let the steam engulf me. Heat softens the edges, washing away the uncertainty of days to come. I hold my head back, letting the water rush down my face and transform me into someone brave.

I've been talking to God more and more lately. Once I'm settled into a new life, I plan to go back to church. There's no point in holding grudges. *Please, God, grant me courage now.*

I dress, dry my hair, put on face powder and mascara, then look in the mirror to practice a poker face before entering the kitchen.

"Well, there she is. Good morning, sweetheart." Alex is dressed in his usual crisply pressed white button-up with dark trousers, only he's wearing my apron over them. He comes over and kisses me on the head, then he eyes his son. "Say good morning, Jack."

"Good morning," Jack says in a timid voice. He pauses then speaks louder. "Good morning, um, Abby." He looks at Alex with wide, uncertain eyes.

"That's fine, Jack. You don't have to call her Mom just yet."

Jack hangs his head like he's let his father down.

"Where's Ruby?"

"Still in bed." He flips a pancake. "Girl problems." He makes a funny face at Jack. "Don't worry. She'll be fine."

My stomach twists as I think about how off she seemed last night. I take the stairs two at a time to her room.

"Lovie, you still have cramps?" Before she can answer, I touch her cheek and forehead and feel fire. "You're burning up." I rush to the hall closet for a thermometer then back to her room to take her temperature: 103.2.

"Lovie, wake up and talk to me. Tell me where it hurts."

She rolls toward me sleepily, her arms around her midsection. "My stomach."

This can't be period cramps. "Have you thrown up?" I take a breath to calm myself.

"I'll be okay. I need sleep." Her voice is weak. She is definitely not okay. She moans.

"Alex!" I yell while sprinting down the stairs. "She's burning up. We need to take her to the hospital."

"Don't be dramatic, Abigail. I'm sure it's just a bug. We've had cases all week."

"Don't patronize me. She's burning up and holding her stomach." Anxiety takes hold. *Five, four, three, two, one...* My arms tingle then go numb.

He tilts his head from side to side and squeezes my upper arms. "You're overreacting."

But I see the concern. "Go look at her right now and tell me that. Go."

Jack sits at the kitchen counter with a plate of untouched pancakes in front of him. His eyes are wide and worried. I reassure him and tell him everything's okay.

Alex heads up the stairs and returns almost immediately, carrying our daughter wrapped in her favorite fuzzy blanket. "I'm going to take her in to run some labs to be safe. Try not to worry." He grabs his keys from the wall hook. "You stay with Jack. I'll call you shortly."

He must be out of his mind. "I'm coming too."

"Meet me there then. I'll get her checked in." He's out the front door and heading across the driveway when he looks back. "And bring Jack."

Of course I'll bring Jack. *Does he think I'd leave him alone?*

"Jack, honey, let's get you dressed so we can go."

"I can do it myself. I'm eight." He's annoyed with me as if my presence is causing all this turmoil.

"Okay, then. Let's hurry."

At the ER, we're taken to the back. I immediately spot Alex pacing. His face is etched with worry and anger. He's never been one to try deciphering or untangling his emotions. Instead, he lashes out at anyone in his path. A wife makes for an easy target.

"Where is she?" I feign calm. On the drive over, I tried both grounding and deep breathing while Jack sat silently in the backseat.

Alex fast-blinks and purses his lips as if holding back from spewing his anger. He looks down at Jack as if he's forgotten the boy is here. "They're running tests."

"Why aren't you with her? What kind of tests? I thought she was only getting labs done." Nervous words spill out.

His fingers massage his temples, and he sucks in a breath. "I know this is difficult, but I need you to get ahold of yourself." His voice is stern, but steady, on the verge of eruption. "They took her back for an EGD. If I could be with her, I would." He snatches Jack's hand, disappears behind the nurses' station, and returns alone.

I follow him down the hall. "An endoscopy for cramps?"

"Her pain is higher up, more in the stomach region. It's been bothering her for weeks, even before Peru. She didn't tell us because she was afraid we wouldn't let her go."

Tears of guilt slide down my cheeks. "I had no idea."

"Neither did I." He pulls me against his custom-tailored shirt, and I let him.

This time, his musky cologne, and even the Cohibas, bring me comfort. He is the only person on earth who loves her as I do. He feels the same guilt for not realizing something was wrong. And I know something is very wrong. I lean in, letting him hold me while I cry. Our solidarity is short-lived. He breaks away, looks down at his tear- and snot-stained shirt, and shakes his head in frustration.

I walk to the waiting room at the far end of the hall and dig through my purse for change. The coffee machine delivers a sludge-filled latte in under a minute. Scalding liquid burns my lips and tongue but calms the shivering. If I hadn't been preoccupied this past month, Ruby might have told me something was wrong. If I wasn't roaming Europe or if I had talked to her more while she was in Peru, I might have sensed she was off and convinced her to come home. But I was wrapped up in my own world, too busy with Daniel. When Ruby was little, I had a sixth sense when it came to her health. I would wake suddenly and go into her room to find her shivering and feverish, her blankets in a bundle on the floor. I should have known about this.

I walk back to where Alex was standing, but he's gone.

"Mrs. Montgomery?" the nurse asks.

I nod.

"Dr. Montgomery is with Dr. Matthews. Follow me. I'll take you."

"Abby, have a seat." The unfamiliar older doctor gestures to the plush chair next to Alex.

Alex's watery eyes meet mine. His face is pale as if he might vomit or faint. His hands tremble. The air is heavy and stale in this uninhabitable room.

Five, four, three, two, one... I try to ground but can't focus. My peripheral vision begins to fade. The men shrink into oblivion. Everything goes black. Distant voices become muffled then muted.

The doctor kneels on the floor beside me. A pretty blond nurse leans down, close enough to kiss.

"What happened?" I blink, trying to remember.

Alex sits in the same place, with his head in his hands. He isn't looking at me. It's not true. None of it. I never heard the words, so I'll take my girl home. I'll make soup and crawl in bed with her. We'll watch reruns of *Gilmore Girls* and snuggle under fuzzy blankets until it's time to leave for college. A mother's love can fix anything.

Whatever this doctor told Alex, it isn't true. Smug and entitled, he even looks like a liar, like an older version of Alex. *Oncologist* is an ugly word. It's embroidered beneath his name. Grim Reaper is more like it. I don't want him anywhere near my girl.

"I'm leaving, and I'm taking Ruby with me."

"I'm afraid that's impossible. She's very sick—" Dr. Death grabs my left arm, and Blondie takes the right. "Let us help you up."

I hiss at them and jerk away. "Don't. Touch. Me."

"Mrs. Montgomery. Abby. I know this is hard to hear, but I need you to listen. We need to discuss treatment options."

My head feels funny, and my nostrils burn from the smelling salts, but I stand long enough to steady myself against the doorframe. Then I'm back in the hallway, walking on the sparkling tile floor. I put one foot in front of the other, rubbing my hand along the lemon-colored walls as I go. If I can't take her now, I'll come back. The hallway is long, and I don't know which way to go. I follow the bright light. That's where I'm going—outside, away from this. Away from Alex. Away from Nurse Blondie. Far, far away from Dr. Death. Maybe I'll be like my mother and leave everyone behind for good.

The sun blinds me and burns my face. Fresh air is even harder to breathe. I walk. I'll walk forever to get away from here. I grab the tree at the end of the lot and heave bad coffee and bile.

Run, Abby. Run. It's just a nightmare. None of this is real. It can't be.

Cars pass by, leaving traffic, noise, and congestion in their wake. It would be so simple to step out and end it all. But no, I have Ruby to think of. *Keep walking, Abigail.*

I pass shopping centers and Chick-fil-A. I cross the Salt Run bridge then turn onto King and pass the ABC store where Alex buys our wine. Then I see Theo's Diner, where we used to take Ruby for breakfast as a kid. I cross the King Street bridge, passing the sailboats docked in the river and the San Sebastian Winery. *Don't think of her. Not yet. Keep walking until you're safe.*

At the Bridge of Lions, I turn right, toward home. I walk along the seawall, past tourists. Their smiling faces infuriate me. I pass the National Guard headquarters and end up in front of my house. It's tall and white with blue shutters—"happy blue." Ruby chose the color when we repainted from "poop-brown." Alex wanted black, but Ruby begged for the blue.

No. Don't think of her yet.

The house is too close to the road, just as I thought years ago when we moved in. The backyard is great, though, perfect for entertaining. It overlooks the bay, with a pool right in the middle, and an outdoor kitchen and bar. I worried we wouldn't use a pool enough to justify the expense, but I was wrong. Ruby and Jess and other girls from school spend weekends here.

At the end of the dock, I lie down on the bare, splintering boards and look up at the perfect blue sky. Cotton-ball clouds hang down. A gaping gash forms in my soul. This is too big for proper tears. Maybe I'll bleed to death, liquefy, and slide between the boards bit by bit. Tears pour from my eyes, and I choke. Still, I laugh. I recognize the hysteria from clinical studies in a past life. I just left my sick daughter, husband, and his bastard son and walked the four miles home. I'm a monster. I should jump in and let all the salt in the sea fill my lungs at once. *No. You're stronger now.*

I'm home. Nothing can hurt me here. This is my safe haven—a place of books, coffee, teenage girls, and lovely conversations. Nothing bad happens here. Not ever.

I can think of her now.

Some early mornings, she and I watched sunrises then walked hand in hand around the corner, past the cemetery, down Saint George Street's uneven bricks, and through the gates to her little Catholic school. I want the time back.

Why her? Why not me?

I need to go back to the hospital. She needs me.

The dock shakes with approaching footsteps. He's here. He lies down beside me and takes my hand, then he looks at me with his red-rimmed eyes. He's about to spew poison. His lips part, and I brace myself.

"How did you get home?"

"Walked."

He exhales loudly. "Abby, I know how hard this is." He clears his throat then sits up straighter, all businesslike. "They've done labs, a CT, an upper endoscopy, and an endoscopic ultrasound. They've set her up with some powerful IV antibiotics and sent a biopsy off to be analyzed. The results will be in tomorrow, but Dr. Matthews is quite sure it's adenocarcinoma, an extremely rare form of cancer, especially in someone as young as Ruby. It looks like, at least according to the ultrasound, the tumor is limited to the lining of her duodenum. They'll do a PET scan and an MRI of the entire abdominal region to be certain."

I try to listen through my sobs, but the details don't stick.

"We're going to transfer her to Wolfson tomorrow. I've already set up a consult with Dr. Franklin. He's one of the best pediatric oncologists on the East Coast. Matthews said the protocol is typically surgery, which will happen fairly soon. They'll go in, clean out any of the areas that may contain cancerous tissue, then she'll probably get a few rounds of chemo to make sure any cells that may have been released into the bloodstream are eradicated."

I sit up and cover my ears, rocking back and forth, feeling the splintered wood pierce my thighs. *This can't be happening.*

Alex slams his hands down on the pier, shaking it. "Abigail, I need you to listen. Our daughter is sick, and she needs you. For Christ's sakes, get yourself together."

I try to stop crying and focus.

"As I was saying, after the chemo, she'll be followed for about five years, so lots of checkups and scans to keep an eye on her and make sure the cancer stays gone"—he looks out across the Intracoastal at the lighthouse then at me—"and it will. We have a solid plan. She's going to be fine, Abby. We're going to kick this cancer's ass, okay?" He pats my leg and rises. "Come on, I'll help you up." He pulls me to my feet, but my legs barely hold me. With his arm around me, he leads me to the house. Inside, he places three tiny pills in my hand. "Take these and go rest for a little while."

I wobble toward the front door. "No. We have to get back to her."

"You're not going anywhere like this. You're a mess. She doesn't know a thing. I told her I'd be right back after I dropped Jack at my parents." He hands me a glass of water. "Go lie down, and I'll be back to get you in an hour. We'll tell her together."

He's right. Seeing me like this would destroy her. I swallow his pills.

Within minutes, my head is pleasantly woozy. In the master suite, I pull back the corner of the comforter and crawl beneath thick gold sheets and drift far away—back to Positano and Daniel's tiny kitchen by the sea. Strong Italian coffee served in tiny white cups tastes like heaven. Smells of fresh croissants and sweet marmalade blow in with the cool morning breeze. In the lemon groves below, an overabundance of mammoth fruits grow. Juices pour out with the lightest squeeze—one lemon is enough to fill a glass. We'll have fresh lemonade every day. Ruby can spend her summers there with Daniel and me.

Morning sunshine beams through the window, rousing me. I'm groggy—and nude. My clothes are folded neatly on the nightstand. My mind races, trying to recall the past twenty-four hours. He was supposed to wake me in an hour. My head splits in two. *What were those pills?*

I yell for Alex and for Ruby. Then I remember. She's at the hospital. The force hits me like a steel beam falling from the sky. "My girl has cancer."

The words singe my heart and tongue. Hugging a pillow to my chest, I rock back and forth, gulping for air. The room spins, and I barely make it to the toilet. I wipe the sweat and vomit from my lips on an expensive white cotton monogrammed towel with a big *M* right in the center—a gift from the Montgomerys. *Fuck you, Margeaux.*

I rest my naked bottom on the edge of the tub. While I indulged myself in a frivolous European fantasy with Daniel, cells multiplied by the thousands and ate away at my daughter. The more alive I became, the more she died from the inside out.

Why would God let this happen? Tommy. My grandmother. I was just beginning to trust him again.

Ruby cannot die.

Please God, I beg you. I'll do whatever it takes. Make me suffer. Take my life. Take anything, except her. I'll give up Daniel and find a way to keep this broken family together if that's what it takes. Just give me a sign.

I reach for my phone to call Alex, but it's dead, and it's the only phone in the house. Why did we get rid of the landline? After throwing on yoga pants and a T-shirt, I head to the front door. I have to get to the hospital. My car isn't here. *Dammit! I walked.*

There's a note on the counter:

Abby,

Heading to the hospital. You looked too beautiful and peaceful to wake. Mark is bringing your car back at ten. We'll head to Wolfson as soon as we get the okay. You can meet us there.

Text me when you wake. Jack is with my parents.

All my love, Alex

I rummage through my bag and find my phone charger. Mark will be here in forty-five minutes. When I have enough of a charge, I try Alex, who doesn't answer. Then I call the hospital. Ruby has already been discharged. After texting Alex, I stare at the phone, waiting for a response. He texts back. They're on their way to Wolfson. He's riding with Ruby in the transport and says I should just meet them there. I try his number over and over, but he doesn't pick up.

Why the hell won't he answer? Ruby has to know she has cancer by now. She must be devastated, and I'm not there. I can't stop crying. I wash my face, pull my hair back, and go into her room to collapse on her bed. With her fluffy comforter all around me, I take in the sweet smell of my girl, coconut and a little lime. Her room has hardly changed in the past few years. The walls are still the crazy colors she chose as a freshman—aqua, pink, green, and yellow with sheer white flowy curtains toning down the brightness. I fill her crazy, colorful backpack with underwear, pajamas, fluffy socks, deodorant, a hairbrush from the vanity, and her favorite pillow that she takes everywhere she goes. I grab her lime toothpaste and toothbrush from the bathroom and tuck them into the side pocket of her pack. Then I make coffee. I'm still nauseated, my head aches, and I'm groggy from whatever pills I took.

By nine forty-five, I'm caffeinated and less woozy. I pace, compulsively looking at my now fully charged phone. Mark should be here any minute with my car. I check my emails, and there are two from Alex, one from last night and one from the night before.

Abby,

First of all, I'm so happy you're home. I've waited patiently for you, and seeing you tonight, walking through that airport toward our family, made me happier than I've been in quite some time. I can't believe the four of us are finally together as a family. You'll adjust to having a little boy in the house, I promise. He's easy to love. Of course he is—he's my son. Our son now! I would be happier if you were in bed beside me. Because you were exhausted, I took the liberty of unpacking your things and came across some clothing I don't recognize. White silk panties that I've never seen before. They're not your style. Where did they come from? I have to tell you seeing them in your backpack was like a punch in the gut for me. By the way, I can't believe you're still using that filthy thing. Apparently, you still don't believe it makes you look homeless.

Also, I didn't want to bring it up when I first saw you, but where did you get the necklace you're wearing? I don't recognize it, and the way you kept touching it seemed strange to me. I didn't see a charge on the credit card, so I'm genuinely curious. Not accusing you of anything, but look at it from my perspective. You coming home with sexy lingerie and new jewelry with no record of charges seems suspicious. You understand, right? I'm afraid my mind will go all sorts of places the minute my head hits the pillow. We'll talk about everything tomorrow.

Good night, my love,

Alex

I don't have the mental energy to dwell on Alex's accusations or behavior, so I delete it and move on to read the second message.

Abby,

I know this is a difficult time, but I need you to keep it together. Our girl will be fine. She is the best of both of us. Strong and genetically gift-ed like me, beautiful like you. She is in the best possible hands, and you know I will scrutinize every test, treatment, and medication. I promise you I will protect her every step of the way. Let us all do what we're trained to do. You should focus on things you can control.

With that said, I've been quite lonely without you and would like for you to start showing me some affection. There's a long road ahead of us, and we will face everything as a family. Ruby knows how much you love her, but honestly, I'm not feeling it. You tensed up when I tried to hold you last night. Did you think I didn't notice? For the sake of every-one, we need to be united now more than ever. And I understand under the circumstances that will take time. I'm hurting as much as you, but we should be comforting each other as married couples do during times of crisis.

I'm looking at you right now, lying in our bed, and it's taking every-thing I have not to crawl in bed beside you. You're so beautiful, even at your age, maybe even more so than when you were younger. I've missed you desperately. You know that my physical needs are greater than most men's. I need release, especially during times of stress, and as a married man, I don't think my expectations are unreasonable.

I'm not trying to pressure you. I just don't want what happened all those years ago to happen again. Please don't assume I blame you, but it's not a complete coincidence that you weren't fulfilling my needs back then when I became vulnerable. I want us to move forward with complete transparency, and I know you want the same. I'm sorry if I seem insensitive. It's just that it has been a very long time since you and I have made love, and we need to reconnect. I'll try to be patient. Watching you and listening to you moan in your sleep is testing me for sure. I imagine you're dreaming of me, with my hands all over you. I want so badly to connect with you right now.

All my love (and lust),

A

His words bring horror. Without a second thought, I'm inside the shower. I let the steaming water scorch me, burning away every possibility and thought of Alex's hands on me. Mark will be here any second, but I take the time to scrub my skin until it is pink and raw and remain until the pain subsides and I'm numb. Alex can't hurt me. Weighted against cancer, he is miniscule.

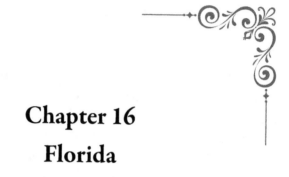

Chapter 16
Florida

Brightly colored kids' artwork and murals cannot disguise the children's hospital cancer ward for the hell it is. Suffering toddlers and teens in various stages of sickness warehoused in one place is enough to break the hardest hearts. After texting Alex, I pace the halls, averting my eyes as wheelchairs carry gowned children past. My denial is deep. I want no connection to these pitiful people. My stomach knots and trembles, and when the phone finally vibrates, I nearly drop it. *7th floor,* the message reads. I hurry past murals of happy circus animals and smiling Disney caricatures and arrive at a set of locked double doors. I hit the buzzer.

"Name, please," a voice says.

I respond, and the doors swing open. A plump, cheery nurse with a mouth full of overly whitened teeth greets me.

"Hi there, Mrs. Montgomery. We just got your little..." She pauses and gives a jolly laugh that shakes her entire body. "Well, not-so-little girl all settled in her room. Right over there." She gestures. "Room 716."

Her cheeriness is unappreciated. I thank her anyway.

Inside the room, Ruby sits in the bed, looking perfectly normal. For a split second, I imagine the tests were wrong. The bleeping monitors and IV lines snaking from her body bring me back to reality.

"Hi, Mom."

I wrap my arms around her neck, bury my face in her tangled hair, and try not to cry.

"Please, don't get upset. I'm feeling a million times better. Dad explained everything."

Alex sits on a blue pleather recliner in the corner, his legs crossed politely. Looking worn, he offers a weak smile. My stomach turns.

I sit on the edge of the bed and rub Ruby's twiggy legs through the blanket. She is the most important thing in the world right now. *Stay present. Don't think about last night.*

"How is she?" I ask Alex.

"She's good. No more fever." He pats her leg and leans up in the chair to stand. "Let's take a walk, so we can talk."

"Hello, parents. I'm right here," Ruby says, waving an arm. "I'm an adult. You can talk in front of me."

I know what she's doing—pretending everything is fine to protect me.

"You're right. Sorry, honey." He looks back at me. "So, the plan is as we discussed yesterday. Surgery first thing tomorrow."

"Wait, what happened to the second consult? With Dr. What's-his-name? I thought we were getting his opinion before we made any decisions."

"It's Franklin. I already consulted with him. He read the reports, saw the scans, and we spoke on the phone during the ride up. He was here when we arrived, so I met with him." He reaches across the bed for me. "Don't be mad, Abby. You weren't here. He agrees with the strategy John Matthews mapped out and is going to be doing the surgery. You'll meet him in the morning."

"What about the biopsy?"

"He's ninety-nine percent positive what the results will be, but the mass has to come out regardless. Look, sweetheart, I studied every test, every report, and I agree with both Matthews and Franklin. Surgery is standard protocol for this type of... issue."

"Cancer, Dad. Not saying it isn't going to make it go away." She looks to each of us and shakes her head. "You both need to like relax. I'm tough. I've got this." She looks at Alex then me. "Seriously, stop with the sad faces. You both look like you're about to have a nervous breakdown. I'll be fine. I promise. I'm a Montgomery, remember?"

We promise to do better.

Instinct kicks in, and I do what needs to be done. I spend the night beside my girl, tossing and turning in the plastic recliner. Dread and regret slosh around my stomach, churning with each flip. I shape and reshape the thin plastic pillows. Alex goes home, comes back, and leaves again sometime in the middle of the night.

Restless dreams have me drifting in and out of sleep and imagining I'm walking along the hills and trails on the Cliffs of Moher in Ireland, something I've wanted to do since I was a girl. In my dream, I look down at the angry sea below and lose traction. The grass is wet and slippery. I'm ill-prepared, wearing shoes with no grip. I slide down the mountain, toward the cliff's edge. My hands claw and dig, clutching at clumps of wet grass to hold on. But it's no use. The clumps break away, and I slide farther and farther, nearing the edge. At the last second, a patch of dirt stops me. In total stillness, I catch my breath and calm my nerves. When I finally get the courage to stand, I lose my balance and fall backward over the edge, onto the jagged rocks below. A millisecond before impact, I snap awake.

An unfamiliar voice startles me. "Good morning. Time to rise and shine."

Squinting against the blinding fluorescents, I see three men. A slight, dark-haired older one who is barely my height speaks. "I'm Dr. Franklin, and I'll be doing the surgery on Miss Ruby here." His voice is loud and more upbeat than necessary. "These guys"—he gestures toward the two younger, taller men, who seem fresh out of med school—"are here to keep me entertained in the OR." He laughs at his own joke. "This is Dr. Young and Dr. Zimmerman."

They give me apologetic looks, for their attending's poor humor, I guess.

"How are we this morning?" he asks me.

I push myself into a sitting position. *How the hell do you think I am?* "Fine, thanks."

"Let's wake our sleeping beauty and get her prepped. The procedure should take about four hours, and we'll have someone come out every once in a while to let you know how she's doing." He takes my hand and smiles. His voice is artificially cheerful. It must take practice pretending to be this jovial when you spend your days slicing open kids. "She's going to be fine, Mom. Don't you worry."

Ruby rubs her eyes, blinking herself awake.

"Good morning, sunshine," Dr. Franklin says. "Are you ready to get this show on the road?"

Alex appears in the doorway, holding two large cups of coffee. He sets them down and reaches for Dr. Franklin's hand. "Good morning, sir." He nods at the other two lesser men, lowly residents for sure.

"All right, then, Alex, Abby. I'll take the absolute best care of her." He looks at Ruby. "We'll see you very shortly, young lady."

"Okay. See ya." Ruby yawns and waves at him. "That coffee smells really good, Dad. Can I have some?"

"No," we say in unison.

"I'm kidding, guys. I'm not an idiot." She smiles a sleepy smile. "Good morning."

"How you feeling, honey bunny?" Alex asks.

"Great. Can't wait to get this over with." Her cheerfulness is forced and fake, something she always does when she's nervous.

I thank Alex for my coffee and take small sips, burning my already-scorched lips and tongue. The nurses come in carrying a blue surgical cap and matching gown for Ruby. They get her changed and jostle the leads and IV lines through the gown while I wait helplessly. They change her bag of saline and inject something to relax her in one of the lines, even though she swears she doesn't need it. I wish they would give me the sedative too.

"Can I please go back with her, just until she's asleep?" I ask the nurse.

She hesitates. "Let me check."

"I'm not five." Already groggy, she slurs her words then laughs. "You're embarrassing me." She laughs again and looks up at me with bright eyes, more blue than green today.

A few tiny golden strands of hair hang out of the cap. I tuck them in and kiss her forehead. Her right hand is already bruised from the IV. The nurse returns with Alex, and I watch as he whispers in Ruby's ear.

A giant smile crosses her face. She wraps her arms around his neck and slurs, "Love you to the moon, Daddy."

"Right back at you, kiddo."

And I know he does. I see the love in his eyes and the worry lines on his forehead.

We walk to the crowded waiting area, where dads hold newspapers and Styrofoam cups of coffee, and moms wear blank stares. Older couples chatter nervously. One lady works a crossword puzzle as another knits. A young Hispanic couple pushes a sleeping toddler back and forth in a flimsy plastic stroller. We sit among the group. I guess we're now members of this club—one no one wants to join, with dues no one wants to pay.

Our lives will be different now. College will be put on hold. Ruby will have to wait until next year, at minimum. Cancer will take the main stage in all of our lives. I should have been more involved in this decision to operate. I should have researched these doctors myself, but I took Alex's pills and checked out. Now I have no choice but to trust him.

He disappears, and I'm just thankful he isn't beside me, trying to hold my hand or suffocate me with words. The waiting is excruciating. I will my mind to take me away. I think of Daniel. I'm sure he's wondering why I haven't called. I planned to be packed and preparing to move out, but I'm here instead. Forty-eight hours ago, I was in Europe. Now, it's a distant memory. A lifetime ago. Every hour or so, a surgical nurse comes out with an update. Everything's going as planned, just as Dr. Franklin promised.

At the conclusion of each procedure, the surgeon crosses the threshold of the room, and all eyes follow in anticipation. Some physicians kneel to eye level with sitting parents. Some stand, waiting for mere mortals to rise to their level. I wonder how Alex speaks to his patients' families. I bet he remains standing. Maybe pediatric surgeons are naturally more empathetic, or maybe they're more detached because they have to be.

I read their faces as they cross from the tile floor onto the carpeting. Most are all business, cutting right to the chase, explaining the outcome of the procedure in layman's terms. I study their body language and gaits. I watch their facial expressions and eye movements. After a few hours, I learn to predict when they come with not-so-great news. Their steps are slower, less deliberate, and sometimes, their thumbs rub over balled fists. Some swallow repeatedly as they survey the room.

I think of the men in dress blues, driving through military neighborhoods. The wives out on the front porch, watering flowers, look up at the oncoming car, their hearts in their throats. The children freeze like salt statues, waiting to see where the car stops, praying it keeps moving. *Don't slow down, not at my house.* They breathe heavy sighs of relief when the death messengers pass by. *Not today, maybe tomorrow or next week, but not today. Not us. Not this time.* Not like when they came to our house to tell us about Tommy.

I watch intently as a surgeon I haven't seen before gingerly crosses the threshold and enters the room of gloom. He stops quietly in front of the Hispanic family. They're oblivious, leaning into the stroller, passing Cheerios one by one to their toothless toddler. The dad shakes a fat set of plastic keys. The energy in the room darkens as eyes and ears rest on the couple, waiting for them to look up and face whatever news is about to come their way.

The surgeon glances around the room and turns back to the seated couple. "Mr. and Mrs. Lopez?"

They look up then stand, optimistic smiles on their faces.

"Can you both come with me?"

They nod and hastily pack up the baby things, still grinning. They don't know what's about to happen. But I do.

Dr. Darkness is about to take them to a tiny room far out of earshot from the rest of us. It'll be basic—a desk and a couple of chairs with tissue boxes all around. He'll have them sit, then he'll shut the door. With an apology, he'll wreck their world. He may ask a staff social worker to be present. If not, someone will be on the way. She'll help with funeral arrangements and transportation of the body. She'll answer whatever questions she can, but most importantly, she'll be the one to stay while the mother wails on the floor. Then she'll be the one to help get her up and back into the chair. She'll stay with the baby while the parents make the appropriate phone calls.

The Lopez family nearly breaks me. I'll never see them again, but for a short while, we were members of the same club. They've moved on to a different club—a club with no name. They won't get to plaster their car with childhood cancer survivor stickers. Instead, they'll buy the ones with angel wings and a memorial date. How strange that there is a name for someone who loses a spouse or a parent but no name for those who suffer the greatest loss of all. A flash of nausea hits me, and my face is suddenly damp with sweat. I run to the bathroom to be sick.

When I return, Alex is fully engaged in conversation with the surgeon.

"The procedure went well." Alex smiles at me, relieved. "Our girl is fine." He turns back to continue his conversation. Alex's sharp brows soften as they chat in doctor-speak, words I could understand if I delved far enough into the reservoir of my mind. But I'm tired and just want to see my baby.

The men shake hands. They'll come get us soon, to take us to see her. Alex's eyes are bright. He hugs me and pats my back in a congratulatory kind of way, as if this nightmare is over.

The recovery room is bright and artificially lit, with pale-blue curtains separating patients. The nurses' station is in the center. Pulse ox and heart rate monitors bleep from each station.

I spot my girl, and my face goes numb almost immediately. *Five, four, three, two, one...*

A nurse tries to rouse her. "Your mom and dad are here, sweetie pie." She rubs her arm.

Ruby rustles her arm away and groans. "My throat hurts."

"That's perfectly normal, honey. Let's take a few sips of water," Alex offers. "It'll help."

Ruby starts to cry. "It hurts. It hurts so much, Daddy."

"I know it does, honey." His face is pained. He rubs her arm then kisses her forehead before picking up her chart. "Can we get another five of morphine?"

"I'll have to check with Dr. Franklin," the nurse says.

Seeing Ruby does nothing to make me feel better. I should be relieved and grateful that the surgery is over. They said she would be okay. But just like me, it's not enough. I need her to be whole and well. Not suffering like this. I can't bear this. I bury my face in her hair, desperate for the familiar coconut scent, but my nostrils fill with hospital antiseptic.

"I'm here, lovie. I'm right here." And I am, in body. Inside, I'm barely hanging together.

She squeezes my arm, shaking and whimpering. She's half awake, half asleep. The nurse returns with a syringe and plunges it into the IV. Tension drains from Ruby's face as she dozes back off, and I begin to breathe again.

In the hospital cafeteria, Alex and I sit facing one another and share bad coffee and stories about our girl. I try to stay present, because nothing else matters in this moment.

"Remember the time she brought home a frog in the pocket of her uniform jumper and forgot to let it go?"

I squirm at the memory. "And I washed it."

"I'll never forget the two of you screaming and her holding the dead bloated frog out to me. 'Fix him, Daddy. Fix him.'"

"That was horrible, and I'm still traumatized by it. But my gosh, she was the most adorable girl, wasn't she?"

There's no question Alex would trade places with our girl in a heartbeat, as would I. I'm grateful that she has two parents who love her as we do. No matter how poor our relationship has been, I can't imagine a better father.

Once we run out of stories, we sit in silence. The uncertainty and unknowing hangs between us. What if she doesn't get better? What if the cancer comes back?

He takes my hand across the table. "She's going to be okay, I promise."

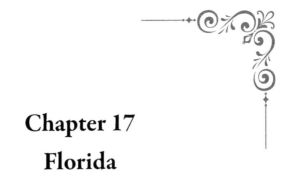

Chapter 17
Florida

Once the initial shock of being thrust into a whole new world of parenting a sick child wears off, Alex and I settle into a groove. We alternate back and forth at the hospital to be sure Ruby is never alone. I take the night shift so he can spend evenings at home with Jack and offer some kind of normalcy in the boy's life.

Ruby surprises us all with her remarkable progress and cheerful disposition. The first few nights, she has a pain pump, which keeps her comfortable and loopy. I question every medication that goes into her IV and keep track in a small moleskin notebook that I carry. While she sleeps, I pore over medical journals, personal blogs, and every website I can find on adenocarcinoma treatments and outcomes. Thankfully, it appears her cancer is the intestinal, rather than the diffuse type, which means it's slow growing.

The surgery was a success, and after a few rounds of chemotherapy, Ruby should be fine. She'll be followed for years, of course. And I will be there every step of the way. The way the nurses at Wolfson speak of Alex, I imagine he spends a great deal of time charming them. At home, he complains, but he knows they run the show.

Daniel leaves voicemails, which I ignore. None of this is his fault, but what if it's mine? I should have been stronger and never run off to Italy. Because I'm not prepared to speak with him, I send a text:

I'm sorry I haven't reached out or responded. Ruby is sick, and we've been in the hospital. She has cancer. She had surgery a few days ago and will be okay, but it's going to take time. I've been a mess, as you can imagine. She got sick the morning after I got home, and it's been pure hell ever since. I hope you can understand this, but I'm going to need some time to focus on her. I'll be in touch when I can.

There's so much more I want to say but can't. I want to tell him I love him and need him. I want him to get on a plane and fly here to be with me. He would come if I asked, but what would that do? Alex and Ruby have no idea he exists or that I planned to file separation papers by now. Plus, I made a promise to God to do whatever it takes to keep her alive. I don't know what I'm supposed to do. I keep praying and looking for signs.

I find the courage to listen to one of Daniel's messages.

"Hey, Doc, it's me." His deep, soothing voice drags out the *hey,* and those few words are enough to make me ache for him. "I'm so sorry about your girl. I'm happy she'll be okay. But damn, I wish I could be with you right now. I know you said to give you space, but I'm worried." There's a long pause. "I'd really like to hear your voice. I'm back in Switzerland. I took that assignment you scouted with me. I'll have my phone on day and night, so please call me back." He hesitates then sighs. "I love you, okay? Don't forget that."

His voice is like a hot bath on a frigid day. I delete the message and the previous three unopened ones as well, then I collapse into a heap and cry. The guilt of ignoring him sends me into a near panic attack. I love him so much, but in reality, what does love matter? It's a verb. It's just a feeling. I need to focus on my daughter. She's what important. I know it's wrong to disregard his heart. He gave it away, only to let me shatter it. Losing me is nothing compared to what he's lost in his lifetime. I'm a speck of dust on the radar.

It is only on the dock beside the water that I feel whole and grounded. Out there, beneath the sun and seabirds, I rewind and imagine earlier years with Alex at work and Ruby still in primary school. Life is as it should be for a moment.

Jack spends his days with Alex's mother. Margeaux despises germ-filled hospitals, and Richard can't be inconvenienced with what little time he has between business trips. Alex makes excuses for them both, but it's obvious he's hurt by their absence.

The day before Ruby's release, Alex and I are alone together for the first time. I bring up the night that continually resurfaces in the corner of my mind—the night he gave me the pills.

"You seriously think I'd have sex with you while you were passed out? Oh, sweetheart, don't be ridiculous." He puts his hand on my shoulder, and I jump. "I removed your clothes because I didn't want you ruining the new sheets I bought to surprise you. They're Italian linen woven with real gold." He hangs his head sheepishly. "But you didn't even notice."

I want to believe him. I really do.

Alex is making an effort to change. On days I'm with Ruby, I come home to a prepared plated dinner in the refrigerator. He's been respectful. He brings red roses as a kind gesture, which just serves a reminder of the disconnect between us. I've never liked roses. They're too much of a cliché. I gave up telling him years ago. I try to be comfortable around him, but even his casual touches during conversations make me shudder. Being under the same roof with him feels like betraying Daniel.

At home from the hospital, Ruby sleeps soundly in her own bed. When I check in every hour or so, I watch for the rise and fall of her chest, grateful to begin putting this cancer nightmare behind us. Her friend Jess visits often, and even though I try to keep the visits short so Ruby doesn't get overtired, I ultimately give in and let Jess stay. Ruby's spirits are always highest when Jess is around. At night, when the house is quiet, Ruby's fear of the future sets in.

"What if Harvard doesn't hold my spot?"

I reassure her, even though the thought of her living twelve hundred miles away knots my stomach. "We spoke with the dean of admissions, and your place will be there when you're ready."

"What if I'm never ready?"

"Then you'll live with me until you're an old woman. It'll be great. We'll make loads of snacks and watch *Gilmore Girls* reruns every week."

That makes her smile.

Jack has become more and more attached to Ruby. Several times during the night, I've found him curled up on her floor with his pillow and blanket. He knows he isn't supposed to get too close with his kid germs.

Chemotherapy is brutal. It sucks light from her eyes and life from our souls. For weeks, she's sweaty and limp. The vomit, diarrhea, and mouth sores are endless and leave us united in our helplessness. No matter what we prepare for her, she cannot eat. When she does, it comes back up or out. After the second treatment, I find her in her room, clutching a handful of her own long golden hair.

She asks me to shave it for her, so I swallow hard against the lump in my throat, then run Alex's electric shaver across my daughter's scalp. To try to cheer her up, I start with the sides and give her a mohawk.

She surveys the new look in the bathroom mirror. "Maybe I'll start Harvard next year like this."

"I think you'd start a whole new trend."

When she's tucked back into bed, I sob into my pillow so that she won't hear me.

Recovery from surgery was the easy part of our cancer journey. Each time Ruby gets her strength back, it's time for another round of chemo, and I don't know if I'll survive it. Alex is strong while I am weak. There's no way I could get through this without him.

"Three rounds is enough," Alex promises. Because I worry he's letting his heart interfere with his judgement, I ask for a private consult with Dr. Franklin, who reassures me Alex would never convince him to change protocol. Franklin is one of the top oncologists in the US. I know this.

In between the agony, we have endearing moments. Alex is supportive and kinder than ever. We're united for once with the common goal of getting our daughter healthy again. Once that happens, I'll revisit my own needs, but until then, I will spend every second with the family that I have, even Alex and Jack. When friends visit, Alex plays the perfect host, husband, and cancer dad. He fawns over me.

"Sweetheart, can I get you another glass of wine?" or "Sweetheart, what would you like for dinner this week?" Either he's a great pretender, or he's become the husband I always hoped for.

On the fourth day after the final chemo treatment, we have a handful of friends and family over for an impromptu gathering. Ruby's feeling better and wants to celebrate the milestone. Her eyes seem even bigger and more vivid since we shaved her head. Her wavy blond locks used to dominate her features, but now her eyes take center stage. We have so much to be grateful for. For the evening, our home overflows with laughter and love.

From the living room, watching him among our children and guests, I can't help but think how easy it would be to slip back into this role as wife and mother permanently. Jack is settled and glued to my side, despite my aloofness. He, Alex, and Ruby are inseparable. Not that I had any doubt, but Alex is a terrific parent to Jack, just as he has been to our daughter. I am the only one out of sorts, the piece of the puzzle that has never fit quite right. Maybe I've been the problem all along. Could his controlling behavior and lack of respect be my fault after all? Can I forgive him? Can I erase memories of Daniel and find a way to start over to keep my family together?

Chapter 18

Florida

In the guestroom bed that night, I think of my bargain with God. I begin and delete a dozen different emails to Daniel. But how can I explain something I don't fully understand? Wouldn't God want me to be happy? I've still seen no signs that giving him up or that staying here in this house is the right decision. Unless, of course, I account for the happiness of my daughter, her father, and his son. Maybe that should be enough.

It has been nearly three months since I've laid eyes on Daniel. During the day, I'm busy and able to push my feelings aside, but the nighttime is different. When I close my eyes, the only way I'm able to fall asleep is to pretend he is there with me.

The following afternoon, Alex is in his leather chair in the study, with a bourbon in his hand. He's relaxed, and it seems, from earlier comments, he thinks we're back to normal.

He's evaded my answers for too long. "Why did Jack's mother leave without a fight?"

The softly lit brass table lamp lights his face. I study him. His eyes narrow, and his jaw sets the way it used to. He sits up straighter, emboldened with pride, and makes a little condescending sound without opening his mouth. It's in that moment, before he even speaks, that I know the old Alex is still there. He hasn't changed at all.

"I made her an offer she couldn't refuse."

"What does that mean exactly?"

"She wanted to live in Paris. I made it happen for her."

"But why wouldn't she take Jack?"

"That wasn't an option. The boy needs a stable life, and she can't give that to him."

"Alex, you separated a child from his mother. Do you know what kind of damage that's going to do? How much damage it's already done?"

He tilts his head and smiles. "Sweetheart, he doesn't need her. You're his mother now."

Alex hasn't changed at all. This is the sign I've been waiting for. As horrible as I feel about it, I cannot be Jack's mother. And I cannot be Alex's wife. My decision has nothing to do with Daniel. Pushing him away has hardened my heart to the possibility of ever having that kind of love again, but my priorities are straight. Ruby came first, but now, she is healing. Her cancer changed us all, but not enough to make me stay in this house of lies. I hope that God will understand.

Without telling anyone, I secure a neglected rental cottage on Vilano Beach the following day. I didn't think it would happen so quickly, but I saw it on Facebook Marketplace and didn't want to lose it. I plan to stay in St. Augustine until next year, when Ruby is one hundred percent and leaves for college. The six-hundred-square-foot wooden beach cottage resembles a tiny yellow box. It has a single bathroom and two bedrooms, both smaller than the Marine Street closets. The salt air has wreaked havoc on everything metal. The owner, Miss Gail, a snowbird from New York, and I agree on five hundred dollars per month if I oversee repairs. She spends half the year in a house next door and says I'll be doing her a favor. She bought the place for her daughter, hoping to entice her to move here, but it didn't work out. We shake on the deal.

At the Marine Street house, I walk across the backyard and sit down in the sand to face the ocean. The sun is high, and the sky a perfect shade of blue. Alex and Jack are gone for the day, and Ruby is with Jess. My stomach knots at the thought of telling everyone, but my decision feels right. I'm taking a step forward on my own without anyone's approval.

For the first time in more than two months, I dial Daniel's number. I have no idea what to expect or if he'll even talk to me. Thoughts of our time in Europe has held me together most nights. I relived our time in Italy and our trips to Paris, Amsterdam, and Switzerland. On so many nights, I've dreamt of him just showing up and sweeping me off to an alternate reality where Ruby is completely healthy and off starting a new life in Boston.

Daniel doesn't answer. My heart sinks at the recording letting me know the number has been disconnected. He probably left a new number in one of the voicemails I deleted, but I will never know. I shouldn't have ghosted him. It wasn't fair. I vanished from his life the way my mother and Tommy disappeared from mine. I know what that feels like. I should have talked to him and tried to explain how conflicted I was about staying for Ruby's sake. Maybe he would have understood if only I'd given him the chance.

I grieve the loss as if it's forever—because maybe it will be. Maybe the whole point of us coming together was to give me the strength to get to where I am now. I've survived the unsurvivable, getting Ruby through surgery and chemo. And after nearly two decades with Alex, I am moving out. I can do this no matter how badly it hurts. I am strong.

I stand and dust the sand from my legs to head back to my car and home. My stomach rolls with a feeling I've gotten used to from all of the months of stress. The undiagnosed gastric ulcer I've been nursing with Pepto and bland foods is finally healing. The vomiting and cramping has stopped. As I adjust my T-shirt, I accidentally graze a tender breast. When it hits me, my knees go weak, and I nearly collapse back onto the sand.

Journal Entry
October 18, 1994

Dear Me,

It's been a while since I've written (I know I always write that), but I usually write when I'm bummed, so a long time between entries is a good thing! It means I'm happy. So many changes since last time...

I finished my first year at Vanderbilt's med school, had a great summer, and started my second, but... drumroll, please.

Now I'm living in St. Augustine (the oldest city), married to the hot resident I used to write about, and having a freakin' baby next month! I keep pinching myself, so I know it's all real. How's that for drastic? As soon as I'm settled with the baby, I'll be back in school, definitely this year. Alex thinks we're having a boy he already calls Jack. Watching a grown man kneel and talk to your stomach is the cutest thing ever.

A baby is a bit of an unexpected detour, but I'm rolling with it. Finishing med school will take a little longer, but I'll get there. Even though I'll lose credits from the first part of my second year since I was too sick to take exams, the credits from the first will transfer to UF. Alex is officially a board-certified MD with a job at St. Augustine Memorial, which is only ten minutes from our new house. He's really great and constantly brings home flowers. Red roses are such a cliché, but I shouldn't complain. He loves them. And at least they're not lilies. I told him all I think about when I smell them is death. Alex's family is well-connected and got him a job right away. They're incredibly happy to have him close. I don't think they're thrilled about me, but they try, and since they are the only family I have now, I try too. As an early wedding gift, they gave us an amazing historic house right downtown on the Intracoastal. Who knows if we'd ever be able to afford something so nice. I wish things were different with my parents. No one has heard from my mom in years, and I don't even know if she's still alive. I still haven't really forgiven my dad, not that he cares. With Tommy and my grandmother gone, there's no one important to me except for Alex and this baby. I'm going to throw everything I have into my own little family. It's all I need. We live in Paradise!

This is irrelevant and probably stupid, but I still don't know how I got pregnant. I know how it sounds, but this baby shouldn't have happened. I was careful every time, and the worst is I was planning on breaking up with Alex. Things weren't going well. He'd never admit it, but he was jealous of my job at Lulu's, the crazy popular place where all the Vanderbilt students hung out. In the beginning, he'd show up every night I worked, then spend half the night flirting with me, the other half flirting with other girls, some from class, some fellow residents. He did it to make me jealous. I'd see the way he'd make sure I was watching, then lean in and whisper in their ears, rub their backs, or touch them in some other suggestive way. I'd get mad but never let him know. If another guy flirted with me, which being a bartender, happened sometimes, Alex would appear out of nowhere, calm as could be, and make some comment like "Sweetheart, when we go home tonight..." to let it be known we were exclusive, which we really weren't. We saw each other at school and at other times. We ate and slept together a few times, but I didn't actually think we were a thing. I assumed he was dating other women, and I was too busy to be a full-time girlfriend. But he was charming and persistent, I think mainly because I didn't give him the attention he wanted. He liked the chase.

Once he convinced me to be his girlfriend, he tried to get me to quit my job, even offering to pay my rent. When that didn't work, he begged me to move in with him. He told me I wouldn't have to work and could focus all my energy on school. He said he had more than enough money between his salary and the trust fund that had been left to him by his grandfather. But I worked too long and too hard both mentally and physically to become dependent on anyone. I manage with school and work and have overcome the stupid panic attacks and blues that plagued me when I was young. My life was exactly the way I wanted it to be. I was taking care of myself. I loved my job at Lulu's three nights a week. Everyone was nice, and I had enough time to study. Once I refused to live with him, Alex stopped coming by, which was a relief. I was tired of his jealous games. Instead, when I got home at three a.m., I'd find him sitting on my front porch, waiting for me. It didn't matter that he had to be at the hospital by seven. He was always there, saying he couldn't sleep unless he saw I was home safely, but part of me wondered if he was making sure I came home alone.

As fate would have it, soon after I decided to break up with Alex, I found out I was pregnant. What I thought was a night of bad crab legs that lingered for days was actually a baby! Alex knew before I did. He went out in the middle of the night to Walgreens to buy a test, came back, and had me pee on the stick. The dreadful double pink lines showed up immediately. I was so upset, I couldn't stop crying. Alex was thrilled. He promised me everything would work out, but I didn't want to hear it. It didn't make sense. We used condoms every single time. He called it a miracle. I said it was a disaster.

I'm telling myself it was divine intervention, but the tiniest part of me wonders if he tampered with the condom. I know how that sounds. A few days after I found out, I emptied the bathroom trash and saw a sewing needle at the bottom. I don't sew. I never have. What a ridiculous thought, right?

The important part is I'm incredibly happy. Now I'm married with a baby on the way. Alex was right. Everything worked out.

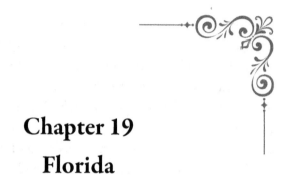

Chapter 19
Florida

Was my last period in Rome or Paris? Definitely not Paris. I would have remembered if I'd had it with Daniel. *There was a small amount of spotting at the hospital with Ruby, but does that count? Oh God! Five, four, three, two, one...* During the drive to CVS, I suck in and exhale the longest, deepest breaths of my life and try to convince myself not to panic. I've been under a great deal of stress, and my cycle is usually in sync with Ruby's, but since chemo, she's been irregular. There's no possible way I can be pregnant, except... that last day in Amsterdam, we didn't use a condom. But I was on the pill.

Oh God! The night of Ruby's diagnosis—Alex's pills. But he swore he didn't touch me, and there were no signs other than waking without clothes. I can't breathe.

Clinging to a triple pack of tests in my shaking hands, I head for the checkout and pray I don't run into anyone I know. The cashier smiles as she picks up and scans the tests. She's eager to say something but doesn't. I take my bag and head for the restroom at the front of the store. Thankfully, it's empty.

Inside the handicapped stall, I cling to the box and close my eyes.

Dear God, I know we just started talking again, and that I've asked for so much lately, but I need one more favor. Please don't let me be pregnant. Amen.

I carefully open the package, pee on each of the three sticks, then line them up on the edge of the sink and wait. The instructions say three minutes, and I try not to look. After one minute, *pregnant* appears, faintly. I watch impatiently for the word *not* to surface. I shouldn't have looked yet. I turn away and wait the full three full minutes. *Pregnant* is big and bold on each stick. *Dammit!*

There is a baby growing inside of *me*—a thirty-eight-year-old soon-to-be-divorced medical school dropout with no means of supporting myself or a baby—a baby I don't even know the paternity of. I dig deep for the strong girl I used to be, for the one I thought I'd rediscovered. She appears every once in a while, and I need her now. Ruby is better and will be on her own in a year. I've finally taken the first steps toward my future. How will I handle raising another tiny human? I've made some questionable decisions lately—starting a relationship without officially ending my marriage and, worst of all, allowing myself to be vulnerable around Alex. *Why did I take those pills from him?*

The strong girl surfaces. No matter what, I'm having this baby. I don't know how I'll manage, but I will. First, I need to figure out how to explain everything to Ruby.

After a good cry and a quick drive, I find myself sitting in the office of my ob-gyn. Imagined reactions from both Alex and Daniel haunt me. Alex will use the baby to try to trap me. I have no idea how Daniel will feel if I ever speak to him again. Maybe he's moved on and is in a rebound relationship by now. Out on the boat with friends and a new girl. Or maybe with Emanuela. I remember the way she looked at him. But if this baby is his, he'll want to be involved, no matter what, though.

After having my vitals taken and giving a urine sample, I disrobe, slip into a pink paper gown, and sit on the exam table. I've known Dr. Kym both socially and professionally for nearly a decade. Years ago, she attended Christmas and social functions at our home, but for the past two or three years, she's been absent from our lives. I used to worry that Alex convinced her I was crazy or that maybe he tried to hit on her. Dr. Kym is tall with beautiful dark hair and porcelain skin. Being an MD makes her Alex's intellectual equal and, therefore, a challenge.

"Well, well, I was about to ask how you've been, but I can see right here." She looks down at the chart, breaks into an enormous smile, and hugs me. "Looks like some big congratulations are in order." She gauges my expression, and her smile fades. "Oh, no, is this not good news? I'm so sorry, I assumed..." Her short wavy hair swishes back and forth as she shakes her head. Then she sits and places her hands over mine. "I'm an idiot."

I feel bad and offer her a smile. "No. It's fine."

"Abby, tell me what's going on." A surprised look comes over her. "Or don't. I'm so sorry, again. I don't mean to pry." She fumbles for the right words, and her genuine warmth makes me feel like I can trust her.

"I do want to tell you everything, if you have a few minutes?"

"Of course. I always have time for you."

Even though I know, I have to ask. "Promise me this will be kept in the strictest confidence."

"Oh, gosh, of course it will be."

I start from the beginning and tell her everything, including the story of Jack. I start to share Ruby's cancer diagnosis, but she already knows. We live in a small town with a close-knit medical community. Chatting with her is so easy. We talk about my imminent divorce and about Daniel. I avoid superfluous details. I tell her about my suspicions that Alex violated me and that no matter what, I want to keep this baby. For a few minutes, we are still—two women from different backgrounds, with vastly different life circumstances, crying together.

We look at a calendar and try to determine a conception date. She marks the days I was away and with Daniel and puts a question mark on the dreadful day I found out about Ruby's cancer.

"Let's take a walk next door and take a peek at the baby. What do you say?"

With knots in my stomach, I nod. "I'm worried because I've been really bad about remembering the pill, but I never stopped taking it completely. I miss a couple of days, then double up. Could the extra hormones harm the baby?"

"Honestly, it happens to so many of my patients, probably five percent or more." She places her hand on my shoulder. "Their babies have all turned out perfectly healthy."

The ultrasound room is no bigger than my bathroom. The slate-gray walls are bare, with no pictures of babies or posters advertising treatments or drugs of any kind. Dr. Kym squeezes the warmed gel on my abdomen and slides the wand back and forth over my slightly swollen belly, the one I thought resulted from my baking efforts meant to entice Ruby to eat. After a moment, an amplified noise screeches like a band's floundering sound equipment. Then I hear *thump-thump, thump-thump*. Our eyes meet, and we both smile as she moves the wand, clicking along the way, measuring the limbs, the heart, and all of the vital organs.

"Look at that little nose." She points to the screen.

I see a face, tiny lips, and nose. The advancement in technology from seventeen years ago is astounding.

"This appears to be a perfectly healthy baby to me. Would you like to know the gender?"

"No."

She takes measurements as I hold my breath. "Looks like you're about fourteen weeks along."

That doesn't help at all, and I find myself in tears again. The shock of pregnancy and the relief of knowing the baby is healthy leave me in a cloud of confusion.

"I'm sorry, Abby. I wish I could tell you what you want to hear." She stiffens and shakes her head. "I'll pray hard the baby doesn't belong to Alex."

The absurdity of her sentence makes me laugh. "Thank you."

She spins a small plastic wheel and smiles down at me. "Well, look at that, would you? Looks like this little surprise blessing is due right around Valentine's Day."

That does nothing to lift my spirits. "How could I not have known I was pregnant? Shouldn't I have felt fluttering or something?"

"Not necessarily. Every pregnancy's different, and you've been dealing with a lot. Plus you said you were vomiting quite a bit in the beginning."

"And I guess I have gained a few pounds. I thought it was from stress eating."

"Your weight is fine, Abby. Quickening usually starts between thirteen and sixteen weeks. I bet you'll be feeling movements anytime now."

In my car, I phone Daniel again, knowing I'll get the same recorded message. I dial his number again and again with the same result. I don't know what I would say if we did connect. I just want to hear his voice. I drop the phone in my lap and sob.

At home, I unlock the front door and call out to Ruby. No response. Alex and Jack won't be home for a few hours, so I'll use this time to talk to her. I find her in her room beneath the covers, with an iPad in her lap, listening to music.

Pushing aside magazines and books, I make a spot on the edge of her bed as she removes her headphones.

"You okay?" she asks.

"Hi, lovie. We need to talk." I rub her arm.

"Uh-oh. Sounds serious."

"It is." I gather my courage. "Before your cancer, you know your dad and I were having problems, and that hasn't changed."

"I knew this was coming."

This is so hard. "I was planning on telling him right when I came home from Europe..."

"But I got sick."

I nod and tell her about the beach house I rented and that she can come and go or live at either place until she leaves for school next fall.

Her eyes fill with tears, expressing what her words won't.

"I know how attached you've become to Jack, and I'm fine with you spending whatever time you want with him."

"This is because of him, isn't it?" A tear spills out, and knowing it's my fault hurts more than I thought.

I open up with her and tell her that things haven't been great for a long time and that it's no one's fault.

Her chin quivers. "I knew you weren't happy, but I thought... Why haven't you talked to me?" She raises her voice. "You keep everything to yourself."

I wipe the tears from her puffy cheeks and pull her to me. "I'll try to do better. From this day forward, I promise I will." She may be grown, but she's still Alex's little girl, and there are so many things she'll never know.

She swipes at my tear-stained cheeks then at her own. "Why can't we look like Rory and Lorelei when we cry?"

Laughing, I look at her red eyes then grab tissues for us both. "I have something else to tell you."

"Oh no, what?" She sits up.

"While I was in Italy, I met someone."

She tilts her head and grins. "A man?"

"Yes, a man."

"Okay. This is a little weird." She scrunches her nose, and I can see the confusion and conflict in her innocent mind. "Tell me, please."

She wants me to treat her like an adult, so here goes. "Remember me talking about my nonna's best friend, Francesca? Well, the man I met is her grandson."

She looks at me, waiting for more. "And?"

"I kind of fell for him."

Her eyes widen.

"When I left, I knew your father and I would never be together again as a married couple. I wouldn't have allowed myself to get involved with someone if I wasn't certain our marriage was over."

"Okay."

"Today I found out—" *Oh, God how do I say this?*

"What? What did you find out?"

"I'm having a baby."

Her shock registers. "Does Dad know?"

"No, and I'd like to keep it that way."

"Is it his?"

"No. Your father and I haven't been together."

She shudders. "Oh God."

I pray Alex was truthful and that my words are true. There's no possible way I could share my suspicions with our daughter. My job is to protect her when I can. Even through the smile, I see the disappointment in her eyes.

She lets out an exasperated sigh. "Do you need a lecture on safe sex?"

"I'm so sorry."

"Does the guy know? Did you tell him yet?"

"No one knows but you. Ugh. What a mess."

"Here, lie next to me."

She breaks into "Three Little Birds."

"Really, it is going to be all right," she says, caressing my arm as if she's the mother bird and I'm her wounded baby dove. "I know Dad has some control issues, and what he did..." She sighs. "Do whatever you need to do. I'll be fine. We'll all be fine, Mom. I just want you to be happy. If it's okay with you, I think I want to stay here for Jack. His mom moved away, and I don't want him to lose both you and me at the same time."

"How did you get so mature?"

She smiles. "I guess I was raised right."

I text Alex and ask him to meet me in the town square after work. A public setting, away from the kids, is a logical place to tell him I'm moving out. Ruby will take Jack and head over to Alex's parents' for the weekend to give us some time. I'll keep the baby a secret as long as I can. I don't know if telling Ruby everything was the right decision, but it's too late now. Besides, I'll be showing soon.

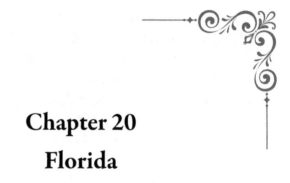

Chapter 20

Florida

On the gazebo stairs in the town square, I sit and wait for Alex. A cold front is coming in, making the weather unseasonably chilly for August. The wind is blowing, and the sun is setting, turning the sky shades of cotton-candy pinks and blues. It's nearly dark. Tourist season will be picking up again in the next few months with Nights of Lights bringing visitors from all over the world. The square and entire bayfront will be strewn with millions of white lights. Ever since *National Geographic* highlighted the event a few years ago, the number of tourists has quadrupled. Soon, the streets will be overrun with trolleys, horses, and carriages.

I hear his voice before I see him. A trail of cigar smoke encircles him.

"I'm here, Abby. What's up with this?" He stretches his neck to the side, flicks the cigar, and folds his arms defensively.

"Thanks for meeting me. Sit so we can talk." I pat the stair below me.

"I'm fine right here."

Knowing it's now or never, I begin. "Alex, you know things haven't been right with us for a long time, and we haven't been happy."

Shifting his feet, he drops then refolds his arms.

I continue. "I'm not saying it's your fault. I know I bear a lot of responsibility for the problems in our marriage. I keep going over that. Maybe if I'd been less needy, less fragile, you would have come to me about Jack. Hell, maybe there'd be no Jack. I don't know. But things are what they are. I've given it a lot of thought and have decided I want to move forward with my life."

"We are moving forward, Abby. Putting the past in the past. Starting over." He uncrosses his arms, tightens his hands into fists, and widens his feet to a battle stance.

Here goes. I'm about to knock him over. "What I mean is I want to move forward on my own." I swallow hard. "I want a divorce. I'm moving out."

He stifles a laugh then looks out toward the water and back at me. "Is this some kind of joke?"

"Alex, listen. I tried. I was going to tell you this as soon as I came back from Europe. But then everything happened with Ruby, and I decided to wait till she was better. I wanted to make it easier for her."

His expression flashes from fury to elation and other emotions I can't read. Spontaneous laughter erupts from him, making me thankful to be in a public place. He goes quiet again, and the wind whistles through the trees, disrupting the silence.

"Make it easier on her?" The words trickle from his lips. "By vacationing in Europe for weeks, coming home long enough to find out she has *cancer*, then abandoning her?" He pauses, narrowing his eyes at me. "You know she won't be living with you, right?"

"I talked to her, and she wants to stay at the house with Jack and you, for now."

"Of course she does. This is definitely all about what's best for her." He smiles. "You're just the doting mother, aren't you, sweetheart?"

"That's not fair."

"Fair? Hmm. Our family has been through hell. And now things are better. Our daughter is better. And you plan to just walk away? Not just from me but from our children?" He takes a deep breath then stabs me in the heart. "I guess that apple really didn't fall far, did it? Like mother, like daughter."

"I'm nothing like my mother."

He cocks his head to the side. "So prove it." After striking that blow, he softens. "Tell me, Abigail, haven't I done everything you asked of me? I've changed. Look at the space I give you. It's been months since we've shared a bed or even a kiss. Yet you're still punishing me. How many times do I have to apologize? What's it going to take to make you happy?"

"You're right. You have changed. And I'm not asking for an apology anymore. This is about you and me and a marriage that should have ended long ago. Maybe never even happened. I don't know. We raised a strong, brilliant daughter. She got sick." I swallow the lump in my throat. "And I'm so grateful that we were there together to see her through. But she's well again, and she's an adult. I can't stay with you anymore. I need to move on."

"No." He shakes his head. "I won't give you a divorce."

I take a deep breath and dive headfirst with a bombshell that's not entirely true anymore. "I've met someone else."

I hold my breath, bracing for impact.

He smiles again, leaning close enough that I can feel his hot, smoky breath on my face. "You must think I'm stupid, sweetheart. Do you think I don't know about your little travel companion?"

My heart pounds against my sweater.

"Former Sergeant Daniel Thomas Quinn. Let's see... He served four tours in Afghanistan, Baghdad, Turkey, and wait, wait..." He looks up. "Israel. That's it. Oh, and his tragic tale—his dead wife and son, burned to death, in an accident he caused."

"That's not true."

"Poor broken guy. Must be the attraction, right? The homeless, the old people, the battered women. You always did like lost causes."

Quaking begins at the center of my core and spreads outward to my fingertips and toes. All this time, living under the same roof, he knew about Daniel. The times I sensed the ghost of his presence. The fear. The cigars and cologne. Remembering a glimpse of a man I thought was him in Paris. He was there. He must have hired a private investigator to follow us and dig up Daniel's past. Why would he keep this secret for so long? Is he that patient and conniving to wait it out, hoping my relationship with Daniel would end? Did he hope in time I'd change my mind and stay?

"Were you following me?"

He doesn't answer.

"Alex, did you come to Europe?"

He smiles, and I know the truth. He was there. It wasn't my imagination.

"Please, Abigail." He shakes his head as if that's the most ridiculous notion he's ever heard.

Shivering, I stand both to appear stronger and to escape, but my legs are granite. Beneath the lighted gazebo, his eyes throw daggers at me. I sense the danger in staying and continuing this conversation. The last twinge of light has gone from the sky. *Where the hell are all the tourists?*

"Let me ask you something. Did sleeping with my wife fix him?"

I force my legs to move and walk away. But he keeps pace beside me.

"Leave me alone."

"I'm your husband. I'll never leave you alone. Where are you going to live anyway? Planning to run home to the daddy who never wanted you? There's nothing in your name, sweetheart. You have no money."

He strikes a nerve.

"I already rented a place. I'll be gone in a few days."

He steps in front of me, grabs my shoulders, forces me to stop, then holds me still. "Just stop. Please."

He won't hurt me. He's not a monster.

We've made it to the seawall near the National Guard Armory. If I screamed, the security guards would come running. I'm safe. The half-moon casts its light on the bay, and the sailboats bob in the water.

"And exactly how do you think you're going to pay for your own place?"

"I have some savings."

"Marital assets. I'll have everything frozen by morning. Credit cards, accounts, all of it. You want out, you leave with what you came with. Nothing. Well, I take that back." He looks up to think. His voice is calmer. "I'll let you have your clothes. Maybe you can sell them at the flea market up there on 207."

I try to step around him. His fingers dig to the bone. He pushes me up against the seawall. I cover my face and prepare for a blow. *Five, four, three, two, one...* My chest and throat tighten.

He lets go. His eyes are filled with hurt and regret. "I wasn't going to hit you. I've never..."

I lean over the seawall and gulp enough salty air to refill my lungs and brain. When I turn around, he's gone. He didn't hit me. I'm okay. I'm going to be okay. But I can't go home. The cottage isn't quite ready, and there's no way I'm involving anyone else. My Tesla is fully charged and parked on the street. The house is dark, but Alex's car is there. I imagine he's sitting in his study with a few fingers of Blanton's, smoking a cigar and contemplating his next move.

Parked in the driveway of my soon-to-be home, I recline the seat as far as it will go and try to sleep. I've always hated this car. Alex surprised me with it a few years ago in a grand gesture in front of many of our friends. He sold my old red Jeep without asking and replaced

it with this Model S. He at least had the decency to add my name to
the title, so hopefully I can sell it and buy something more affordable.
Despite the terror of tonight, the weight is off, and somehow, I allow
the sound of ocean waves to lull me to sleep.

I wake to the morning calls of hungry gulls hunting for breakfast
and step out to stretch and survey the tiny place that will soon become home. She definitely needs some more work, but the prospect
of moving in soon and living independently gives me a slight thrill.
A short walk on the beach clears my mind further.

Hopefully, Alex is at the hospital. On my drive to Marine Street,
I pray the house will be empty so I can slip in, pack a bag, and leave
for good. Alex's car is gone, thank God. I slip my key into the lock,
but instead of turning, it sticks. I pull out and try again. At the back
door, I get the same result. It infuriates me that he's had the locks
changed so quickly.

I ignore the camera above my head, pick up a small river rock
from the flowerbed, and smash the glass door panel closest to the
deadbolt. I reach through and unlock the door. Of course, the alarm
blares immediately. He forgot to change the code. I disable it and
sprint upstairs to the guest room, grab my old backpack from under
the bed, and fill it as quickly as possible. I run outside, pop my trunk,
and toss my pack inside, locking the car door behind me. Next, I dart
to the laundry room, grab a basket, and fill it with essentials for the
cottage. Two forks, two knives, two spoons, two plates, two cups,
two towels, a set of bed linens, a down blanket, and two pillows.

Adrenaline, along with the tiniest bit of exhilaration, surges
through my body as I rob my own house. Sudden terror seizes me,
and the hairs on the back of my neck rise. I sprint out of the front
door, leaving it wide open behind me, and race to the car.

Stomping on the gas pedal, I'm nearly to the end of the driveway
when the black Range Rover blocks my way. Through the rearview

mirror, we make eye contact, then he throws his door open and rush-
es toward me. My heart implodes. I scream.

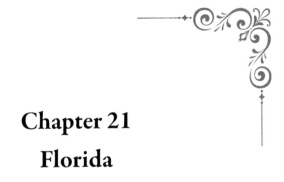

Chapter 21
Florida

In the driveway, my body trembles uncontrollably. Alex's fists bang on the car window hard enough that I worry it will shatter. "Unlock the door, Abigail."

I'm afraid and don't know what to do.

He scream-whispers, his angry breath fogging the window, "Unlock the fucking door."

I make my voice strong. "Move your car, or I swear to God, I'll hit it."

His jaw shifts as if he's grinding his teeth. "We need to talk."

"I'm leaving. Let me go. Please."

He takes a step back and bends to pick up a large rock, bigger than the one I used. After studying it, he narrows his eyes, contemplating his next move. He will bust my window, then what? My skull? Without taking my eyes off him, I dial 911. My finger hovers over the send button. If I press it, everything will change. I'll set things in motion that can't be taken back. The police will come and possibly arrest him. He's the chief of staff at our local hospital. The news will be everywhere. He could lose his job. Ruby will be humiliated. I need to be sure. Maybe I'm just overreacting.

He looks in the window then at the screen of my phone. "You think I'm going to hurt you"—he holds up the rock—"with this?" He shakes his head in disgust and lowers his voice. "I was thinking of how we chose these rocks instead of mulch. I never imagined you'd use one to break into our home."

He walks away with his head hung low and his shoulders slumped. After getting into his car, he backs up and lets me go.

I pull off on Avenida Menendez to calm myself. *Five, four, three, two, one...* Once I stop trembling and feel grounded, I replay the scene in my mind. Alex watched me break the door. Of course he was angry. All these months, he thought I was going to stay married to him. Our daughter won't be in the clear for a few years. There's so much stress on us all. It's going to take time for him to adjust to my leaving him. I say these things to convince myself he would never hurt me. He just loves me so much, he can't imagine being without me. There's no way he was following me in Europe. He couldn't have stomached seeing Daniel and me together. He would have reacted and revealed himself.

I spend the following day cleaning and clearing the cottage of all the debris left behind by the electrician and plumber. The landlady gave me three thousand dollars to update the plumbing, electric, and install new countertops.

"The work needed to be done anyway," she said. "You did me a favor by supervising."

I know she was just being nice.

Because of limited options, I move in before the work is complete. I phone Ruby to explain the circumstances.

"How upset was he?"

I spare her the details. "He's going to need some time to adjust."

"Should I sleep over at Grandma and Grandad's a few more nights with Jack?"

"Good idea."

"But I'm coming over to help you during the day, okay?"

I agree.

THROUGHOUT THE WEEK, Ruby helps finish readying the cottage without doing anything physically exerting. She fights me, though, insisting she's perfectly fine, but I win. We scour Craigslist and local thrift stores for secondhand furniture and get lucky enough to find a white slipcovered sofa just as it was being put out. I pour myself into renovations, trying to think only about the now. I hear my grandmother's words. *The past is the past. No sense dwelling.*

We paint the shabby old kitchen cabinets and dark wood-paneled walls a creamy shade of linen white. We buy bright white cotton sheers then marvel at the way the ocean breeze blows them around. For the living room, Ruby chooses an aqua-blue rug and tropical-colored throw pillows. Together, we transform the tired little cottage into something out of *Coastal Living* magazine with bright, fun colors Alex would never approve of. There's no dishwasher or dryer, and the crazy aqua-colored refrigerator and plain-white coil range appear to be older than me, but they work. Newly installed white Carrara marble countertops, deeply discounted remnants left over from a big job, make the biggest difference. Countertops and installation took up almost half the budget, but they're worth every penny. A rusted old bistro table and two chairs sit on a small patio outside the living room. Salt air heals souls but maims metal. I scrape away the rust and paint them bright shades of coral. Ruby ties two new aqua- and mango-colored cushions to the seats.

With everything complete, we sink into the new-used sofa and admire our hard work. We did it! Ruby and I renovated and decorated this little cottage in a short time, on a tight budget. The project was a great distraction for us both. The aftermath of cancer has drained us—her physically, me emotionally. But things are working out. My anxiety has quieted, and Alex seems to have accepted our separation. In the daylight, the future feels hopeful. In the night, the moment I lay my head on the pillow, sadness over losing Daniel slips in.

On my first evening alone in the cottage, the weather app confirms a nor'easter just off the coast. The sun has already set, and the wind has picked up, whistling through the palms. Angry waves pound the sand in the backyard, making me uneasy. I try oils, deep breathing, and meditation. This is my first time living directly on the ocean during a storm. The living room lamp flickers a few times then goes out, leaving me fumbling through the darkness, in search of matches. A panic attack looms. *Five, four, three, two, one...*

If only I could see. I find my cell phone and use it to light the way to the finicky kitchen junk drawer. After several tries, I'm able to shimmy it open and retrieve matches. I light the Yankee jar candles I took from the house and place them around the cottage. Their familiar beachside scent brings the slightest comfort. I wrap myself in Ruby's fuzzy aqua blanket and curl up on the sofa to practice breathing techniques again. This time, they seem to help.

In the darkness and solitude, I try to be brave and hopeful. There's nothing to be afraid of. Ruby is healed. Everything will be all right. I'm stronger than before and am going to be a mother again. Daniel and I once found each other thousands of miles and an ocean away. If we're meant to be, maybe he'll cross that ocean again and find me.

With the relentless wind howling outside, I climb into bed. The evil twins, melancholy and anxiety, take turns occupying my head. I shouldn't feel this way. I should be grateful for the blessings I have. But I'm the loneliest person in the world. For the first time, I feel the baby fluttering inside. With a medley of joy and sadness, I cry myself to sleep.

Through the unsettling darkness, Alex's eyes are upon me, watching from above.

It's only a dream. I blink my swollen eyes open and focus. Alex is there, towering over, watching me.

Panic seizes my throat. "Is Ruby all right?"

His eyes are distant and glazed. He doesn't respond.

"What the hell are you doing?"

He sits down on the edge of my bed.

Clutching the sheet to my neck, I scoot back against the wall.

His face offers no expression. "I wanted to watch you sleep, one more time." His voice is flat. He reaches for me, placing a hand on my leg. "I won't hurt you."

My insides knot as I plan an escape. My voice is high-pitched and all wrong. "I need the bathroom."

"Tell me the truth." He licks his lips and leans in with his reddened eyes. "Are you pregnant?"

The lie on my tongue would be easier, and it tastes right, but he must already know.

I nod, but it doesn't register. "Yes," I whisper.

He puts his head in his heads and rubs his face slowly, methodically. Then he pushes his hands through his thick dark hair and comes back to life. "It could be mine."

"No, it can't," I say, needing the words to be true.

He shakes his head. "Yes, it can."

His confession turns my insides to ice. I tremble. How much more can my body take? I close my eyes, praying he'll disappear, but when I reopen them, he's still there. "Get out before I call the police."

He snaps back. "Do it. What would you tell them? Your husband's upset because you fucked someone else, or because you lied about being pregnant and moved out?"

I think back to that awful night of Ruby's diagnosis. "I'll tell them what you did to me."

"First of all, sweetheart, you wanted me. You were in my bed, moaning and begging for it. When I got in beside you, your hands were all over me."

My voice shakes, but I scream anyway. "You're a liar. You drugged me."

"I gave you something to relax, Abigail. Big difference." He shrugs. "But call the police. Tell them what you want. You've been to therapy. There's a documented history of mental and addiction problems in your family. Think they'll take your word over mine?" He laughs. "By the way, did you think your boyfriend was going to come rescue you when he found out you're knocked up?"

I don't dare tell him Daniel doesn't know and that he's no longer my boyfriend.

"Next time you talk to him, if there is a next time, tell him the baby is mine." He turns on the light and holds out a manila envelope. "Also here, you might want to talk to him about this. I brought you a present."

"It's three o'clock in the morning. Just go," I plead.

"This can't wait." He sits back down on the bed and pulls out a stack of eight-by-ten black-and-white photographs. The first few are Daniel: him alone sitting at a table at an outdoor café, him leaning against a building, and him looking out across the street. The next is of a tall woman with shoulder-length light hair, an infinity scarf wrapped around her neck, wearing a short leather jacket and tall boots, coming toward him. In the next, he stands, arms outstretched. Then they're tangled together, embracing. His smile is big and bright. He looks happy. In the next, he's pulling her back, looking into her face. Then he's hugging her again. My stomach drops, and the baby moves for the second time. I flip through the images, tossing them aside as I finish. He's having coffee or tea then walking away with the woman. Next, they're going up steps, and finally, into a house.

Alex's eyes are on me. "Seen enough?"

I tear them from his hand in one swift swipe, knocking them to the floor. I will not show weakness by crying. I want to accuse him again of stalking me in Europe, but I can't. I just need him gone.

"Sorry to hurt you." Alex puffs out his lip in feigned sympathy. "I just wanted you to see the kind of garbage you fell for."

"Get out!"

"Don't be angry, sweetheart. I'm looking out for you."

"There's something wrong with you."

He pats my leg and smiles. "Just protecting my family." He winks then stands, looking around the room, a sour expression on his face. "You won't last long in this dump. See you, sweetheart."

He slams the front door and vanishes into the night, leaving behind the smell of cologne and Cohibas. My shaky legs take me to the front door, to lock the door. Like that'll stop him. Tomorrow, I'll change the locks and add deadbolts. Tonight, I curl into the fetal position, wrap my arms around my plum-sized baby, and weep again. Daniel didn't waste any time finding someone new. I figured he wouldn't, but seeing the proof guts me. Did I really think he would wait?

Chapter 22
Florida

Sunlight and the sounds of hungry gulls fill my bedroom and bring a new day. I wake as if Alex didn't break in hours ago, terrifying me and bringing proof that Daniel is with someone else. It's just after eight in the morning. I blink my stinging eyes to focus then grab my phone to check for messages. There are two from Alex. Feeling sick, I open the first, sent at four in the morning.

Abby, poor, poor, stupid Abigail,

What did you do? What the hell were you thinking? Slipping up and letting another man inside you! That's hard enough to forgive, but the possibility of his seed being planted in you sickens me! If this wasn't such a fucking tragedy, it would be funny. Do you not remember how babies are created? Were you so busy obsessing over me in medical school that you weren't paying attention, Abby? Was that the problem? I knew something was up. The way you've been acting since you came back, so distant to me! No wonder you wouldn't share our bed. Guilt was eating you up, wasn't it? You couldn't look me in the eye because you knew what you'd done. You've been knocked up and don't even know who it belongs to. I was so naïve thinking we were working things out. I don't understand how you could do this to me.

That stupid necklace. I should have known it was more serious than fucking. All those years I begged you to have another baby, and you refused. But you went out and fucked a stranger, and now you're hoping the baby is his. I can tell you it is not. I can feel it, and my instinct is never wrong.

I want to blacken the eyes that looked into yours and bloody the mouth whose lips you kissed. The rage in me is blinding. This is killing me, Abby. Killing me! How will I ever forgive you?

Shivering, I pull the comforter around me and force my fingers to open the second email, which he sent an hour ago.

Abby, my brilliant, sweet Abby,

I was awake all night when it finally hit me. You're hoping this baby isn't mine so you can get even for Jack. I didn't think you had it in you. Bravo! Very well played, sweetheart. I couldn't have thought of anything better. Whether or not this baby belongs to another man, I'm relieved. All this time, I was thinking you ran off and fell in love with someone (other than me) you wanted to share a life and child with. I cannot stop laughing at the absurdity of the whole game—ours, mine, and maybe just yours. Hilarious! I've had time to think it all through, and I want you to know, I forgive you. And of course, I still love you, more than ever actually. I'll even learn to love the little bastard if it turns out not to be mine.

Once it's born, we can do the test and go from there, but I won't give you a divorce. Not when I'm certain you'll change your mind, especially now that you need me more than ever. When you come back home, we can sort through everything. You can continue to stay in the guest room, for now. There will be no worries about me pressuring you for lovemaking in your condition. Even I have my limits. I promise to be patient, take things slow, and continue to give you whatever space you need. I just want you home with us. Please consider my words. You and the children are my everything, and I need us to be together as a family.

Love,

A

P.S. I pray you'll forgive my email from last night. I was typing out my thoughts and may or may not have been under the influence of fifteen-year-old Pappy. You know how I love my bourbon. Anyway, I should never have hit Send. Those were irrational thoughts never meant to be shared. You're the one who says getting private thoughts down helps. You know how I feel about the Hippocratic oath. I would never harm anyone.

I toss my phone and burrow beneath the blankets. After waking with him in my house and reading his twisted words, I don't know what to think or do. He was so angry. And he broke in. If I try to get a restraining order, it'll be his word against mine. His parents know all of the judges in St. Johns County. If he's told them about the baby, no one will believe anything I have to say. I have no choice but to move forward and try to forget this night ever happened. In the morning, two dozen red roses arrive. Into the trash, they go.

TWO WEEKS GO BY WITH no contact from Alex. Maybe he's worried I'll stain his stellar reputation by calling the police or his parents. I plow forward with my life, grateful for the silence and the new beginning. Beach yoga, meditation, and sounds of the ocean waves soothe my spirit. Staying grounded helps me delve deep and focus on my inner strength. I'm going to be a single working mother, so I'll need every ounce. To make a divorce happen, I'll have to file the legal papers on my own. Each attorney I've called wants at least five thousand dollars down, and I don't have that kind of money to spare. My savings is low. Thankfully, Alex didn't freeze the accounts as he threatened. I accepted a job for *Social*, a local magazine, writing short articles and taking photographs. The pay isn't terrific, but the hours are flexible enough to allow me time with Ruby and to volunteer. Thankfully, Ruby was able to convince Alex to give me my old DSLR camera.

During our travels, Daniel taught me enough, mainly how to use flash properly. I hadn't realized the difference a Speedlight made, so a few weeks ago, I bought one and have been practicing ever since. My photos are actually pretty good. Twice a week, Ruby and I volunteer at the Betty Griffin thrift store and at an organization called Pie in the Sky. We drive around our community, delivering fresh produce to food-insecure seniors.

Ruby spends most overnights with me and early evenings with Alex and Jack so she can help with dinner and homework now that Jack is in school. I'm grateful Alex doesn't try to dissuade her from sleeping at the cottage, because having her brings comfort. I know as long as she's with me, he won't show up unannounced. Newly installed double deadbolts and a do-it-yourself alarm system are extra reassurance.

"Dad says to tell you that he still loves you and wants you to come home." Alex only communicates through Ruby now.

I know his words tug at her because she doesn't know everything. I didn't tell her he broke in while I was asleep, that I think he was in Europe, or that he hired a private investigator. I let her think her father is a saint, because that's how a mother protects her daughter's heart. She tells me that Alex has become quite the cook. All the years of marriage, and he never showed any interest before.

"He's learning so he can spoil you. You know, in case you ever decide to go back."

"You know that's not going to happen, right?"

"I do. I just feel sorry for him sometimes."

I hug her. Her wishes are the same as his. She claims to understand the separation, but no one really wants to see their parents divorce. There's been enough upheaval in her life, and my claim to independence just makes things even more unsteady for her. I guess it'll be a while before I can lay down that guilt.

Some mornings before dawn, I sit with the stirrings of the new life inside me. It's then that I allow Daniel to flood my mind. When I wake, I sense him. When I drift off at night, I dream of how he loved me and the way his skin felt against mine. He's in my bones. We still lie beneath the same stars and moon. He is out there somewhere, even if he's with someone else. Maybe he's just filling a void. Sex and love don't have to be synonymous.

Alex's silence is out of character. I would have expected him to behave the way he always has, doing whatever it took to obtain his goal. Because he still hasn't tried to contact me, I imagine he's accepted our separation and is ready to move on with the next step, so I call him.

"I wanted to let you know I went to the courthouse and filled out paperwork on my own."

He seems genuinely surprised. "For what?"

"So we can get a divorce."

"Oh, Abigail, why would you do that?"

The call disconnects. When I redial his number, the call goes to voicemail. I keep trying, calling several times a day. When that doesn't work, I have him paged at the hospital. He finally agrees to go to mediation, but only to satisfy his parents, he says. Publicity from a messy divorce would be an embarrassment to the Montgomery name.

It takes dozens of phone calls to attorneys' offices, but I find someone willing to squeeze us in. Alex fails to show. He also ignores my calls and hospital page. Two dozen red roses arrive, with a message that reads, "Sorry I missed the appointment. Maybe next time. A."

The following Thursday, I'm waiting in the attorney's office. Once again, he doesn't show. I apologize and hand them my debit card to charge the three-hundred-fifty-dollar fee that I barely have. I'm livid enough to sit in the parking lot and dial Alex's number again and again. I send texts and leave voicemails that go unanswered. Again, he sends more roses, three dozen this time. This message reads, "I won't give up on us. A."

He's accustomed to the weak version of me and thinks I'll just give up on getting this divorce, but he's wrong. Living by the sea has a magical calming effect, and despite its age and state, the cottage finally feels like home. Life is moving along, and I'm mostly content, except like a bruise that won't heal. At night, when all is quiet, my thoughts still turn to Daniel. I Google him, and at first, I find nothing except credits for a few images. Daniel Quinn is practically a ghost. Eventually, I find a wedding registry listing his name and that of a Georgia Hart. Georgia, I remember, was his wife's name.

I search "Crosby Quinn" and get several hits, all about the accident. The first article is short, with basic information with no mention of Daniel.

A five-year-old boy and his mother were killed in a fiery crash on South Street in Manchester Saturday evening. The car was stopped on the shoulder for unknown reasons, when, according to a witness, a truck slammed into the car, pushing it down the ravine. According to Manchester police, the car burst into flames, immediately killing the occupants.

Police identified the deceased as five-year-old Crosby Quinn of Manchester and Georgia Hart, also of Manchester. Before police released the names, the Manchester Public School superintendent sent a letter to families, identifying one of the deceased victims as a current student of the district. The accident is still under investigation, and police are asking anyone with information to please contact them.

The second article breaks me:

At only five years old, Crosby Quinn's young life was cut short in a horrific accident over the weekend. Thursday night, hundreds of grieving community members came together to honor him. Crosby attended Manchester Elementary School. He was well-liked by the teachers and students, and tonight, some of his young classmates and their parents shared stories about him.

One classmate's parents tell us Crosby and her son were best friends. "He was the nicest boy, so polite and serious. He'd do anything for my son and any of his friends."

"It's hard to imagine that the little boy is gone. At least he's with his mother," said one of his teachers. Police tell us his mother was killed as well but his father survived the horrific accident, which remains under investigation.

Reading the words on my screen puts me right back in that kitchen in Paris, where I forced him to relive this hell. I see the agony in his eyes and his shaking hands. God, how badly telling the story hurt him. Right now, I wish I could wrap my arms around him and heal the hurt I added. But we can't be unbroken.

God and I are still talking, but lately, he's on thin ice. I spend the early evening on a blanket on the sand, meditating. It's hard but important work for my mental health. Tonight, Ruby is staying at Marine Street to help Jack with a science project, which means I'll be alone. I'm going to do everything I can to keep my mind calm.

Heading back to the house, I spot a fat manila envelope on the bistro table beside the sliders. Next to it is a small vase with a single red rose. The envelope is filled with ugliness, I suspect.

Pushing the curtains aside, I storm through the cottage, opening and slamming the doors, searching for Alex. "Don't play games with me," I yell, my Zen long gone. "I know you're here."

I return to the bistro table and sit. The cottage is empty. The envelope isn't. Dozens of photographs spill out onto the table. I choose one where Daniel faces the camera, though he doesn't see the lens. God, I miss him. I hold his face to my chest.

I lay it down and stare. In the next shot, he's on a park bench, coffee in hand, scarf wrapped tightly around his neck, looking very Italian. The background is familiar. I flip through the next few photos, same park bench, zoomed out a bit, a mosaic tile wall behind him. I study the buildings and the architecture. He's on a hill somewhere. For a moment, I can't place it. Then it hits me. He's at one of the most famous UNESCO sites I've seen in *National Geographic*—Park Guell. Daniel's in Barcelona with the same woman. She's dressed as she was in the other photos—in a leather jacket, infinity scarf, and big sunglasses. They sit side by side, in a repeat of the last photos. This time, though, something is different. A young boy who looks very much like Crosby runs toward them.

My pulse races.

Next, Daniel is crouched down, scooping up the boy. Then the woman kisses the boy's head. These must be from before. I flip the photo over, searching for a date, but my heart sinks when I find they're only a week old. Could he have another family? His constant travel would make it easy enough. But it seems impossible he would keep that from me, unless they were estranged. He walks hand in hand with this boy, carries him, and watches over him at the playground, with happiness beaming through his eyes. He's certainly involved now.

Five, four, three, two, one... It doesn't work this time. Before full panic sets in, I race across the sand, photos in hand. I hurl the pictures toward the ocean, but the wind catches them. They soar through the air, circling around and around until the tornado of truth swirls down upon my feet. With hurt too big to contain, I drop to my knees to cry, but I'm empty. Life is a continuous cycle of torment. How could he love me the way he did and keep this from me? It doesn't seem possible, but the proof is in front of me. I don't deserve this.

With the moon above me, I lie still in the sand beneath the stars, listening to the crashing waves, and remind myself how small I am in this big world. I breathe and wait for a calming numbness to flow through me. My ego begins to fade. I've spent a life allowing self-pity to rule. I've allowed the men in my life to determine my happiness, only to get crushed by them. I've built walls to guard my anxious heart and made myself believe I was unworthy of love.

I am good. I deserve better.

Leaving the scattered photos, I brush the sand from my body and go inside. On the ground beneath the table, there's a photo I missed. The three of them are going into the front door of a row house. Daniel unlocks the door. The house number and street name are visible, 208 La Rambla. I'm always looking for signs, and now there's one right in front of me. I've been waiting for months for him to reach out, and he hasn't. Even though I've left Alex, and Ruby is better, my life still feels unsettled. I love him, even though I lost him, and there's unfinished business between us, regardless of the baby. I know what I must do.

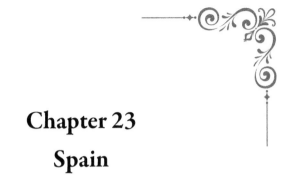

Chapter 23
Spain

With determination in my mind and fire in my soul, I will fly to Barcelona to see Daniel. I won't spend my life wondering about the woman and child in the photos. I want answers and cannot continue to sit and wait for something to happen. For once in my life, I'll be proactive instead of reactive. I'll lay it all out and tell him everything, about Ruby and about Alex. He deserves to know why I pushed him away in the beginning, and I deserve to know why he gave up so easily. I'll tell him about the baby. Hiding the pregnancy is no longer an option.

I text Alex: *Stop using our daughter to communicate. Stop coming to my house uninvited. If you want to meet, call and ask.*

Alex: *Did you get the pictures of Casanova?*

Me: *Stay away from my house.*

Alex: *Just come home, sweetheart.*

Me: *I'm leaving town for a few days, so I'll be dropping by in the morning to bring some of Ruby's stuff. Tell her I'll call her tomorrow.*

Alex: *Let me guess, going to confront Loverboy in Spain?*

Me: *I just wanted to let you know. Goodbye.*

The next morning, as I pull into the Marine Street driveway, Alex is sitting on the overstuffed wicker porch rocker with a cup of coffee in his hand. It's been nearly five weeks since I've seen him in person, and I do my best to hide my expanding belly. "Well, good morning, sweetheart." He raises his mug. "Want a cup? I just made it."

He does a double-take and averts his eyes from my stomach. "I've always thought you were most beautiful when you were pregnant."

"Where's Ruby?"

"Out like a light. Why don't you have a seat so we can talk?" He gestures to the rocker beside his.

I set Ruby's duffle bag down beside him. "No thanks. I need to go."

"Abigail, please. I haven't bothered you at all. I keep hoping time away will make you miss me and miss us. We all want you to come home." He uses the *we* to guilt me.

"That's not going to happen, and the sooner you realize it, the better off we'll all be."

He shakes his head. "I don't understand you."

"You never have. That's part of the problem."

"You're wrong. I know you like a book."

"Alex, I hate red roses. I've told you that a dozen times, and yet you still send them."

"Most women—"

I cut him off. "Most women would love them. I know, I know. You always say that. I'm not most women."

"Abby, I've changed. We've had almost twenty good years together. Why would you throw it all away now? If it's about the baby, we can raise it, together, even if it's not mine. I love you, sweetheart, and I'll love that baby the same way I love Ruby and Jack. Just give me the chance."

"I'm leaving."

"Wait." He stands and hands me a folder. "Take these with you. Read them on the plane."

"What are they?"

"Termination of parental rights."

"What?" I raise my voice. "What the hell? She's eighteen."

"Relax. They're not for you. They're for Danny Boy to sign, just in case. I had the attorneys draw them up."

"You can have your attorneys do this, but you can't agree to a legal separation?"

"I told you already, I'm not giving up on us."

"We're finished, Alex."

"Just take the papers with you when you dump this loser. I'm doing you a big favor. Last thing you want is this guy with rights to the kid, just in case."

"Tell Ruby I'll text her when I arrive."

He leans in and tries to kiss me on the mouth.

I step out of his reach. I don't have the energy to fight with him. "I have to go. Can we talk later?"

"Okay, sure. But you've got a long flight. Give some thought to what I'm saying."

I bite my tongue and walk away.

"Just get him to sign those papers, then come home to me, sweetheart," he yells after me as I climb in the car.

I pretend not to hear him and drive off.

He must be delusional. I'd sooner live on the streets than under the same roof with him again. I'm grateful to be separated, even if it isn't yet legal.

AT THE JACKSONVILLE airport, I browse the books and ultimately settle on *The Alchemist*. The primary theme of the story is pursuing our dreams by focusing on our own journeys. Living our lives to please others is a miserable existence. I was living proof. It was different when Ruby was young and I put her needs ahead of my own, as loving mothers often do. But now, I'm starting over. The choices I'm making are my own. I'll have a baby to think of soon, but this time, motherhood will be different. I'll be stronger and a better example for this child. He or she will grow up looking at me with admiration instead of pity. One of the greatest takeaways from the story was the importance of action. It's the only way to learn.

On the approach to Barcelona's El Prat, I dry my eyes. It's been a long flight, nearly twelve hours, and I'm feeling brave and proud of myself for taking it. No matter what happens when I see Daniel, I'll be okay. If I spend the rest of my life with only the love of my children and myself, I'll be happy.

When the plane touches down, reality rattles me. I'm a truth seeker who flew almost four thousand miles to confront my former lover. Whether it's bold or crazy, I deserve answers. Why did he let me fall for him when there was someone else? The little boy hurts the most. All the secret boys. Jack, Crosby, and now this one. It doesn't make sense. I place a hand on my round belly. What will I tell this child?

One thing at a time, Abby! I just want this all to be over so I can move forward. I'm so tired. I text Ruby to let her know I've arrived and will be back in a couple of days.

The Aerobus drops me in Barcelona's chaotic city center. Gray skies and heavy clouds douse my fire and add somberness to my already-conflicted emotions. Gusts of frigid wind cut through the long wool coat I'm wearing. I take shelter inside a busy café on the main drag, squeezing myself into a small booth by the window. The warmth, the noise, and the smells of coffee and baked muffins bring comfort. Soon I'll be face-to-face with Daniel and his second wife or longtime lover. Knots form in my stomach. If he's gone, I could be forced to wait for days. Maybe coming was a mistake.

Get it together, Abby. Be brave. Just breathe. You've got this! A sliver of light appears through the clouds, beaming its way to my window, bringing the tiniest sign that I'm doing the right thing.

La Rambla is only half a mile away. I memorize the route and begin—sixteen blocks to the left, then a right. Despite the frigid cold, the streets are crowded and lined with musicians, parrot sellers, clowns making balloon animals, and dozens of other vendors. The address I'm looking for is on the left. In front of the tall house, a brightly colored stained-glass door stands out against the charcoal siding. The fat trim is bright white. The house is exquisite. Fear seizes me as I contemplate my next move.

Five, four, three, two, one... I take a deep breath, ascend the concrete stairs, and ring the bell.

An eternity passes without an answer. When I give up and turn to go, the sound of clicking deadbolts stops me. A petite blonde with a dancer's body, the same woman from the photographs, appears.

"*Hola, sí?*"

I suck in my stomach and stand taller. "Hi. I am looking for Daniel." My shaking hands fumble for my coat pockets.

Her brows furrow, confusion on her face.

"Daniel Quinn," I say. "Is he here?"

"And who might you be?" she asks, with a heavy Irish or British accent I can't quite distinguish.

"I'm an old friend from the States," I lie.

"Well, sorry. He's not here." She looks down at my backpack beside the stairs and folds her arms. "Have you traveled all the way from America to see him, *friend*?" Her eyes narrow. "Might I ask what business you have with him?"

I had a fling with him, fell in love, and am having his baby. Maybe. There's nothing I can say that won't break this woman's heart too.

"I'm... I'm passing through, and I thought I'd just..." I start over. "I'm a photographer."

Her eyes narrow again as if to say, "Don't patronize me."

Coming here was a mistake. A huge mistake. I realize that now, seeing this woman in the flesh, the absurdity of the whole situation.

I'm getting the hell out of here. "I'm sorry. I'll catch up with him later."

I step back down the stairs. Dizziness overcomes me and I miss the last step entirely. Humiliated and flat on my back, I assess the situation and pray for the sidewalk to swallow me whole.

"Oh Christ," she says, shaking her head. "You all right?"

"Yes." I think so.

"Come on then." She reaches out her hand and pulls me to my feet. "Let's go inside. He'll be back soon." She smiles down at me, seemingly taking pleasure at my discomposure.

"No. I'm fine. Forget it." I pick up my pack and turn to walk away. But the dizziness causes me to stumble again. I steady myself against the railing. "I just need a minute, and I'll be gone." Tears of embarrassment and exhaustion sting my eyes. Cold winds freeze them against my cheeks.

"Come inside, Abby," the ballerina says. With her hand on my shoulder, she guides me up the stairs and into her home. Creamy white-paneled wood walls extend upward to high ceilings, twenty or more feet tall. Silk cream curtains pool at the base of each window, while white sheers hang in the center. An enormous turn-of-the-century carved limestone fireplace is the focal point of the room.

"How do you know my name?"

"Daniel told me about you. He'll be back soon, and it looks like you two have some things to discuss." She nods toward my stomach. Vanilla and fresh flowers waft through the room. A wave of nausea hits me.

Her face is stern, and mine, I imagine, twists in confusion. Why would this woman invite me into her home when she knows about Daniel and me?

The ballerina shakes me out of my introspection by offering her hand. "I'm Claire."

I nod, unable to bring myself to shake her hand. This is all so bizarre, it makes my head spin.

She gestures toward the sofa. "Have a seat. I'll grab us some tea, and we can chat." She forces a smile. "We have a lot to chat about, Abby, you and me." She disappears into the kitchen.

Even though she also deserves answers, I don't want to tell her anything.

Candid snapshots line the mantel: a close-up shot of her and one of the boy alone on a wooden rope swing. Then there it is—the woman, Daniel, and the boy, all smartly dressed, at a play or concert, maybe. The boy is looking up at Daniel. The photos are recent. Both Daniel and Claire look as they do now.

My face flushes with angry heat.

Claire returns, carrying a tray of cups and saucers, a silver teapot, and small containers of cream and sugar. I remain in front of the photographs, clutching my coat protectively in front of me.

She sets the tray down, walks around the table, and stands beside me with a forced smile that falls short of her eyes. "Please have a seat." She fills our cups, and when I hesitate to take mine, she adds, "Don't worry, it's decaf."

Satisfied it won't upset the baby, I take a small sip. "Just so you know, I'm not here to interfere with anything. I just need to talk to Daniel, then I'll go."

"Oh, so you're here to finish the job, then?"

"What job?"

"Of breaking his heart once more." She shakes her head and looks away toward the window. "Never mind, then."

My head swims, and I blink, trying to refocus. What the hell is going on? There's no way I'm talking to her. I stand to go and am hit with another wave of dizziness. I guess I'm just exhausted, both mentally and physically.

"You don't look well, hon. When's the last time you slept?" She tilts her head with a look of concern.

I try to remember but can't. It wasn't last night. And maybe not the night before.

A second later, she's beside me, leading me down a hallway. "Let's go get you to lie down."

I stop and open my mouth to protest, but she swats her hand at me. "It's just for a wee bit. I'll have him wake you when he gets here." She looks down at her wrist. "Should be quite soon."

Her kindness moves me. "I'm so sorry. I traveled through the night to get here."

"Ah, of course you are, hon." She opens a bedroom door at the end of the hall.

Embarrassingly, I lean into her, too unwell to read into her words.

She peels back the thick heavy quilts, patting the sheets of the king-sized poster bed. "There you go. Rest up now."

She wouldn't have poisoned me. The thought is ridiculous, not that I would blame her. Unsure if I'll ever wake, I close my eyes for a moment and drift off.

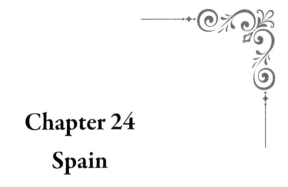

Chapter 24

Spain

In the home of my former lover and his ballerina, I wake with a fogged brain, unsure how long I've been asleep. Rolling to my side, I open my eyes. He's there in a plush oversized chair beside the bed.

"Hi, Doc," he says, his voice gravelly and low. He leans in, a warm smile across his face, and slow blinks in a way that melts me. Even in the low light, his eyes are so blue. With the back of his hand, he strokes my cheek and whispers to me, "I can't believe you're here."

I soak in the touch of his skin on mine, then the bizarreness of the situation hits me. I pull away. "Where's the ballerina?"

His brows knit together in confusion.

"Your wife or girlfriend or whatever she is." I sit upright.

"You mean Claire?"

Who else would I be talking about? Fury hits. "Yes, Claire."

He spits out a laugh. "Why would you think—"

"Who the hell is she, then?"

He puts his hands on my cheeks and leans in until his face is inches from mine. "Doc, she's my sister."

I never even considered the possibility. "She lives here? But her accent..."

"It's Irish. She and her mom are from Dublin."

"Why didn't you tell me about her? Why didn't she tell me who she was?"

"I'm sorry you thought that we were together. I didn't tell you because before a few months ago, I never knew her. My dad had an affair with her mom. I'd heard rumors when I was a teenager but ignored them. I didn't wanna believe my dad would do that to my mother. It seems he had a thing for European women."

He lowers his eyes. "A few months ago, Claire tracked me down. Her husband had surgery then got himself addicted to opioids, and she didn't know what to do. She needed help and just wanted to connect. She definitely should have told you who she was." He pauses, thinking. "I'm just getting to know her, but she can definitely be catty when she wants to. And I might have had a little too much to drink when I first showed up a few months ago, and oh, hell..." He hangs his head. "I may or may not have been a little busted up about you. I didn't think I'd see you again. Otherwise, I would never have told her—"

"What about the boy?"

"You mean Josh? Her son."

Her son. Not his. "What happened to her husband? Where is he now?"

"He's still in rehab. He came a few weeks ago but relapsed."

I sit with his words.

"How did you find me anyway?"

"It's a very long story."

He touches his forehead to mine. "I can't wait to hear it." He sits back up. "I guess your being here means you went through with it and aren't with that asshole anymore?"

"I moved out months ago. Why did you change your number? Why haven't you called?"

He lets out a sigh and sits straighter. "Abby, I called so many times. I left messages. I knew you went back to him. I..." He takes a deep breath. "I have a confession. I was in Florida twice. When you left me that message about your daughter, I booked the first flight I could get and drove to the hospital in St. Augustine. I guess I thought you'd be alone and might need me. I was walking down the hall when I saw you and your husband. He was holding you. Your head was in his chest, and you were crying." He closes his eyes. "My heart split, and I knew I was wrong. You had him."

"Daniel, please. I did need you, so much. I was a wreck. She was so sick in the beginning, and I was weak. He was only hugging me."

He hesitates for a second, smiles, then takes my hands in his. "I believe you, but why didn't you return any of my calls?"

I sit up, pulling the covers with me, and think of a way to gather the past few months' feelings into words that will make sense. "I guess I just felt like my daughter getting sick was punishment—"

He cuts me off. "For what? Being happy?"

"Yes. I was desperate and praying so hard. I made a promise to God—" I choke on my words. "To sacrifice anything if she got better."

"Jesus, Abby. God doesn't work like that. I'm sure he wants you to be happy and your girl to be well."

"I know. I see that now. I was just desperate and lost. I wanted you to show up and take me away from everything."

"Why couldn't you at least talk to me? You just ghosted me."

"I know, and I'm sorry. It was all so hard. I was confused and wanted to focus everything I had on her."

Leaning back in the chair, he says, "There was another time. I took an assignment in Cassadaga, a little hippy and psychic commune a couple hours from you. I drove by your house and sat out front for a while looking at it, thinking about you and your family inside. I figured you were staying with him, and I'll be honest..." He shakes his head. "It fucking killed me. Understand, it doesn't mean I didn't think about you." He stares at me with an intensity that makes it impossible not to feel his words. "I've never stopped missing you, but I wasn't going to interfere, no matter how much I wanted to break that door down and take you away." He leans closer again, rubbing my hand. "When I got back, I knew you were done with me, so I changed my number."

"There hasn't been a day that I haven't thought of you and wished we were back at your place in Italy or traveling somewhere together. I've never stopped loving you. Not for a second. I had to stay in the house until Ruby was well."

It occurs to me that he hasn't mentioned my pregnancy, and because I'm burrowed beneath the quilts, he can't tell. Claire must not have told him.

"I missed you every fucking day." His eyes are wet with tears. "But I knew you were gone." He stands and, in a swift motion, peels back the covers and pulls me to my feet, to him. "What the..." His voice cracks. "Holy hell is that?" He points to my stomach, then a nervous laugh escapes. "You're pregnant!"

His face contorts. His lips move as if unsure how to begin. "Is it, um..."

God, I'm about to lose him again. "I think the baby is yours. I haven't been with anyone else." I want to believe my own words.

He swipes at his wet eyes. "You think so. What the fuck does that mean?"

"Sit back down," I say.

"I'm good." He folds his arms defensively and takes a step back.

I tell the story about the afternoon of Ruby's diagnosis. I explain how I fainted then walked four miles home, completely out of my mind. I tell him about the pills Alex gave me that knocked me out and how I woke up without clothes.

His jaw goes taut, and his fists ball. "Jesus Christ, he fucking raped you." He paces the room and expels a groan. "And you still stayed there..."

"I didn't know. He swore he never touched me until I'd already moved out. When I told him I was having your baby, he confessed."

"This fucking guy is going into the ground. To jail at least."

"It would be his word against mine. There's no way I'd win."

He paces the room then sits back down. "What kind of monster is so hard up he finds out his kid is sick then takes advantage of his unconscious wife?" He blows out a breath.

"I know. I hate him for it. But for my own sake, I'm not going to dwell. I just want to continue to move forward."

"So what you're telling me is this may or may not be my baby?" He shakes his head. "We were careful."

"That last day in Amsterdam. You didn't use anything, did you?"

He pauses, looking back. "No, but it was just that once, and you said you were on the pill?"

"I was, but I forgot to take it a couple of times. Sometimes I'd take two pills together when I remembered. It's not that uncommon." I put my hand on his. "I had an ultrasound, and I believe with all my heart this baby belongs to you."

He falls back in the chair, dropping his head into his hands, and lets out a long, loud sigh. My heart and head tangle together. This is all too much for him, and I understand. I came for an explanation about the woman and boy, and I got it. Now it's time to leave.

"I'm sorry about everything." I slide out of the bed and stand to go. "Where are my shoes?"

He grabs my arm and pulls me against him. "Don't go. I need some time."

I spot my shoes in the corner and pull away to grab them.

"Abby, you broke my fucking heart. Then you show up after all this time, pregnant. Maybe, maybe not with my kid. Can I get a minute?"

He's right. "I'm sorry, again." I lean against him and start to cry.

"It's okay." He rests his chin on my head, stroking my back. "Everything's gonna be all right."

I think of "Three Little Birds" and smile.

"You never did tell me how you found me."

Hesitantly, I tell him about the pictures.

He drops his hands. "I don't get it. How did you see pictures of me?" A knowing look registers. "Your ex had me followed? That's hilarious." His hands slam down, smacking the chair, making it clear he doesn't find it funny at all.

"I saw you and Claire hugging and the little boy, and I thought—"

"You thought they were my—" He doesn't finish. "Oh, Doc, that asshole has put you through hell, hasn't he?"

I shake my head then look into his eyes, still feeling all those familiar feelings and knowing he feels them too. The months apart vanish, like time stood still. He lays me down on the bed, his face nuzzles into my hair. His mouth runs gently along my neck, ear, and cheek before connecting with my lips. "You're beautiful."

"I'm as big as a house."

"Abby, I love you. No matter what."

"I love you too."

The baby jabs at his arms, causing him to jump. "My God. I forgot how much of a miracle this is." He rubs at the little protruding bump. "Do you think that's a foot or a fist?"

"I'd say a fist or maybe an elbow. I think the head is over here." I move his hand to just under my left breast.

"When will the baby be here?"

"According to my OB, Valentine's Day."

"Wow, that's only a few months away," he says, nuzzling into me.

We sleep soundly through the night, his body pressed behind me and his arms around me protectively.

I wake at first morning light to voices outside the door.

"Morning, Sleepyhead." He enters, carrying a tray. "Freshly squeezed OJ, a croissant—not like Paris, so don't get too excited—and some coffee, but I'm not sure if that's all right."

I sit up. "Wow. You're sweet. Thank you."

He sits on the bed, placing the tray over my lap.

"And, yes, it's fine. I can have a cup a day."

He leans in and kisses my forehead. "How long do I get to keep you?"

"I fly back tomorrow."

He sticks out his lip in a pout as Claire appears in the doorway. "Sorry about yesterday, hon. I didn't mean to be such a bitch. It's just this one here"—she squeezes Daniel's arm—"is my big brother, and I just found him, so I'm a wee bit protective. He's had a rough go."

"I totally understand," I tell her.

"But for feck's sake, don't go breaking his heart again. Otherwise, you'll have me to contend with."

I promise her I won't.

"I'm off to work. Nice to meet you, and congrats on the baby." She smirks. "Whoever's it turns out to be."

Daniel shoots her a look, and she stares back, a condescending smile on her face. "See ya."

"You told her?"

"Don't be mad. I couldn't sleep last night, and you were out cold. I told her how I felt about you and want to be with you, even if it turns out"—he raises his voice, imitating Maury Povich—"I am *not* the baby's father."

I force a smile. I need this baby to belong to him. "I'm glad you and Claire found each other."

"It's been great being here for her and Josh." He smiles. "Being around him reminds me what it was like..."

The thought of his son makes me instantly sad.

"Hey, hey, no. It's okay. No long faces today." He rubs my arm. "Let's go check out the city. I'll take you to the craziest market you've ever seen, and... I can't believe you're only staying a day. Any chance you could change the flight?"

I would love to, but knowing a subpoena with a court date could arrive any day, there's no way I'm missing out on making my separation legal. "I have to get back to Ruby."

I fight the urge to ask him to fly back to the States with me. I know it wouldn't be ideal right now. He's here helping his sister and nephew, and I'm still not legally separated.

"Let's make the most of our day, then."

Tomorrow, I'll head home and, once again, move forward with my crazy life. Today, we'll play happy tourists.

While riding through the crowded streets on a double-decker bus, we stop at the Sagrada Familia, one of the most famous churches in the world. Sadly, it's undergoing heavy construction, covered in scaffolding and tarps, so we stay put. At Plaça Catalunya, the main square, we disembark and wander a bit before boarding the bus to Park Guell, the place I've seen in Alex's photos.

Gaudi's colorful tile mosaics reveal both his eye for beauty and his patience. My stomach twists as I remember the feeling I had thinking of Daniel here with his lover. Parts of the park are deserted, and around nearly every turn, disheveled foreigners sell trinkets and knock-off purses on worn blankets. Their feet and eyes shift back and forth nervously. When uniformed men appear, they gather their blankets and scurry away.

Back on the bus, we ride to La Boqueria market and disembark into a sea of people. Destitute beggars hold their paper cups high to the smartly dressed businessmen and tourists who pass. Daniel drops coins in each cup, lighting the weary faces each time the sound of change jangling against the few coins inside.

I pull Daniel toward a candy stall with brightly colored displays of sweets. The sugary smells of black licorice and peppermint sticks remind me of childhood, of days when Tommy was still alive and our parents would take us to Pop's, the old candy store on Main Street, to let us fill brown paper bags with sweets from the barrels.

Octopus and big inky squid stare blankly from their ice beds. I breathe through the queasiness. Butcher stalls offer up pork, beef, and other cuts of meat I don't recognize. Spain's beloved *Jamón Ibérico* hangs from several stalls. Fruit stands overflow with ripe, fragrant fruit, some unrecognizable. Daniel buys me a small fruit cup and himself a few slices of ham to tide us over until dinner.

Back at The Hotel Lauren, he draws me a warm bath and runs out to grab dinner. Alone with my thoughts, I wonder where we'll go from here. Like Alex, Daniel says he wants to be with me regardless of the baby's paternity. Does he mean it, though? I know Alex well enough to know that he could never love a child who isn't his. Is Daniel capable? Could he love a baby from a man he detests?

I will not allow delusions of sailing off into the sunset seduce me. Not this time. I will protect my children—and myself. Before Daniel and I are together full-time under the same roof, I need to be certain we will be able to make it work. We both need to tie up loose ends—he with his sister and her family, me with Alex. I would like to take things slow and wait until the baby arrives. Empowered with the clarity of my decision not to rush things, I climb out of the tub to wait for dinner.

Daniel arrives carrying two brown paper bags, leans in, and kisses me. "Sorry I took so long, but I got the best paella in town."

I wrap my arms around him.

"You realize we've been together in five countries now," he says. "How crazy is that, especially since we've never been together in the States?" He winks. "Hopefully that'll change soon."

I squeeze him, thinking of my decision.

"I can't wait to wake up beside you every morning."

I smile to avoid the topic a little longer. Nerves lessen my appetite, but the outer edges of saffron rice are crispy and delicious, so I eat, passing over the clams, mussels, and other bits of unrecognizable seafood. I try to unsee the glaring shrimp and lobster eyes.

Daniel eats my discarded parts. "How awesome is this paella?"

"It's great."

"All right, let's get down to business and chat," Daniel says.

I've been dreading this necessary moment. "So I've been doing a lot of thinking today while we were walking around."

"Uh-oh," he teases.

"We really rushed into things the first time around, and I need us to go a little slower this time. I'd like to have my divorce settled and maybe even wait until the baby's born before we move in together."

"You're right, Doc. As much as I want to get on that plane with you tomorrow, I feel like I need to see things through for Claire and Josh. Her husband should be coming home in a few weeks, and I'd like to stick around to make sure everything's okay."

I expected more of a protest.

"I'm not having second thoughts, if that's what you're thinking."

How does he do that?

"Any idea when your divorce will be finalized?"

I tell him about filing the papers and about how I expect a court date very soon.

"Once Claire's husband is back and things are settled, I'll come to Florida."

I imagine Alex popping over and seeing Daniel at the cottage. "I'd like that very much, but my place is pretty tiny."

"I'll rent a place for us then. Maybe eventually we can move in it together? As long as I'm within an hour's drive of an airport, I can live anywhere."

"I'd like that. Next fall, when Ruby leaves for school, I'll go anywhere with you."

He leans in and kisses me. "I look forward to that day."

We spend the next hours talking about Ruby and our future together. We go to sleep with a solid plan.

Daniel's whispers rouse me before dawn. "Did I wake you at all?"

Somehow, I'd forgotten about his PTSD nightmares. "No. Have the dreams stopped?"

"These past two nights, they have." He kisses my cheek then climbs out of bed. "I have to get going."

"Why? It's still dark."

"I have an assignment and a flight out in a few hours." He looks at his watch. "You still have plenty of time before you need to get up. I ordered a car to take you to the airport, but for now, close those eyes and rest."

And with that, I'm left alone in a half-empty bed while he showers. I try my best to stay awake to say goodbye, but when I wake hours later, to my phone alarm, he's long gone.

PART 3

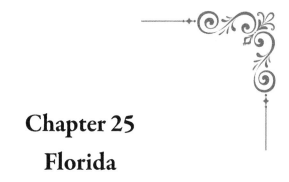

Chapter 25
Florida

Just after midnight, my jet from Barcelona touches down at Jacksonville International Airport. After driving with poor visibility through sheets of rain for two hours, I arrive at the beach cottage. As soon as I open the front door, I sense something is off-kilter. Hints of cologne and those stupid cigars linger in the air. I go from room to tiny room, surveying everything, my pulse quickening. Did I leave the throw pillows arranged like that? My dresser drawers are closed properly, but the closet door is slightly ajar, and I'm certain I didn't leave it that way. If he isn't still here, he was. I check the locks on all the doors and windows, but everything looks okay.

I'm pregnant and exhausted but unwilling to ignore my instincts. Then I see it—a five-by-seven photo in a white weathered frame sitting on the end table, a single red rose beside it. The photo was taken Christmastime in the town square about five years ago. Ruby, Alex, and I are huddled together, smiling. It's a close-up, a selfie Alex took. I'd downloaded it to my laptop but never printed it. The flower and photo are messages so I can see he's broken in again. Without words, he's telling me we belong together and that he'll go to any lengths, follow me anywhere, and come into my home uninvited anytime he pleases. He's letting me know he's in control, like always. Why didn't I leave him years ago? Why did I let him dominate me? I could have stopped him months ago. If I had, this would all be over by now.

After a restless night, I wake. I let Ruby know I've returned, and she tells me she's planning to go to the movies and sleep over at Jess's.

It's well past noon, there's a warm breeze blowing, and the sun is shining. Conch shells, remnants of last night's storm, litter the beach. I walk a mile or so, gathering them, even the broken ones, in my overstretched T-shirt. I'll add them with the others Ruby and I have been collecting. After each storm, we go out in the early morning, before the tourists arrive, to collect Mother Nature's gifts. We study the shells, turning them over to try to determine their age. My favorites are battered down to the core with only a skinny spiral remaining. They're resilient. No matter how many storms have tossed them about year after year, the most beautiful part is preserved. They're beautifully broken. We line our little patio with favorites and toss the rest back out to sea.

With each step along the coast, my anger over Alex's invasion fades. I make a plan to set firm boundaries. I'll tell him the next time he pulls a stunt like that, he'll be arrested. I'll call the media and make sure his face is splattered all over the news. I'm finished dealing with his nonsense.

With my sliders open and a warm breeze blowing in, I unpack and clean while blaring Maroon 5.

Singing, I scrub the shower then dance my way to the kitchen to grab some water, still belting out lyrics. A dark figure looms outside the door, and my voice cracks with fear.

The curtains part, and Alex steps inside. "Nice singing." He smiles. Freshly applied cologne drifts in with the breeze.

"Didn't mean to scare you, sweetheart." He steps forward and kills the music. He's wearing a crisp white shirt and classic gray trousers, too dressy for a Saturday. The devil in disguise, he smells and looks nice, trying to hide the poison inside.

"What the hell are you doing? You have no right to keep coming here uninvited. You broke into my house, Alex. I could have you arrested right now."

"Oh, relax. You need better locks. A child could pick those cheap Chinese-made deadbolts. I'm not staying long. I just want to know how Danny Boy took the news." He plops down on the sofa and crosses his leg, giving me a "You're being hysterical" look. "And if you got him to sign the papers."

I cannot bring a baby into this world while still legally married to this smug, arrogant man. "I need you to get out, and the next time you show up here, I'm calling the police."

He laughs like I told a joke, letting me know my threats are exactly that. "Calm down. I'll go. But first, tell me what happened."

"It doesn't matter. I don't want to be with you. I'm not asking for anything. I need you to leave me alone and just sign the damn separation papers. I know you have them. They've been sent certified twice now."

He looks at the floor then back at me. His eyes are sad and glassy. "I told you, sweetheart. I'm not giving up on you. You'll come to your senses sooner or later."

I already have. If he didn't have such an enormous ego, I might pity him. But his arrogance, even after all this time, is inexcusable. "Look, our separation is going to get granted with or without your signature. I would greatly appreciate if you would just stop fighting it."

"Abigail, I know you're smart enough to have dumped Danny Boy. You wouldn't have gone all that way if you hadn't. You're going to need me. There's no way you can afford to raise a baby on your own. You're barely getting by."

"Alex, please. Just let me go."

We're both silent long enough for me to think my words are sinking in. Then he smiles and steps closer. Taking my head in his hands, he kisses me hard on the mouth. His tongue forces its way between my teeth and fills my mouth with the taste of mint and cigar. I push him away and grab my phone from the coffee table. He's gone with the breeze, back through the curtains, the way he came.

"911, what is your emergency?"

I tell them it was a mistake. What would I say? I'm afraid of my estranged husband because he broke in and left me flowers and a family photo? Or that he just came over and kissed me?

The rest of the day, I do what I do best—try to forget what happened. He must have believed I would come home, rid of Daniel for good, and jump into his arms. I couldn't have made it any clearer that I no longer want to be with him. I will not allow this to go on any further. I know the divorce will eventually be granted with or without his approval, but his cooperation will make the process so much easier. I swear if he bothers me at all after we're divorced, I'll get a restraining order.

The following morning, I find myself in the office of a new therapist. I should have made this appointment long ago. I kept telling myself I could manage on my own. Melody is strong and quick-witted, and I appreciate her candor right away. She takes notes until I stop her, not wanting to take a chance they'll be subpoenaed during our divorce hearing.

"I've worked with plenty of women suffering from this type of domestic abuse," she says. "What you call charming and taking charge, I call manipulative, narcissistic, vindictive, sociopathic even. These men are used to getting what they want, and when they don't, they can be dangerous."

"Wait." I stop her. Hearing the label coming from an outsider seems dramatic. "I know he's been cruel at times and consistently controlling, but he's never laid a hand on me. We've had a lot of ups and downs. He was really good to me while Ruby was sick."

"You mean after he raped you?"

My cheeks flush with heat and embarrassment.

"Please, Abby, take some time to think about the whole picture, about his behavior through the years, especially these past few months. He committed a heinous crime against you, and now you're pregnant. He's dangerous."

My mouth opens instinctively to protest. Instead, I consider the possibility that she's right.

"You think you're placating him by asking for nothing from the dissolution of the marriage, but that isn't what this is about. It's about control, about keeping you with him, about keeping his picture-perfect family intact."

"I don't know what to do about my daughter. I'm not sure if I can keep her from staying with him. Some nights, she stays there with her half brother. Honestly, though, he'd never hurt them, not in a million years. He adores them both, and he's an excellent father." I need her to understand the truth of my words. His erratic behavior with me has nothing to do with the kids.

Melody shakes her head. "Well, you know him better than I do. But I am worried about you. I wish you would consider filing an ex parte to keep him from coming to your home."

"I've researched it and been over it in my head a hundred times. I don't have any proof. My accusing him of being dangerous will infuriate him and further delay the divorce. I just want this to be over. Can't you understand?"

She nods. "Well, it sounds like your mind's made up. Promise me you'll be careful and keep in touch to let me know how things progress."

WINTER APPEARS IN TYPICAL Florida fashion—overnight. There's a slight chill in the mornings and evenings, but mild sunny afternoons. Ruby and I celebrate her excellent lab and PET scan results by going shopping for Christmas decorations. There continues to be no sign of cancer in her body. She is going to go on to graduate college, get married, and have children someday. A normal, healthy life is in her future. After Christmas, she'll begin online classes to get a head start at Harvard.

For dinner, we make strawberry-and-Nutella crepes, then we turn on Spotify and dance in the living room. We decorate then bicker over which cookies we should bake. She loves quadruple-chocolate everything.

"Sugar cookies are so boring. And messy."

But I have such fond memories of rolling out dough and cutting shapes of stars and trees with my grandmother. "What if we compromise and make chocolate sugar cookies?"

"Is that even a thing?"

"It'll be our thing."

"If there's chocolate involved, you know I'll eat it."

"Can I make some extra batter to take to Jack? I want to make cookies with him too."

"Of course you can."

"You know he keeps asking if he can come over here with me. I feel so bad telling him no."

My heart breaks for him. First, his mother left, then I did. If I thought spending time with him would ease the transition, I would have Ruby bring him over. But I know it would only cause confusion and encourage Alex to continue fighting the divorce.

In the evening, we take a stroll on the beach to look for shark's teeth and seashells for our collection. Most days, we take turns cooking, alternating between breakfast for dinner or soups and salads. When I'm not working and we're not volunteering, we ride our bikes through uptown to browse the boutiques and antique stores. We walk all over town, like we used to, talking about life, the stars, and the baby who will arrive in two short months. I cherish every moment with her, knowing my attention will soon be divided.

My girl will get to be around for the first six months with the new baby before heading off to school. Harvard gave her no trouble at all deferring her start date. Not exactly a typical gap year, but she's already matured light-years ahead of her friends. I guess cancer and divorcing parents will do that to a person. Life is settling into a light and peaceful lull for us. Daniel and I talk on the phone each night, ending our calls with loving sentiments that give me hope all will be right in this world. His brother-in-law is back home, and everything seems to be going well. It's taken a lot of conversations to ease his anger toward Alex for taking advantage of me. Because I don't remember anything, the whole thing doesn't seem real. Again, I just want everything to be over between us, and it seems we're so close.

When a video text arrives, I realize Alex hasn't come around the way I hoped.

Got your precious papers, sweetheart. The video shows a close up of the front page then Alex sliding the packet through the paper shredder.

A week later, I open the door and sign for certified mail. The separation was granted even without Alex's signature. I thought this day would never come. I call Daniel, who sounds ecstatic.

Ruby continues to visit the Marine Street house and also spends Sundays with her father and Jack, but she no longer stays overnight.

"I'm worried about Dad. He seems bummed lately and hasn't been spending much time with Jack. Grandma has been taking him to soccer practice and staying with him until bedtime. It's weird. I've never seen so much of her in my life. She seems kind of like a normal grandmother."

"Well, she wasn't around much for your dad, so I guess she's making up for that. Try not to worry about him. He'll be okay. The holidays are hard for a lot of people. He has a great support system with lots of friends and colleagues. Not to mention a pretty amazing daughter."

Chapter 26
Florida

Daniel's Airbnb beach house is quadruple the size of mine. It has a sleek, modern kitchen with white concrete countertops and floors. East-facing rooms have floor-to-ceiling windows and full ocean views. The house sits on Vilano Beach, one-half mile from the cottage. I was able to go check it out before Daniel booked it. When he arrives, I run, although it's more like a waddle, to greet him.

"Hey, you," he says when I open the front door. He takes me in his arms and squeezes. When he pulls back to survey my expanding waistline, there's an ear-to-ear smile. "My God, your belly is huge!"

"I know. I look like a whale."

"The most beautiful whale I've ever seen." He kisses my lips, sending that old familiar current of electricity surging.

I cannot believe we're finally together, here in Florida. I pull him through the house excitedly and show him all the rooms. We sit out on the balcony and walk the beach. He is calm and relaxed and has trouble saying goodbye.

"I'll be back bright and early," I promise. As tempting as it is to stay, I don't want Ruby alone—not if I can help it.

The following morning, Daniel is in the kitchen, shirtless and barefoot, holding a steaming cup of coffee. Ruby and I walk up the stairs, and she leans into me and whispers, "Way to go, Mom. He's hot."

My cheeks burn.

"I didn't expect you so early. Give me a sec," Daniel says before disappearing down the hall. He returns a minute later, wearing, of course, a gray T-shirt.

He smiles, but his nervousness is palpable as he reaches for Ruby's hand. "Nice to meet you, Harvard," he teases.

She steps in to take his hand. "Nice to meet you, secret boyfriend."

"Ruby," I say.

He grins. "I see you're cheeky, just like your mother."

"Cheeky? Where are you from again?"

He looks at me. "I'm from all over."

"Okay then, world traveler, you want some coffee?" she asks before disappearing into the kitchen.

The banter between them is instant, and I know they're going to get along just fine.

Because it's a warm day, we take our mugs out to the second-story deck. Seagulls and pelicans swoop by, almost eye level with us. The ocean view from high up is even more magical than below. We chat easily. Daniel tells Ruby about some of his favorite cities, and she tells him all the must-see places in St. Augustine. The Alligator Farm and Farmer's Market are top of the list. The thought of walking around town, seeing all the touristy sites makes me uneasy. Even something as simple as eating out is going to be impossible without running into old friends or people Alex knows.

Being in foreign cities together felt completely natural. Having him here, though, causes a shroud of anxiety to cover me.

IT DOESN'T TAKE LONG for Alex to learn Daniel is in town. He fills my voicemail with dozens of silent messages and bitter, spiteful digs that convince me to try to keep Ruby with me.

"Your behavior is unacceptable," I tell him one afternoon when I accidentally swipe up instead of down, answering the call.

"Don't think I don't know what you and your boyfriend are doing."

"What?"

"The two of you. Poisoning my daughter against me," he spits into the phone.

I try to reason with him, but it's no use. I refuse to say anything negative, even when Ruby complains. My patience is tested over and over. I should have seen this coming. I guess I hoped to keep Daniel's visit a secret.

A few days before Christmas, Ruby, Daniel, and I are on the upper deck of the beach house, rehanging garland and lights that had fallen, when Alex pulls into the driveway.

"It's Dad!" Ruby says, a look of horror on her face.

Daniel looks at me. "How the hell does he know where I'm staying?"

My stomach lurches. "I have no idea."

Alex gets out, leans against the Range Rover, and stares up at us, squinting against the afternoon sun.

"Enjoying playing house with my family, Danny Boy?"

Daniel locks his jaw and takes a step toward the stairs. "If you want to talk, I'll come down, and we can do it man to man."

I grab his arm to stop him. "Please don't let him bait you."

"Dad, what are you doing here?" Ruby yells down.

"I was driving up to Ponte Vedra and saw your car."

"Okay," she says nervously.

"Do you want to take a ride with me?"

She hesitates. I know she doesn't want to go, and I don't want to let her. "Can I just stop by the house later?"

"Sure." He climbs into his car and squeals the wheels backing out, nearly hitting an oncoming car.

"Oh my god, what was that about?" Ruby asks me with crimson cheeks.

"I don't know, lovie."

Daniel is visibly on edge. I try to pretend it's no big deal, but now that Alex knows where Daniel is staying, I'm worried about what may be coming.

Two days later, I open the front door of the cottage to a young man in a suit.

"Abigail Montgomery?"

"Yes."

"You've been served."

He hands me an ex parte stating I cannot visit the Marine Street house or go anywhere within five hundred feet of Alex. The paper-work says he fears for his life. How was this processed without a hear-ing? My blood boils. I have no idea what he'll do next. I take some deep breaths to calm myself and phone the attorney Daniel insisted on hiring. She assures me the order is temporary and that nothing will come of it.

"He's just trying to upset you. Don't let him win."

During our visit, she tried at length to convince me to go after half of the assets, and even alimony. I refused. "I just want to cut ties as painlessly as possible. If I try to take anything, it'll just delay this process." For my own mental health, I need the divorce to happen now.

She agrees to disagree but promises to do everything she can to get the proceedings expedited.

The following day, after Ruby leaves, I go to run errands and meet Daniel for brunch in Ponte Vedra, where no one knows me. In the driveway, I find all four of my tires completely flat. The key neck-lace Daniel gave me in Amsterdam is gone. I left it hanging from the rear-view mirror. According to the AAA serviceman, someone pur-posely released the air, and I know just who that someone is. I have the tires filled and meet Daniel for lunch. I only tell him about one of the tires because I'm certain there will be a confrontation between Daniel and Alex if I tell the whole truth.

Later that evening, a voicemail from Alex makes my skin crawl. "Sweetheart, I heard about your tires. What a bummer. Hope you weren't too inconvenienced."

Alex's teenage pranks will not get to me. Sometime during the night, though, he steps up his game. I wake in the morning to discover the Tesla gone. In a rage, I dial his number.

He answers the phone laughing. "Now, now. You know you shouldn't be calling me. Did you forget about the no-contact order? I wouldn't want to have you arrested."

"Why are you doing this? Grow the hell up!"

"What is it exactly that you're accusing me of now? Choose your words carefully, sweetheart. I might be recording."

"Why would you flatten the tires then steal my car?"

He snickers. "You mean the car I bought and paid for? If you and your boyfriend truly believe I'm doing these things to *our* vehicle, why doesn't he do anything about it? Guess he's not such a tough guy after all."

I slam the phone down. He's baiting Daniel—through me. He hopes to get him to make a move so he can have him arrested. Alex is clever. I may have lost my cool, but I won't let him win.

Hours later, the police find the Tesla two blocks away, half-sunk in the marsh. The front and rear windshields are both smashed, but nothing inside was disturbed. My key necklace is back in its place but covered in mud. *Why would Alex take it, dirty it, then put it back?*

I've had it! I photograph my ruined car, upload the pictures to Facebook, and write, "Who would steal my car, destroy it, and leave it two blocks away? First one to guess wins a prize!"

Maybe shaming him publicly will make him stop. This time, I'll have no choice but to tell Daniel about the car and the ex parte against me.

"This fucking guy has to be stopped."

I know he's right, but I feel powerless to do anything. The police say they'll do an investigation but tell me not to get my hopes up.

Daniel puts his fist through the living room wall of the beach house. "I can't take it, Abby. He's playing dirty and needs the piss beat out of him."

"That won't solve anything."

"Trust me, I know guys like this, spoiled arrogant bastard. It's the only way to teach him a lesson."

"No." I'm firm with my answer. "No violence. Get a grip on yourself. He's Ruby's father. Beating him up like some thug would destroy her. It'll all be over soon."

He groans in frustration then holds me by the shoulders. "I hope you're right. This has to end."

He apologizes for his temper and spends the afternoon repairing the hole.

Bottling up anger, then exploding, is one of the hyperarousal symptoms of PTSD. Daniel and I research more constructive ways to deal with his issues, like running and meditating. I know he has a lot of healing to do and that it will take time.

"What happened to seeing a therapist?"

"I swear I was going to start seeing someone in person, but then Claire needed me. I did find a guy online who specializes in PTSD. He says Special Ops guys are more than twice as likely to develop issues. The accident, losing Georgia and Crosby probably multiplied everything." He shakes his head. "I'm in better shape than most. A lot of guys end up drunks or junkies, and some off themselves."

I know he's right, because back in Europe, when Daniel was waking me with his nightmares, I spent a ton of time researching PTSD and its effects. Repressing anger causes a lot of problems.

"As soon as we're settled, I'll go to therapy every day if that's what it takes. I want to be the best possible person I can be for you, for your daughter, and for the baby."

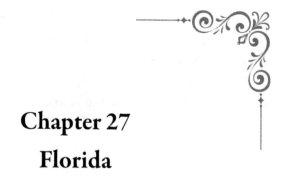

Chapter 27
Florida

In the week after his arrival, life unravels. While happy to have him, I'm constantly on edge, torn between spending every minute with him and Ruby before the baby comes and worrying what Alex will do next. Tension electrifies the air. Daniel tries to help relax me by massaging my back and taking me for long walks on the beach.

I've lost the ability to meditate. Each time I try, my mind fills with grim possibilities. There's no way to unwind. How do I explain my deepest worries to him about the baby? I'm terrified it belongs to Alex. What will our lives look like once we know the truth? Daniel reassures me that it doesn't matter. Of course it does, though. I'm holding out hope that once he goes back to Italy, things will settle down with Alex. Our divorce should be finalized very soon, and I truly believe that finality is what he needs.

At dinner, Daniel surprises me by taking my hand in his and say-ing, "Guess what?"

Oh no. I'm not prepared for any surprises, but I smile anyway. "What?"

"I extended the rental so I can be sure to be here when the baby is born."

I thought he was planning to leave the day after Christmas. The longer he stays, the more opportunities Alex has to provoke him—but I try to hide my frustration. I understand why he wants to be here.

His eyes study mine. "I thought you'd be happy. What's going on, Doc?" He drops my hand.

No way can I explain my—probably irrational—fear that Alex is a ticking bomb.

"Is this about your ex?" He shakes his head then leans in closer and lowers his voice. "I'm not tiptoeing around, letting that asshole dictate our lives anymore."

The last thing I need is for him to challenge Alex. "I'm sorry you're involved in this mess."

"We've waited so long to be together. I'm not letting him stand in our way."

To avoid further upsetting Alex, I limit the time Ruby and Daniel spend together, but it doesn't seem to help.

Dread gives way to terror each time I pull into the driveway in my rental car—I haven't even tried to work with the insurance company payout. Most days when I return to the cottage, Alex has been there. He doesn't try to hide it, leaving my dresser drawers and kitchen cabinets open. I've changed the locks three times now, but it's obvious that isn't going to stop him. I share the truth with the attorney, who continually urges me to file my own ex parte, but I know that little piece of paper would only infuriate Alex further. I keep his invasions secret from Daniel.

On the blustery evening of December twenty-third, Ruby and I are curled up on either end of the sofa, playfully fighting over one small fuzzy throw she insists is hers. *Sweet Home Alabama*, our favorite chick flick, is nearing the end. Jake and Melanie are about to be reunited in the middle of a thunderstorm.

Ruby's cell phone rings. "No problem. I'll be right over," she says, then ends the call. She turns to me. "It was Dad. There's an emergency at the hospital, and he needs me to stay with Jack."

"But you know there's a big storm coming in tonight, and I'll be scared," I whine. "Why can't Grandma go?"

"He couldn't reach her. You know he wouldn't ask if it wasn't an emergency."

A nor'easter off the coast is coming in soon, and I have a foreboding feeling. The rain hasn't yet started, so I can't use that as an excuse, but I desperately want her to stay. When she's away from me, I am less than whole. When I'm alone, my anxiety spikes. Muscles around my neck and chest tighten, and my nerve endings are raw, like live exposed wires dangling millimeters apart. Alex will be at the hospital, so everything should be all right. I could drive to Daniel's, but he's already gone to bed. Besides, I still have presents to wrap. "Please text me the minute you get to the house."

"Don't I always?" She wraps her lanky arms around me and kisses my cheek. "I love you to the moon," she says, giving my belly a rub. "You, too, little one."

Tomorrow is Christmas Eve. Ruby will have dinner with Daniel and me at his place, then she'll spend the night at Marine Street with Alex and Jack. I tried everything to talk her out of it, but I couldn't change her mind. Jack wants her there when Santa arrives. I begged her to get up super early and go. I even offered to drive her myself, but she's a stubborn adult now, I remind myself. Alex's parents will join them for Christmas brunch.

The wind is strong, and the steady rhythm of raindrops ping the metal roof. I'm both too anxious and too tired to wrap gifts and nearly nod off while waiting for word from Ruby.

My phone vibrates on the nightstand, and there's a message from Ruby: *Back safe. Nighty night. <3*

I bury myself beneath the covers and pray I'll somehow sleep through the storm. At some point, exhaustion wins.

Loose shutters banging against the cottage walls jolts me from deep, disorienting sleep. Heavy rain pelts the metal roof. Outside sounds like a war zone. Fear causes a chilly sweat to coat my body. I wrap the comforter around me tightly. Wind howls and whistles through the rickety windows and doors. I've never been more afraid.

There's nothing to be afraid of, Abby. It's just a storm. I keep my eyes squeezed shut, waiting for the calm to come. *Five, four, three, two, one...* Lightning flashes, and I see a window, dresser, curtains, the shape of my legs beneath the covers, and my hand held close to my face. *Four.* I feel the sheets, the warm comforter tucked around me, the soft downy pillow beneath my head, and the tight ball of flesh with the baby tucked safely inside. I reach under the pillow beside me and touch the phone hidden there, just in case. *Three.* I hear the angry ocean's churning waves pounding the sand. I hear the wind howling and the thunder cracking and rumbling through the sky. *Two.* I smell the salty air permeating through the walls of this beach shack and the remnants of a vanilla candle I burned earlier. *One.* I lick my lips and taste popcorn from earlier. *Deep breath. It's working.*

Thunder cracks, and lightning flashes illuminate the room. Alex is there—standing at the edge of the bed, staring down at me. His swollen eyes are bloodshot and empty, like before.

I scream. "What the hell are you doing?"

He doesn't blink. He doesn't answer. He sits down then rubs his hands along the sides of my face and across my hair, like he's petting a dog about to be put down.

I reach for the cordless phone tucked beneath the pillow, but he snatches my wrist and slams it to the headboard. His anger doesn't surprise me, but the roughness of his movements do. His eyes are glazed and blank. My voice and my touch go unnoticed, as if I'm a ghost.

I swing at him with my free hand, striking the side of his face. "Let go of me!"

He's holding the white linen scarf I bought in Sorrento. With little effort, he ties my hands to the headboard, making each knot tighter than the last. I kick, thrash, cry, and scream. But it's no use. He leans his weight across my thighs. He's too strong.

"No one can hear you."

"What are you doing?" I hear the desperation in my voice.

He leans over my exhausted body and kisses my mouth.

I lie frozen, letting him kiss me, tasting bourbon, smoke, and hate. *Five, four, three, two, one...* I breathe deeply, fighting not to black out.

His kiss is urgent. His tongue probes deeper, then he breaks away. "Is this how you like it?"

I close my mouth, turning my face away.

He reaches down and squeezes his groin. "Do you know how long it's been for me?"

He removes my panties. I beg him not to and squeeze my legs together. It's no use, though. He'll have this last dance.

He spreads me wide, forcing my legs over his shoulders. My thighs tighten around his neck, but he's unfazed. He puts his mouth on me then thrusts his tongue, warm and wet, inside.

I sob, but my body responds in the ultimate betrayal.

"No one can make you feel like I can." He pants and wipes his mouth with the back of his hand.

Searing pain surges through my groin and into my back. My abdomen contracts. I dry heave. He stops, stands with a satisfied smile, and removes his pants. I hear the sound of his belt buckle hitting the floor and the sloshing as he strokes himself harder.

I cross my legs and plead again, begging him to stop. He's not yet past the point of no return. "Please, Alex, what about the baby? What about Ruby?"

My cries go unanswered. He climbs on top of me, pushes my legs apart, and thrusts deep inside. The storm is direct-

ly above us now. There's hardly a break between thunder
and lightning. The room is bright when I scream again.

With every thrust of his hips, I want to die.
"Is this how Danny Boy fucks you? Is this what you beg for?" He
lifts my hips and rams himself inside, deeper and harder. He yells between breaths, "Does he enjoy it, knowing my baby is inside you?"

He looks at the ceiling, at the wall, everywhere but at me. "I
guess I should have been giving it to you like this all along."

"Alex, look at me!" I scream, hoarse. "Look what you're doing.
The baby."

My abdomen tightens again with another contraction. *Long
breath in, long breath out. Repeat.* I squeeze my eyes closed to escape
this horror.

His body stiffens, and he groans. He throbs and fills me with his
poison. His movements slow then stop. His face is inches from mine,
his exhausted breath blowing my hair. I open my eyes and meet his.

He runs his eyes over my body with a look of disgust. Then he
stands, turns on the light, wipes his still erect penis with my comforter, then steps back into his trousers. He avoids looking at me as I
lie there, empty and shattered.

"Untie me, please." A sob erupts. "I won't tell anyone."

He paces the room silently then lies down beside me, leaning his
forehead over to meet mine. He strokes my cheek then unties me.
His eyes convey what his mouth cannot—desperation and anguish.

"I love you so much, Abby," he cries. "I tried to be without you. I
tried to forgive you. I honestly did."

His wounded expression disappears. Then he sits up and strad-
dles me. My belly—the baby—separates us.

"But I saw you. The way you slept. With him in that shitty little
hotel in Switzerland. Your body draped over his. You never slept with
me that way." He shakes his head in regret. "I should have bashed his

skull right then. This would all be over." His eyes meet mine. "Don't you understand? You belong to me, sweetheart. You always have."

It wasn't in my head. He used a PI to find me. He was there in Wilderswil.

Waves of searing pain flow through me. My body implodes. I try one last time. "Please. The baby."

His fingers slide up on either side of my throat. "There's no saving this baby. It's ruined."

Each digit presses deeper into the back of my neck. His thumbs find the hollow groove at the front. They connect with my windpipe.

I swing and scratch at his head and neck. I claw at his eyes, but it doesn't matter. I'm weak. My left hand scours under the pillow again, desperately searching for the phone.

Warm liquid gushes between my legs, soaking the sheets. *The baby is coming. It's too soon.*

"The baby," I squeak from my constricted throat.

He pretends not to hear then releases the pressure for a moment, stroking the hollow of my throat. He reaches down and caresses the gold key I forgot I'm wearing. He presses it into the groove over my windpipe. It lasts almost a minute. I gasp and plead. He could make this swift and easy. He doesn't. He prolongs my suffering.

He moves his thumbs, relieving the pressure enough to allow me to take in a strawful of air. Then he presses back down again. He does this, over and over, stopping each time before I lose consciousness.

The sharp edges of the pendant pierce the skin, and blood pools in the hollow space between my collarbones. My body convulses.

He cries, "You did this to me. I never wanted to hurt you." He hisses, "This is your fault. You drove me to this."

Bile and blood fill my throat. I retch.

His teardrops fall, join mine, and roll gently down my cheeks. "You are *my* wife. This is my city."

His thumbs spread and settle on the perfect spot. He presses down. I struggle, clawing at his face with one hand. With the other, I continue the search.

In the final moment between light and darkness, my fingers grip the phone beneath the pillows. I press three digits then the talk button. From far away, I hear a voice, but it's too late. Darkness pulls me. I release my grasp and give up the fight to stay in this world.

The baby crowns, splitting me in two. It doesn't happen at all like I expect. I thought I'd float above and watch the scene play out. Instead, a burning sensation passes through my throat and chest. That's it. There's no light. No one from the other side. Not my grandmother. Not Tommy.

As I pull in the last sips of air, the only thoughts crossing my mind are greedy and selfish. I want for nothing, except oxygen. I fight to keep my eyes open, even after the pressure makes it unbearable. Vessels swell and burst. I stare up at Alex until the very end. I want him to look at me. To remember my eyes. The way he made them bleed. But his soul has departed. Soon mine will too. He is broken, like me.

I dream of sirens and blue lights. I dream of banging on doors and windows, of the front door being kicked in. They are too late. They can't save me. They can't undo what is done.

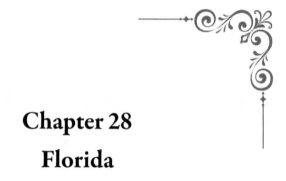

Chapter 28
Florida

"Where am I?" I cry to the empty room. I smell bleach and urine that I hope isn't my own. I am curled in the fetal position, struggling to break through the heavy fog in my mind. I must be sedated. The room is stark and white with no furniture. The door holds a tiny pane of glass. I am safe—in a hospital, perhaps—but I don't know why. I rest my eyes again, allowing the tension to release from my body and my mind to drift.

Time passes. I know because they bring meals—pale-yellow eggs and toast with gelatinous lunchmeat slices on white bread. After dark, they bring mashed potatoes with yellowed gravy and thick slices of meatloaf. The smells are repulsive, and I leave the trays untouched.

When I wake, they bring the pills to make me sleep. "Open your mouth. Lift your tongue."

I obey.

Clinking keys unlock my door and rouse me. The rhythm of familiar footsteps, hard leather meeting concrete, near my head. Through the smallest slivers of my eyes, I try to be lucid when I see him. He is hazy, but his shoes are not. Brown polished Berlutis that cost more than my first car stop at my bedside. They are his favorite. Alex is here.

"I'm going to give you something to wake you up, sweetheart."
His voice is a million miles away.

I try to move my lips to thank him, but they are frozen, my
tongue weighed down like an anvil. I reach for him to hold me, but
my leaden arms disobey. I need him to help me understand. A pin-
prick pierces my right hip and sucks me into another atmosphere.
I bolt upright, gasping for air. Vomit fills the back of my throat. I
choke it back.

He sits down beside me. My knees are tucked tightly against my
chest. He rubs my back the way he used to, long ago. "Calm down,
Abigail. Breathe. Take some long, slow breaths," he says, undertones
of annoyance in his voice. "Keep breathing, and you won't get sick."
He speaks to me as if I were just another of his patients.

I swallow the bile and wipe my burning, watery eyes. "Where am
I? What happened?" I reach for his arm, clinging with both hands.
"Tell me, please." My voice cracks.

Tenderly, he rubs my cheek with the back of his hand, and I look
into his eyes for an answer. He pulls free of my grasp and towers over
me.

"You're in the hospital." He crosses his arms and smiles down at
me. "My hospital."

I study him. His second-day stubble and clothes are all wrong.
He's always clean-shaven. His shirt is loose and wrinkled. His pants
are stained. Alex is always meticulously dressed. For him to look like
this, something terrible must have happened.

I need to know why I'm here. "What happened?"

"Oh, sweetheart, you did this to yourself." He sighs and cocks his
head to the side. "You've been struggling lately."

Think. What is he talking about?

"You tried to hurt yourself."

My mind races as tiny flashes of memories flood my brain. A
heavy thunderstorm. Sitting on my grandmother's front porch swing

in Franklin, Tennessee, my legs curled beneath a knitted blanket. A baby with outstretched arms toddling toward me. Standing on a balcony overlooking the sea in Sorrento. Sitting at the kitchen table in a tiny apartment in Paris. Telling Daniel about the baby.

Daniel. The baby. My head spins. I reach down to my stomach and press my palms harder and deeper into swollen flesh, searching desperately for signs of life. But there's nothing. My womb is soft and empty. Cries of a desperate animal build then escape from my vacant abdomen. At once, every emotion I've ever held unleashes. Fear, regret, and mostly rage flood me and commandeer my body from the bed, shaking my core. I scream at him, hoping my words will cut him to shreds.

His eyes widen in surprise and maybe even fear as he turns and knocks three times on the glass pane. I charge him, tearing at his shirt and scratching his face. I scream the words over and over. "Where is the baby? Where is my baby?"

Before I see them, I hear them coming. Footsteps thunder down the halls, echoing against the concrete walls. The door slams open, and their shadows fill the room. They surround me. Their arms take hold, bending and twisting me away from him. I fight with everything in me until a jab in the arm renders me useless.

Once I am subdued, he steps closer and leans in. "You shouldn't have left me, sweetheart."

Later that day, maybe the next, I wake. The sun is gone, and I'm alone again. Clips of memories flood my head like scenes in movies seconds before the character dies.

Before the people with the pills come, I remember something, and it stays. A man is in my head. He's been there before.

He's young, barely grown. Shaggy blond hair hangs over one eye. He flips his hair to the side and smiles at me, then he fades. He reappears. His eyes are strangely beautiful, like colored gems.

He's with a girl. Her eyes are the same. She dances and twirls on a beach, tossing her head back in laughter. He joins her. They reach for me to dance with them. And I wish so desperately I could. Her golden hair catches the sunlight and blows in the breeze. She's beautiful and I am drawn to her.

I won't forget this time. Not when they bring the pills. Not ever. I'll hold on. The next time I wake, I remember them. Tommy is the man. His face is dim, barely there. It fades.

The golden-haired girl remains, vivid. Ruby. She once moved inside me. She was plump and round when they first placed her in my arms, sticky and wet. Her cries filled the room.

Everyone laughed. "Nice lungs," they said. My lips crack in remembrance.

Is it real?

Another memory comes, more recent, closer to the surface. Suction sounds and gurgling. "Born too soon," someone says.

"Come on, baby girl. Breathe," a voice says.
A tiny cry. Gurgling. More suction. Beeping monitors.
"That's it. You're doing it."
"She's hanging on."
"This one's a fighter."

They come again, with more pills. Saltwater courses through my veins. I'm in the deep end of the ocean. I'm breathing it in. I'm drowning. No one can save me. Thoughts and nightmares blend. Whether they're reality or dreams, I can't tell.

Finally, the fog lightens. *Don't think too hard this time. Stay awake. Focus.*

The ocean comes to me. A cottage on the beach—it's mine. Waves and palms rustle in the breeze, and the air smells of salt.

The man with the gemstone eyes is gone. He's been gone for days now. But the girl with the golden hair is there. I think she's my daughter.

Curled in a fetal position, I doze. Next time, they bring the pills, I'll fight harder. I'll kick and scream and bite if I have to.

When I open my eyes again, a lady doctor looks down at me.

"Hi, Abigail. How are you feeling today? Do you mind if I talk with you awhile?"

I nod.

She wears a white lab coat and holds a clipboard in her hand. "My name is Dr. Alexandrov. But you can just call me Dr. A. Everyone does. I'm here to ask you a few questions."

Maybe she can help stitch these tiny memories together.

"Can I help you sit up?" she asks, leaning in and placing her arm around my back.

My face brushes against her lab coat. She smells of bleach and fabric softener. With her help, it still takes all my strength to right myself.

"I'm married to a doctor," I say with sudden lucidity. His name comes to me. "Alex."

If I keep stitching the threads together one by one, soon I'll make a blanket.

"That's excellent, Abby. Do you know why you're here?" She scribbles something on her clipboard. "Do you remember what happened?"

I squeeze my eyes closed and try, but I don't.

"That's all right. I've taken over your case and am going to work with you until your memory comes back. You've been taking a lot of very strong medications, and I'm in the process of weaning you off of them. Everything will be clearer, and I have a feeling your memory will return in no time. For now, just rest."

She is pretty. Her sandy hair is sleek and cut to her shoulders, and her amber eyes are kind. "I'll be back to see you this afternoon, and we'll chat more then."

I slide back down, curl into a ball, and drift away again.

"ABIGAIL, IT'S ME, AGAIN. Listen, I need you to wake up and eat a little something. If you don't start eating, they're going to put in a feeding tube, and we don't want that."

She rolls a tray toward me. On it is a plate of French fries, apple-sauce, and a leathery-looking burger. I blink my eyes open. My head is clearer. This time, I'm able to get into a sitting position on my own. I lift a wilted fry to my lips and take a small bite.

I cough. My throat is coated with dust. My tongue is thick and heavy. "Water, please?"

She hands me a plastic cup filled with metallic-tasting lukewarm water.

I force myself to eat the applesauce. It soothes the rawness of my throat.

"I'm so glad you're finally eating. How are you feeling now?"

"Confused."

"I understand. Do you know what city we're in?"

"St. Augustine." That comes easily. I drink the rest of my water, ignoring my burning throat. My voice is hoarse, and I don't sound like myself. "I have a daughter. Ruby."

"That's great progress." She's clearly pleased. "What else do you remember?"

Trapped beneath the icy surface, concern breaks through. "Where is she?"

"She's fine. I promise. Tell me more about you first, then we'll talk about your daughter."

"I'm from Tennessee, but have lived in Florida since..." I try but can't remember how long. "Since I got married. I met my husband in medical school at Vanderbilt. We got married after he graduated, and I quit school. He's the chief of staff at St. Augustine Memorial." I speak slowly, my throat dry and scratchy, as if I'm hearing these things for the first time. *Have I done it?* I wonder. *Have I told her enough? Will she tell me about Ruby now?*

Her eyes narrow, and her brows come together. She looks worried. "That's great, Abigail." She pats my leg.

"Abby. Everyone calls me Abby."

"Okay, Abby, do you know where you are or why you're here?"

I look around the room with the tiny glass window.

"Did I do something bad? Did I hurt someone?" Panic rises in me. *Five, four, three, two, one...*

"Do you remember anything that happened the last time you were home?"

I shake my head.

"This is going to be difficult, but I want you to take your time and try to remember. You're safe now. No one can hurt you. I'm here with you. You can trust me." She puts her hand on my shoulder.

I try but can barely remember the inside of the cottage. The curtains were blowing in the sea breeze, and that's it. The rest is blank. I shake my head. "I don't remember."

"It's okay, Abby. I'm going to help you. I might say things that make you uncomfortable, but it's important." She looks at me. "Tell me you understand."

"I do."

"Okay. The report says your husband—" She pauses. "Dr. Montgomery came by your home on the night of December twenty-third to bring some gifts. That was a little over a week ago." She looks up. "I understand the two of you are separated. He claims he found you unresponsive in your bed and promptly called for help. The report here"—she looks down at her clipboard then back at me—"says he believes you attempted to take your own life. He says you've made attempts in the past. Is that true?"

I shake my head. He's lying. I may have considered ending things, but I never actually tried.

"Okay then, let's move on." She makes a note. "Do you remember being pregnant?"

I pause and pull myself out of bed to stand. The room spins.

She looks at me worriedly then places her hands on my shoulders. "You had a baby, Abby."

Blackness pours in, blocking my peripheral vision. And just like that, my knees give out. I grasp for her as I crumple to the floor.

Chapter 29
Florida

"Whoa. It's okay," she says, pulling me up. "Abby, look at me. Everything is all right. You have a beautiful baby girl."

I press my hands deep into the folds of my abdomen. It's soft and empty. "I do? A girl, and she's alive?"

"Yes, a girl, and yes, she's very much alive."

"Is she okay?"

"She will be. She arrived a little early and had a bit of a rough start, but she's fine."

I ask if she's sure, my mind spinning once again. I know what she's saying is true. It came to me in a dream.

Her warm eyes are genuine and filled with pity. "I'm sure."

"Can I see her?"

"Not yet. We need to make sure you're okay first, and we need to figure out exactly what happened to lead up to your alleged"—she makes air quotes—"psychotic break. I really want to help you, Abby. Dr. Montgomery has given some conflicting reports, and I don't believe he's being honest about what happened. The psychiatrist who had your case has had you on some heavy-duty stuff. More than necessary. But I'm in the process of weaning you off everything."

Can I trust her?

"Abby, you were in bad shape when you came in. The report says you coded on the ride in and had to be resuscitated. Once you were stabilized, you were moved here to the psychiatric wing." She pauses and presses her lips together. "I'm going to be straight with you—Dr. Montgomery had you Baker-Acted. When I got your file, I raised some questions, and he changed his story. He's now saying your estranged boyfriend is the one who hurt you."

"Estranged? I don't understand. We're together."

She scribbles furiously on her notepad.

I close my eyes. Beyond the fog, I see Daniel's face. I see his eyes above me, and his lips kiss me tenderly. He mouths those three words. He would never hurt me—this, I know is true.

Anguish surges through me, causing pain to fill every crevice. A sob seizes my raw throat. I place my fingers there, feeling the tenderness beneath my touch. "Where is Daniel?"

Dr. A looks pained and unsure of what to say.

"Please tell me," I say.

"Abby, I'm sorry to tell you this, but he's in jail right now. Just until everything gets sorted out."

Despite the pain, I sob harder. "Because of me?"

"Once the reports came back saying you couldn't possibly have done this to yourself, Dr. Montgomery—" She swallows. "He suddenly recalled seeing Mr. Quinn leaving your house in a hurry."

"And the police believed him?"

"I know." She closes her eyes, shaking her head. "Dr. Montgomery claims he was so traumatized by finding you unresponsive, he had a breakdown and is now suffering from a rare form of PTSD. He even has his"—she again makes air quotes with her fingers—"'condition' documented from a very well-esteemed psychiatrist, a colleague of his, I suspect."

The memories keep coming. "Daniel loves me."

"Is there anyone who would want to hurt you?"

My head is heavy. "I don't think so."

She continues, "The police have been here several times to question you, but you wouldn't speak to them."

"Why can't I remember?"

"You've been through a great deal of trauma. Someone tried to kill you, and you gave birth. Sometimes our bodies have a way of protecting us, our minds in particular. What happened is all there. When your mind and body are ready to face the truth, it will surface."

I rub my hands through my unwashed hair and wonder if this could be any worse.

Dr. A puts a hand on my shoulder. "There's something I need to tell you." She hesitates. "Dr. Montgomery has petitioned the courts for custody of the baby."

"She's his?" I recall the uncertainty of not knowing.

"Was there doubt?"

I don't respond.

"Well, his name is listed on the birth certificate as the baby's father." She flips through a chart. "And it seems there was a paternity test, so yes, it looks like she belongs to him."

My body is heavy. Breath hitches in my throat. My heart implodes. "No." It can't be true. I remember now. I prayed so hard. Bile rises in the back of my throat. "I'm going to be sick."

She hands me a plastic bowl, and I pant through nausea, my head reeling with emotions. I want to see my daughters!

I curl back into bed. "Please go away."

"I'm sorry. I'll give you some time." I hear the clicking of the door closing behind her.

I try, but tears won't come. There is nothing left in me.

HOURS, MAYBE DAYS, blend together. There's a knock then a voice. She's back.

"Hi, Abby. I may have some news."

I am awake but refuse to roll over to face her.

"This may be nothing, but I had someone check the baby's file. The actual paternity test results were not in there. Just notes. Dr. Montgomery refuses to produce the paperwork."

A tiny glimmer of hope emerges. "So there's a chance she may not belong to him?"

"That's what I'm saying. I tried to get him to resubmit a sample to an independent lab, but he refused. He says he ran the test himself, which isn't even legal."

"I didn't sleep with him. I think he may have—" I cannot finish my sentence. "She can't belong to Alex. She just can't."

"Listen, I know this is a lot to handle. We need to get this mess sorted out. Please know I'll do whatever it takes, including going to the board, to keep the baby with you." She places her hand on my arm. "Abby, please try not to worry. I'm going to help you remember. I promise."

"Why would you do that? You don't even know me."

She smiles. "I'm a close friend of Katherine Kym's. She's distraught over this whole situation."

Dr. Kym is my ob-gyn. I don't know what to say.

"Frankly, Abby, this is unprofessional of me, but I know a sociopath when I see one."

"But my daughter—my older daughter—I need to see her."

"According to the notes, she's been to see you several times while you were up in the ICU. Let me do some digging and see what I can find."

"I want to talk to Daniel."

"Soon, you will. I promise. For right now, though, neither of you has phone privileges."

I'm a prisoner, held against my will. "Can I at least see the baby, please?"

"Tell you what, let me go see if there are any strings I can pull."

More determined than ever, I fight to clear my head. I swallow down Styrofoam cups of cold black sludge from my lunch tray, praying it'll clear the cobwebs. When the nurse comes, I ask for more. With each passing hour, I swim closer to the surface, closer to the truth, and closer to meeting my new daughter. My daughter. The words settle on my tongue. I have a baby girl. I should have been there to witness her take her first breath.

Her birth was traumatic. I sense it. She's been more than a week without a mother to bond with and feed her. She's been alone. *And where is Ruby?* A mother's most important job, my job, is to be there and protect the children. *How could this happen?*

The more coffee and water I consume, the faster the medication works its way out of my body and the clearer and angrier I become. I spend the afternoon pacing my tiny locked cell. I want to see my baby. I want to talk to Ruby and to Daniel. I haven't committed a crime and shouldn't be held prisoner. At the door, through the tiny glass pane, I see Dr. A.

"I'm sorry it took me so long, but I have great news. You can see the baby. First, though, I need you to promise to remain calm and do as I tell you."

My head is clearer, but the caffeine and surging emotions have me irritated. "Why am I being held captive, like some kind of murderer? Why are my children being kept from me? Why can't I talk to Daniel? Where is Alex? This is his hospital. I don't understand why the hell all this is happening."

She carefully weighs her words then touches my shoulder. "I know, sweetheart. I'm so sorry." They sound like Alex's words on her tongue.

I swat her hand away. "Don't call me that," I snap then apologize. "Please."

She takes a step back, wrinkling her brow.

"Alex calls me that." I try to explain, but I shake, and the words won't come.

"Abby, I'm sorry for what you're going through, but I need you to listen to me carefully. I'm trying hard to get you out of here. I'm risking my career. Please understand that. I know you're frustrated and angry. I get it. But I can't help you if you don't pull yourself together. This means no outbursts. No matter how warranted they may be. I'm working to get you and the baby transferred out of here to Methodist Hospital. Dr. Montgomery has no working relationship with them."

"Get me transferred? I don't understand. Why can't I go home?" My insides quiver. "I need to be with my daughters. I need to get Daniel out of jail."

"Listen to me." Her hands are on my shoulders. "I'm trying my best. I have some very good people working with me behind the scenes, but Dr. Montgomery and his family are powerful people. I don't want you to do something impulsive without thinking it through. We need a plan. What we need most, though, is for you to remember what happened that night. So, for now, I think the best thing is to have you placed under a voluntary hold at Methodist. This means you have the ability to check yourself out, if you want. My hope is for you to stay—with the baby, of course—until your memory returns. I will be there through every step."

"But what about Ruby?" I cry. "I don't know how long it's been since I've seen her or how long I've been here."

"Four days in this department, the first four days in the ICU, and two in an intermediate care unit. I spoke to your daughter this afternoon. She said to tell you she loves you and that she and her—half brother, is it?"

I nod.

"They're staying with your in-laws. She said everything's fine and that she's been going to the nursery to hold and feed the baby each afternoon. I promised her I'm taking very good care of you and that she'll be able to see you soon." Dr. A tucks her hair behind her ear, takes a step back, and smiles. "She's a sweet girl."

I desperately want to see Ruby. I can't imagine what she's going through right now, knowing someone tried to kill me. She has been through hell and doesn't deserve any of this. My ears pound with rage that has no place to go.

I take solace in the image of the new baby in Ruby's arms. I beg Dr. A to get the paternity test results.

"I will do my best to get a court order. Also, I almost forgot to mention—I found your father in Tennessee. He's helping us. Apparently, he's pulling strings with some judge friend of his."

My father, an old retired Franklin beat cop, is friends with a Florida judge. "I haven't had much of a relationship with him since I was a kid."

"Well, it seems he's trying to make up for that. He's been advocating on your behalf and stirring up trouble every chance he gets."

That sounds like George West. The man was once a Franklin, Tennessee legend. The man I remember used to chew his moustache crooked when contemplating an important decision. It's been years since I've seen or spoken with him. I'd like to say we drifted, but that isn't really true. I've had so much anger toward him that I made it impossible for him to have a relationship with me. He finally gave up. Who could blame him? Thinking about him makes me realize that for the first time in a long while, I ache to hear his drawl or even his quick-witted off-color jokes. I miss the way he smelled of Old Spice, applied with a heavy hand, and of Wrigley's spearmint gum. I long for my dad.

"Dr. Montgomery isn't happy. His attorneys are filing injunctions as quickly as we file on our end. He even attempted to file an ex parte against both your father and me to prevent us from seeing you. Thankfully, it was denied."

She shakes her head in disbelief. "But Dr. Montgomery did manage to have your father barred from hospital grounds, even without the ex parte. Don't worry, once you're transferred, you'll see him." She smiles and hands me a robe and brush like I should be thrilled at her news. She has no idea. "Put this on and run the brush through your hair. I'm going to grab a wheelchair and take you to meet your new daughter."

Dr. A uses a key card at three different sets of locked doors to exit the ward. The hallways are long, brightly lit, and smell of industrial cleaner. While waiting for the elevator to open, she makes small talk, but I can't focus. I'm too nervous waiting to meet my nameless baby girl. Daniel, Ruby, and I never got serious about names. We joked about some ridiculous ones like Finn, Vin, or Lynn Quinn. We wanted the baby's name to mean something, and I thought we had more time.

But what if she is Alex's? I push the thought away.

Dr. A gets us buzzed in through the double doors of the Mother-Infant Unit and wheels me into an empty room lit by cool fluorescents. "Make yourself comfortable. I'm going to see if we can get that little girl in here to meet her mom."

I stand from the wheelchair and open the blinds, allowing the warm sunlight to stream in. In the bathroom, I glare at the reflection. The person with hollowed cheeks and greasy hair cannot be me. I look closer at the dark circles beneath my eyes and notice tiny ruptured blood vessels in the whites. In the center of my neck are two distinct yellowish-brown spots with raised red scabs the size of my key pendant. I turn my head to the side, lift my hair, and expose four finger-length lines of the same color on both sides of my neck—bruises from the attack. I trace them with my fingers and come undone. Why would anyone hurt me like this? Other than Alex, I have no enemies. As quickly as the thought flashes in my mind, it vanishes into the darkest depths of my being.

After a knock on the door, a hazel-eyed nurse with a warm smile wheels in a plastic bassinet. I quickly splash water on my face, pat it dry, and step out to meet my daughter. She is tiny and swaddled in a generic pink-white-and-blue hospital blanket, with a Pepto-pink hat snugly on her head.

"This little girl is four and a half pounds of perfection." Nurse Bonnie passes the sleeping bundle to me, eyeing me with a merciful look. She must know my story. Everyone probably does.

My heart nearly bursts open at the sight of my baby girl. In that moment, who fathered her or how it happened doesn't matter. Tears roll down my cheeks onto hers, causing her eyes to open. She blinks slowly, trying to adjust to the sunlight.

"Hi, beautiful girl."

Hearing the sound of my voice, she opens her eyes wider and studies me. Through the slight haze of tears, sea-blue eyes look up at me. Alex's and mine are both brown.

Removing the knit hat, I run my hands through her hair, thick and dark—like Daniel's. She looks different than Ruby did as a newborn. So much smaller and darker.

I bring her tiny head to my nose and take in the intoxicating scent only a newborn can offer. Having her in my arms is more soothing than any type of meditation.

"I think this girl has more hair than me," the nurse says, running her fingers through her own fine fiery-red hair. She's holding her clipboard, standing beside the bassinet, with a smile so warm, it makes me wish she was my own mother. "Nothing in the world smells better than a new baby."

"Are they sure she's okay?" I ask. "She's really completely healthy?"

"She sure is. She had a little extra help breathing the first few days. That's why she's been in the NICU, but she's strong and ready to go over to the regular nursery. Only thing is, we don't know what to call her. Do you have a name for her, hon?"

I look down at my blue-eyed angel baby and think of all she's endured in her short life. She's a light, brighter than I could ever imagine. I know the perfect name for her, but I'm not ready. Not without Daniel. "Soon."

I forgot Dr. A was in the room, sitting in a chair beside the window, doing paperwork.

She stands and heads for the door. "Abby, I'm going to give you some privacy, but I'll be right outside. I'd love to leave you alone with her for the afternoon, but I'm afraid—"

A commotion outside the door startles us both. Dr. A steps out and threatens, in a booming voice, to call security. Unsure what's happening, I hold the baby tightly against me and breathe. Alex steps inside and closes the door behind him.

"Hey there, sweetheart," he says, his voice off-kilter, his clothes wrinkled. "I see you've met our girl."

The hair on the back of my neck rises. My heart races. I squeeze the baby tighter to my chest, causing her to squirm. My mouth is too dry for words.

"Listen," he says, pacing the room. "They're trying to get you moved out of here, for some reason." He laughs hysterically, without smiling. "Tell them you don't want that. Tell them you want to stay here, with your husband." His hand rests on my shoulder. "Okay?"

My body quakes, and the baby nearly falls from my arms.

"Give me my daughter, Abigail."

"Please help." I try to scream, but only a squeak comes out as he snatches the baby from my arms and heads for the door.

Nurse Bonnie swings the clipboard hard, making contact with the side of Alex's head. She rears back and does it again and again. "Give that baby back to her mother, you bully bastard."

"Help!" I scream, and the baby's lungs open up.

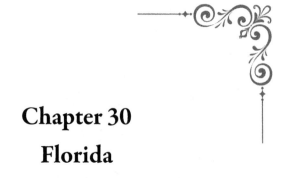

Chapter 30
Florida

The door opens with a bang. Security guards flank Alex. Nurse Bonnie snatches the baby from my arms and huddles in the corner, shielding the baby's body with her own.

"Dr. Montgomery, if you don't get out of this room right now, you will be forcibly removed," Dr. A says.

"This is my hospital. You leave. Remove her," he tells the guards.

They look from doctor to doctor, unsure whose orders to obey.

"I am the head of this hospital, and you"—he looks at the poor nurse—"are fired!"

"You don't scare me, tough guy," she retorts.

"Why don't both of you come with us," the bigger of the two guards says to Dr. A and Alex. "We'll straighten this out downstairs."

"Let's go." Dr. A is at the door. She opens it, gesturing for the others. "After you, gentlemen. I'll be right back, Abby."

Once they're out of the room, Nurse Bonnie hands the baby back to me. I try to settle the both of us. *Five, four, three, two, one...* The baby stops crying, and I take a deep breath, trying to understand what just transpired. Alex has obviously had a psychotic break. I have to get us out of here, away from him.

The nurse leaves then returns. She places her hand on my shoulder and says gently, "Hon, I'm going to take her and get her ready for transfer."

"Transfer? Where?"

"The paperwork just got expedited." She smirks. "You're both going up to Methodist. You'll like it there. My sister Laurie works the ER, and she's going to watch over you."

I think about Alex threatening her and wonder if she forged signatures to get me transferred. "What did you do?"

"Don't you worry about a thing. If he's going to have my job anyway, I might as well go out with a bang."

Within minutes, the transfer team wheels in a plastic isolette and tries to take the baby from my arms. How could I hand her over with everything that's happened? I won't.

"I'm sorry. We have our orders. The baby will be there when you arrive."

The old me might have complied, but this me is a fierce fighter. This past year has cost me so much. I nearly lost Daniel, Ruby, and my life. I have to protect my daughter. "No. I'm not leaving her side. Someone tried to kill me and nearly killed her. I'm staying, and we're leaving this hospital together."

Both guys' eyes widen. "We'll have to go talk to the supervisor."

"Tell your supervisor and your supervisor's supervisor. I'm not handing this baby over to anyone. Tell them I'll sue this hospital and each person that tries to take her from me."

Nurse Bonnie yells after them, "Damn right, she's not."

Dr. A steps in, just in time. "I'm the one ordering the transfer, and I insist mother and baby stay together."

WHEN I ARRIVE AT METHODIST, my sweet Ruby is there waiting. I fall to pieces the minute I see her. She doesn't miss a beat and runs over to greet me with a squeal and an armful of pink balloons. "I'm so happy you're awake."

Her spiky hair tickles my neck, but having her there, in my arms, I can breathe again. Self-consciously, I fumble with the pink linen scarf around my neck, thankful Dr. A gave it to me.

"Mom," she says with her eyes on mine, "I've been so worried."

"It's okay. Every little thing—"

She forces a smile then rakes a hand through her short hair.

"We have so much to talk about."

"And we will. We'll have all the time to do that later. Let's just be happy right now. Please."

I have no choice but to honor her wishes. She's matured so much, but I know she's going to need a lot of help getting past what has happened. We spend the afternoon together with the baby. We count fingers and toes and take turns feeding and changing her. I'm still weak, so Ruby does most of the work. I try to get her to open up, but she refuses to talk about anything that isn't happy. I wish I could erase everything bad that has happened to both of us, because, other than Daniel, everything I love is in this room.

Ruby leaves to pick up Jack from soccer practice, and I'm left alone with Dr. A. I beg her to find a way to contact Daniel. I'm desperate to hear his voice and know he's okay. Two hours later, I pick up the ringing phone and hear his voice on the other end of the line. It nearly breaks me.

"I promise we're going to get you out of there." I inhale then exhale to calm myself. "I'm so sorry, for everything."

"I thought I'd lost you." His voice quivers, then he sobs.

"I'm tougher than that," I try to joke. "I'm fine, Ruby's fine, and so is the baby."

"Are you sure you're okay? Tell me everything. What does she look like?"

My heart knows she belongs to him, but until there's a paternity test, doubt will linger in the shadows. "She has your eyes and your hair and the cutest little nose."

"She does?" I hear the excitement in his voice.

"I can't wait for you to meet her. I miss you."

"Did you give her a name?"

"Soon. Once we're together."

"Abby, tell me, please," he says. "Tell me you know I had nothing to do with hurting you."

"Of course I know you would never hurt me."

"Listen, Doc, my time is up, but I can call you again tomorrow." He speaks quickly. "Please stay strong, and don't worry about me."

The line goes dead, leaving me in silence and making me more determined than ever to get my memory back and get Daniel free.

Dr. A has a guard stationed outside of my door and papers filed. Alex isn't allowed on hospital grounds. I have no idea how she pulled it off. I only wish Ruby could stay here with me. She promises she's safe with Alex's parents and Jack. "Grandad is making Dad see someone, to talk."

The Methodist doctors are kind and understanding. But Dr. A is my saving grace.

"What about your other patients?"

She smiles. "Business is slow at the moment."

"I don't believe that."

"I promised Katherine I would take care of you."

Our relationship has crossed to another level, like we're old friends. Last night, she sat with me while I cried about the mess my life has become. She helped me understand that my reluctance to move forward stems from abandonment issues. I never got to say goodbye to my brother. My parents left me, and my grandmother, the only one left to care about me, died. According to Dr. A, my reactions are pretty normal.

"I'll continue to help you as long as you need me."

With morning comes news. "We weren't successful getting the test results from Alex…"

My shoulders droop.

"But your attorney has petitioned the courts to force him to submit his DNA, and the good news is we do have a sample from Daniel. But it could take a while for the results—sometimes up to eight to twelve weeks."

Waiting will kill me. "Thank you. I don't know how I can ever repay you for helping me."

"How about by remembering what happened the night of December twenty-third."

"I want to. I swear, more than anything, I do." I reach up and run my fingers along the raised scab on my trachea. The touch brings a brief flash of terror and threatens to bring forth something I'm not ready for. I remember the gold antique key and chain necklace I was wearing. "Dr. A, can I ask you something?"

"Anything."

"The night of the attack, I was wearing a necklace with a key. Have you seen it?"

"No. Your belongings came over with you. Just a nightshirt I don't think you'll ever use again."

My mind drifts back to the last time I can remember. *Sweet Home Alabama* was ending. Ruby was leaving… My father's loud voice echoing down the halls snaps me back to the present. There's no mistaking that Texas drawl. Dr. A heads him off in the hall before he comes in.

"I'll wring his goddamn neck and kill that son of a bitch as soon as I see him." A few seconds later, he says, "What the hell do you mean 'Don't upset her'? She's already upset. That goddamn lunatic tried to kill her." There's a long pause. "I don't need her to tell you a goddamn thing. The whole damn world knows it was him."

Dr. A's responses are too soft for me to hear. Minutes pass as I fight the urge not to run out into the hall. As I take a few deep breaths, preparing for the Texas tornado, my father swaggers through the door, as calm as can be. He's wearing cowboy boots and a big smile, carrying an armful of wildflowers.

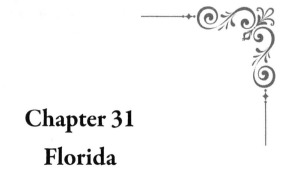

Chapter 31
Florida

"Sugar," my father says, stifling a sob, "I brought you these. When you was just an itty-bitty thing, you loved these crazy ol' weeds." He lays them down and wraps his arms around me. His hands are rough against my skin, and he smells of Old Spice, like always. When he stands, his eyes are wet with tears.

"Don't cry, Daddy. I'm okay." The sight of him stirs long-buried emotions. Through the years, I've built impenetrable walls, growing so calloused and indifferent to my parents. I've only recently begun to realize Alex helped secure those walls. Whenever I spoke of trying to reconnect with my father, Alex convinced me not to. He would remind me how my father never tried to get me back from my grandmother. He said being in my dad's life would only remind him of everything he'd lost. Back then, I thought he was being protective out of love, but now I see he was keeping me isolated. Seeing my father with a head full of thinning gray hair and wrinkles around his eyes makes me feel small again.

"I'm so sorry, baby girl. I have so much to say, and I didn't know if you'd throw me out of here."

I dab my eyes. "No. Things are different now."

My father sits in the chair beside my bed, and we spend hours catching up on a lifetime of missed moments. He tells me how the Nashville screwballs have crept right into Franklin and turned the place into a yuppy circus. He rants about the traffic on Liberty Pike and how he can't even buy a plain cup of coffee anymore.

"They make it in some damn test tubes while you watch," he says. "Who the hell needs to watch their coffee dripping? Damn yuppies, that's who."

I can't help but laugh at his fury over the most ridiculous things.

He shakes his head. "And forget Nashville. Some rich sons of bitches came in and turned it into the goddamn Las Vegas strip. You couldn't pay me to go there. It's a crying shame."

I haven't been back to Franklin since my grandmother died. Dr. A helped me see my father was not only ill-equipped to deal with his own grief, but he also didn't know what to do about my mother or me. That's why he let me stay with Nonna.

"Sugar, I'd give my right eye to go back." He hangs his head then looks at me. "I should've done better by you and by your mama. I wish I'd tried harder."

"I know, Daddy. It's in the past. Have you heard from her?"

He pulls out his billfold, takes out a photo, and hands it to me. "Your crazy mama's still living with the damn hippies. She makes jewelry in an art colony over in New Mexico. It's some dusty old mountain town called Madrid. But not like the one in Spain. It's pronounced Maaa-drid." He bleats like a goat, making me laugh.

I look at the photo of my mother, expecting to feel angry, but it doesn't come. Her skin is weathered from the desert sun; her dark hair is longer and peppered with gray. She looks weak, like she always was. I can't imagine ever leaving my daughters. But I've never lost a child, so what do I know? I don't hate her. Maybe she did what she had to do to save herself from drowning.

"She writes me from time to time and always asks about ya." He smiles a melancholy smile. "She loves ya, you know." He pats my leg. "We both messed up everything for ya. I hope one day you'll be able to forgive us."

"Like I said, Daddy, what's done is done. All we can do is move forward. Forgive yourself, okay? For everything."

"I swear I'm trying, darling." He leans back in the chair, chewing on the corner of his mustache, just as I remember. "Bet you never thought you'd see the day ol' George West went and had his head shrunk."

"You did?" I put my hand to my chest, exaggerating my surprise. "I'm so proud of you. Did it help?"

"Damn straight. That head shrinker had me write letters to y'all, even Mama and Tommy." He stands taller, yanking up his pants like he does when he's about to tell a joke. "I told him that idea was dumber than tits on a bull."

I laugh. "So, did you write us letters?" I don't recall ever getting one.

"Sure as hell did, and I'll be damned if he wasn't on to something."

"What did you do with them?"

"That head shrinker wanted me to bring them in, read them to him, but I told him no way in hell. They were none of his goddamn business. He told me to send yours if I wanted, and to burn Mama's and Tommy's. Some kind of transcendental bullshit, if you ask me."

"Transcendental, Daddy?" I laugh again.

"You like that? I knew you would." He slaps my knee. "That was the head shrinker's word. I wrote it down so I'd remember. I mailed yours. I mailed you a bunch, so did your mama, but you never wrote back, so we just figured—"

I cut him off. "Daddy, I never got a single letter from either of you."

He shakes his head and stands, pointing a finger at me. "That son of a bitch. He did something with them."

A quake begins spreading from my core. "Please, I don't want to talk about him."

"No, darling, of course you don't." He steps in to hug me then sits down on the edge of the bed. "Don't you worry. That SOB will never hurt you again." He lifts my chin. "You hear me, sugar? I'll make sure he pays."

I want to argue, to tell him I can take care of myself like I always have, and that I don't even know if Alex hurt me, but I stay quiet and small. My big strong father holds me against him, and all at once, I'm a frightened little girl from the sticks. I tell my dad about Daniel, and when I share that Daniel is a Nowhere native, George West says exactly what I knew he would say. "You have got to be shittin' me."

Reconnecting brings a peace from my past I never imagined. All these years, I kept thoughts of my parents buried along with my brother. Dead to me. Funny thing is, no matter how many times rust gets covered, it always resurfaces.

I try not to think of Daniel in jail, wrongly accused of hurting me. We haven't spoken today, and I can't help but worry. According to Dr. A, after my last conversation with him, his phone privileges were revoked for not following the rules. She tried to explain his PTSD issues to the sheriff, but he wouldn't budge. In order to stay sane, I trick my brain into believing Daniel is simply back in Positano, visiting Francesca and his cousins.

I'M LYING IN A DARKENED room on a soft leather chaise, still in the psych ward of Methodist Hospital. The room is considerably cozier than mine. There are curtains, carpet, and a potted palm by the window. Dr. A sits in a chair next to the unlit lamp. Soft classical music plays, and candlelight flickers around the room, meant to help me relax.

"Okay, Abby, I need you to close your eyes. You're in your cottage alone, in bed, nearly asleep. There's so much on your mind. Daniel is in town. You're trying to get Alex to stop harassing you."

I interrupt. "I don't see why this will work this time." This is our second shot at hypnosis. I'm frustrated. I know what she wants me to say, and I know she's probably right. But I can't ruin Alex for something I can't remember.

"Abby, please be patient with the process. This time, I'm going to do things differently. I'll read back your account of the events from that night. I'm hoping something will trigger your memory. The sooner you remember, the sooner your life will get back to normal. You know how badly I want to help get Daniel out of jail and get his name cleared, but more than anything, I want you to remember what happened that night. So let's try again, please." Dr. A told me earlier she wants me to stay until my memory comes back. "Once you leave here, your mind will callus over the trauma, and the chances of you remembering will decrease substantially."

With a low voice, she begins. "You're in your bedroom. It's dark. The wind is blowing, and there's a storm on the horizon. The wind picks up, and the surf is pounding the sand. You're worried about how Ruby is handling everything. You think of Daniel and the secrets you've been keeping from him. Your home was broken into. Your car sabotaged. The tension between Daniel and Alex is taking its toll on you."

My eyes are heavy.

"Ruby is on the sofa with you, watching *Sweet Home Alabama*, when Alex calls. A nor'easter is coming in, and you're anxious. Ruby's leaving to go watch Jack. You kiss her goodbye, go to the bathroom, then into your bedroom, where you undress and slip on a nightshirt. You pull back the comforter and crawl into bed while waiting for Ruby's text. Once you know she's arrived safely, you sleep."

Her voice gets softer. "You are asleep, Abby. Sound asleep. Tell me what happens next."

I'm quivering and afraid. The wind and thunder are so loud. The lightning strikes so closely.

"What are you afraid of, Abby?" she asks, her voice soft. "What else is happening?"

"He's there, standing over me. I smell him—cologne, bourbon, cigars. I haven't yet opened my eyes, but I know he's there." My body trembles as I relive his words to me: "You are mine. You belong to me, sweetheart."

I feel his hot breath against my face and his tongue in my mouth. "His hands are on my hips. He thrusts inside of me." I feel his palms and his fingertips slide across my breasts, across my clavicle, then around my neck. "His thumbs press in the hollow of my throat into my windpipe." My throat burns. I feel the key break my skin and the blood pool. "I hear the sounds of swallowing, gurgling, and crying."

"Who's crying, Abby?"

My body tightens and splits in two.

"Who's there with you? Tell me."

It was him. I open my eyes and gasp for breath. "Alex."

I pull my knees to my chest to stop my body from convulsing and bite hard to stop my teeth from chattering. The truth has surfaced.

All this time, he claimed to love me. All he did was try to possess me and control me. Why would he rape me? Why would he try to end my life? Why would he hurt a baby he thinks is his? What kind of love is that?

He never loved me at all. Love is doing whatever it takes to make the other person happy, even if it means letting them go. If Alex loved me, he would have released me. If I loved myself, I would have gone long ago.

The truth is out. We can move on now.

Dr. A turns on the lights. She stares straight ahead, quiet. Her jaw is taut. When she looks at me, her eyes burrow into mine. "He raped you. I didn't know."

I am raw and edgy, all nerves. I open my mouth to speak but come up empty.

"That's all we need." She touches my arm and stands to go. "It'll all be over soon."

"Wait. Don't tell anyone. Please. It would destroy Daniel and Ruby. Please?"

"But, Abby, this would put him away—"

I cut her off. "I never want to speak of it again."

She nods, disappointed. "That's your choice, and I'll honor it if you're certain."

"I am." After nearly a year of rebuilding the broken shell of a person I was and spending months helping Daniel get over Alex taking advantage of me on the night of Ruby's diagnosis, I will not allow Daniel to know about this. No matter how much he loves me, it will change the way he sees me. We'll never be able to make love without him imagining Alex violently raping me.

"Do you really think it's over?"

"I know so." She kneels and hugs me.

"Dr. A, I don't know your first name."

"It's Grace," she says. "Why?"

"Of course it is." I smile through chattering teeth.

AFTER ELEVEN DAYS BEHIND bars, Daniel reenters my life through the hospital room door. All charges have been dropped. Deep lines I haven't seen since Paris etch his face. Despite the hell he's been through, his eyes are still bright Mediterranean blue. He buries his face in my hair and presses my forehead to his. "I've missed you."

"We have a lot to talk about," I say.

"I know we do, but not tonight. Let's let tonight be about you, me, and that baby girl."

His lips meet mine, and for a moment, time stands still. The world around us and all that has happened disappears. He wants to celebrate a baby that may not be his.

"I want you to meet her," I whisper, picking up the call button.

"Wait." He lowers the bedrail and squeezes in, enveloping me. "I want to hold you for a minute. I didn't know if I'd get the chance again."

His wet eyelashes press against my cheek.

I pull back and kiss them, tasting salty tears. He pushes my hair away and traces the bruises along my neck. And just like that, he tenses, stands, and empties his lungs with the force of a hurricane. "I will fucking kill him."

"Shhh, it's okay." I reach for him. "He's going to prison for a long time."

"Prison isn't enough. He tried to kill you." His voice cracks. "I cannot fucking live with that." His forehead veins bulge. He paces a few steps with clenched fists.

"Please stop it," I beg. "I need you to calm down. You don't have to do anything. He'll pay."

Daniel takes a few deep therapeutic breaths and sits back on the bed. He shakes his head and presses his lips together. "Damn right, he'll pay."

I wrap my arms around him and hold him until his breathing slows. He leans in, touching my face. "I'm sorry, Doc. I won't let him ruin this for us." He sits back up, pressing his fingers against his closed eyes. "Can I meet our baby now?"

Our baby. A nurse brings her in, and my heart melts as Daniel leans down to look at her. He inhales sharply then bites down on his palm to keep from crying. He reaches into the bassinet and scoops her up, bringing her face inches from his.

"God, she's beautiful." He sits back on the bed, unwraps her, and kisses her tiny toes. Then he looks at me. "She's so small." He swipes away his tears, and when his spell finally breaks, he says, "Abby, I can't tell you how I know this, but she belongs to me. You and I created this beautiful little person."

Praying he's right, I wrap my arms around them both.

"I was thinking of calling her Grace." The name of Dr. A, my saving grace.

"Hello, Grace," he whispers.

"I was hoping we could make her middle name Thomas, after both yours and Tommy's," I say.

"Grace Thomas Quinn, hmm." He looks up. "I love it."

"Look at this," Daniel says. Baby Grace has her fist wrapped tightly around Daniel's finger. He looks into my eyes. "I swear to God, no matter what, even if she isn't mine, I'll love her as if she is." He slaps his free hand to his chest. "She has my heart already."

Leaning back beside me, he holds our tiny daughter between us. For a moment, my heart overflows. I lean my head on his shoulder and say a silent prayer. God is back in my good graces.

After a firm knock at the door, two Saint Johns County deputies step inside. My stomach twists.

Chapter 32
Florida

"Abigail Montgomery?"

Daniel is quick on his feet in a defensive posture.

"I'm Officer Nichols, and this is Officer Bowen from Saint Johns County."

My mind races. *Is Daniel about to be arrested again for something he didn't do?*

"We're here to notify you that Alexander Montgomery has been arrested and charged with attempted murder. He's being held and awaiting arraignment."

Relief washes over me.

"Do you have any questions, ma'am?"

I do. I have so many questions. "Can he get out? I mean, will he be able to post bond?"

"With the charges he's facing, bond is unlikely."

Alex cannot hurt us anymore. The lights suddenly seem way too bright and the television in the background too loud. Alex deserves to rot in a dirty prison cell. But emotions are perplexing, and my thoughts freeze up. I need time to sort through my feelings. For Daniel, I smile and pretend to be elated. Then I think of Ruby. How will she take the news? How will Alex survive prison? His career is over. And what will happen to Jack? I swallow against the lump in my throat.

OUT OF THE HOSPITAL, I say goodbye to the makeover cottage Ruby and I worked so hard to create. At first, I decided I would never step foot inside, but after talking with Melody, I changed my mind. She thought it might help give me closure on that chapter of my life. The kitchen and living room look the same. The door to the bedroom, where the attack happened, is shut. I hesitate then open it, unsure what I'll feel. Someone cleaned the room. It doesn't look like the crime scene I imagined was left. The curtains are open, and the sun is shining in. Through the thin walls, I can hear the ocean's crashing waves. I hear the laughter of little kids on the beach. I sit on the bed to let whatever emotions come forth. I close my eyes and wait for the fear and terror that doesn't appear. I find an ephemeral peace here.

Other than personal belongings, I leave everything. I tell the landlady she can have it all. Miss Gail says she's planning to turn it into a vacation rental and promises we can use it for free anytime. I know we never will.

With all the chaos surrounding us and no place to live, Daniel managed to convince the AirBnB host to give him a discount rate for the next six months. She's happy to have a single family instead of large groups cramming in and making messes.

Life is finally going smoothly, as it should. But, sometimes, when contentment flows in, panic surges behind it, like some rogue wave. *How does one move on for good? Damn you, Alex, for causing so much pain. Damn you for stripping away the youth of our daughter. Why couldn't you just let me go?* Half my heart is full with Ruby, Daniel, and Grace. The other half is scarred and stained.

No matter how often Dr. A tries to convince me, I know if I were stronger in the beginning, I would have made better choices. If I'd divorced Alex right away, our lives might be different. He wouldn't have tried to kill me and wouldn't be in jail right now.

No matter what future I imagined for myself, becoming a statistic was never one. Now I'm a member of another new club—the one in five victims of severe physical domestic violence. I am a battered woman.

"No one talks about domestic abuse. Victims are embarrassed and blame themselves, just like you, but I'm here to tell you, this is not your fault," Dr. A says.

Alex faces fifteen years for attempted murder. That hardly seems like enough time. But the prosecutor calls it a crime of passion, and because he is rich and attractive and *was* an upstanding member of the community, a jury will never see him as a monster. If they knew about the rape, he would probably get double the time, but that secret will go to the grave with me.

After his arrest, the expedited divorce becomes finalized. When the moment finally arrives, all I can do is erupt in tears. Joyful tears.

AS THE DAYS PASS AND each night as darkness rolls in, I worry Alex will find a way to hurt me again. He has nothing left to lose. Ruby is finished with him, and Jack's mother is taking her son away to Paris soon. Even after Alex's release, his life will never be okay. He's not cut out for prison. Maybe an inmate will smell his weakness. Maybe he would be better off dead. But in the daylight, when I think of Ruby and Jack, I want nothing more than for Alex to get help, to heal, and to find a new normal. I pray after his release, he'll move far from here and start a new life.

Ruby says she'll never forgive him, and I worry holding a grudge this strong is going to continue to damage her emotionally. Until a couple of months ago, her entire life had been lived in one house, and now, in a short time, she's been in three different places. Her world has been turned upside down. How will she get through this unbroken?

When Daniel finds out how little time Alex is facing, he nearly punches a hole through the bedroom wall. He stops himself and opts for a run on the beach instead. The PTSD therapy he's started attending has stopped the violent nightmares, but his flares of anger concerning Alex are a work in progress.

At Dr. A's urging, I attend a domestic violence group she promises to be therapeutic and healing. There, I listen as women bare their souls and share heartbreaking tales of being beaten and held against their will. Many say they went back—or are still there—living with their abuser. Without money, they have little choice. They're afraid for their children or afraid that without a place to live, they'll lose custody.

During the first two meetings, I keep to myself, closed off. Socioeconomically, I have little in common with these women. Alex wasn't unemployed or an addict, and other than the night of December twenty-third, he never physically harmed me. It's at the third meeting that the internal fissures begin to spread, and I finally get it—I'm no different.

I listen to a woman named Melissa share a story that sounds very much like mine. Her boyfriend was charming and attentive and made her grateful to have him. He put a roof over her head and reminded her often that she would be nothing without him. When she enrolled in community college to better herself, he snapped, knowing she would eventually leave him. Before that day, he'd never harmed her with anything but words. Her story strikes a chord, and while unlike us, they weren't well off, inside we were the same. She spent years battling anxiety and depression, exasperated by living with a controlling partner.

My life may have looked better from the outside. My physical wounds weren't evident, but inside, I was bruised and bleeding. My abuser may have dressed nicer and had a better career than many, but his story is the same. He used fear to control me as long as he could, and when that stopped working, he tried to finish me. Full of fear, I stand up and share my story. It is then that I truly become one of the brave ones.

While Daniel is out for a run, I gather the courage to read the police report I've had hidden for days. It shows that the sheriff's office, along with the St. Augustine PD, showed up on December twenty-fourth at three in the morning after receiving a 911 hang-up call. They pounded on the door for approximately two minutes then forced entry. Paramedics followed and found Alex kneeling on the foot of the bed, covered in blood and fluid as he pulled the baby from my unconscious body. He explained that he was my husband and though we were taking some time apart, we were cordial. He'd dropped by with some gifts and found me unconscious and crowning. He insisted I was gone, but thankfully, the paramedics followed protocol and checked for a pulse. Finding a faint one, they bagged me. The paramedics took the baby and me away, and that's when, according to the report, Alex fell apart. "Extremely distraught" was their wording.

The first officer on the scene knew Alex and wrote down that he was in shock after finding me unresponsive. The initial report said Alex told them I had a history of suicide attempts and that he believed I tried to hang myself using a scarf. The necklace that punctured my throat must have gotten caught in the scarf.

Alex flashed his credentials and performed well enough that they believed his story. The report noted that Alex made no effort to resuscitate me. He didn't call for help or open the front door when the police arrived. He explained that away by insisting I'd been gone too long and that he was in shock.

Later, when investigators became suspicious, Alex changed his story—he suddenly recalled a man dressed in a gray T-shirt with an American flag emblem and running shoes fleeing the scene. No one jogs in the middle of the night, so he knew the man must be responsible for hurting me. When pressed further for a description, Alex told the detectives he had a muscular build and tight-cropped dark hair. He said he'd seen him once before and believed it was my estranged lover. That was all that was needed to issue a search warrant for Daniel's beach house. Because Daniel couldn't prove his whereabouts and they immediately spotted a pair of tennis shoes and gray T-shirt with an American flag, he was taken in for questioning. If it weren't for Alex's status, I don't believe the officers would have taken his word as gospel.

When Dr. A appeared and pressured the police department to take a closer look at Alex, they did. They may have suspected him and probably would have eventually learned the truth, but they weren't moving fast enough. Once Alex fell apart at the hospital, he became a suspect. It was my memory of that night, though, that ultimately led to a warrant for his arrest.

Chapter 33
Florida

O n the first day of spring, as the sun sinks into the sea, Daniel and I stand on the beach hand in hand, sharing a moment I never thought would come. The most important people to us are all here.

Ruby is beside me, barefoot in a flowy white cotton gown with baby Grace in her arms wearing a tiny version of the same dress. Headbands of tiny daisies adorn their heads and mine. Ruby made them herself, replicating a photo she saw on Pinterest. My dress is simple white cotton, similar to the girls', only it stops midcalf. I carry a small bouquet of wildflowers, another of Ruby's Pinterest creations.

My father is here, dressed in a cowboy hat and boots, wearing his favorite silver Lonestar belt buckle. From the looks of him, no one would know he'd been gone from Texas most of his adult life or that he was attending a beach wedding in eighty-degree weather. Daniel's cousins from Italy and his best friend, Michael, are here as well. Since arriving, Stefano has been arguing loudly with Luciana, then erupting into laughter over every little thing, ranging from who gets to hold the baby to who gets to cook breakfast. I can tell she's ready to drown him in the ocean. Watching Stefano and my father try to communicate is priceless. Neither understands the other, yet they keep trying, getting louder and louder.

Each time Stefano sees my father, he yells, "Giddyap, cowboy," and makes a lassoing motion. Before the day ends, my dad may be ready to drown him too.

Preacher John officiates our short, sweet ceremony. I'm thankful he encouraged us to write our vows.

When it's Daniel's turn, he glances down at his creased paper, and with a shaky voice, he begins. "Abby, from the moment I met you, I was taken. I never thought I'd find happiness again. I certainly wasn't looking for it." He pauses, folds his piece of paper, tucks it into his pants pocket, and takes my hands in his. "I'd pretty much given up hope and was going through the motions, living day to day the best I could." A tender smile spreads across his face. "As you know, I've loved and lost before. Everything that mattered to me was taken." His voice cracks, and he turns his face toward the setting sun. "I was barely alive before you showed up out of nowhere and breathed life back into me. You gave me a reason to smile again. You gave me the most beautiful baby girl and *best teenager*, if that's even a thing." He winks at Ruby. She laughs. Daniel looks down at our adjoined hands then back up at me. "Abby, you make me whole, and I can't wait to live my days with you and with the girls. I owe you my life. My love. My everything." He reaches back into his pocket and produces a yellowed slip of paper that I instantly recognize. "I want to read a small passage from one of the letters from your grandmother to mine." He leans forward and touches his forehead to mine. "This letter is from 1945," he tells our friends.

After the move, I tucked the letters away in a drawer and somehow completely forgot about them.

"It is my greatest hope that one day we will become family. In my dreams, I will one day have a son, and you will have a daughter. They will marry, have children, and our blood, our people, will be joined together for eternity."

I wipe my tears. Although we're a generation late, we came together despite all odds. With fate and love, two families are now united. How could she have known that her wish would be my destiny?

When it's my turn to speak, Ruby hands me my vows.

"Daniel, when I first met you, I was lost and broken." My voice comes out shaky. I take a deep breath and continue. "I didn't know how different life could be. How it was meant to be lived. I didn't know love like this was possible or that there was someone out there so perfect for me."

I pause to look into his eyes. They brim with tears. I hand my vows to Ruby and take his hands. "You are everything I've ever imagined in a partner, a father, and a soulmate." I blow out a breath, overcome with emotion. "I don't know how the stars aligned so perfectly on that day that led me to the Amalfi coast, up that mountain, and straight to you." I lean in and put my arms around him and look out at the faces of our guests, knowing I have to finish. "I look forward to every day from here until eternity with you." I reach up and pull his head down so that I can whisper into his ear. "Also, I got the test results."

He pulls back with wide, expectant eyes.

I bite back my grin and savor the moment. "Grace is yours."

He smiles then hoists me up in his arms. "I already knew it in my heart." He looks at the suddenly overcast sky. "Thank you," he says before pressing our faces together and kissing every part of mine.

"I guess it's time for me to pronounce you man and wife," Preacher John says with a smile.

Our guests cheer. Out of nowhere, Stefano barrels toward us, speaking rapid-fire Italian I can't make out. He grips us in a bear hug then trips backward over his own feet and falls into the sand. This overgrown toddler is now my family too.

My father laughs a big belly laugh and dabs his eyes with a hanky. He hugs me and says, "I'm so proud of you, sugar," then turns around, his arm outstretched, holding his flip phone. "Now let's you and me take one of them there selfies so I can send it off to your mama."

I haven't yet been fully ready to reconnect with her, but I know I need to start somewhere. So I lean in close and smile for his picture.

"Well, I'll be damned." Daddy fumbles with the keys. "It worked."

And with his words comes an unexpected crackle of lightning. Thunderheads roll in over the dunes in the distance. The wind whips out of nowhere, ripping the folded paper from my hands. Our guests begin scurrying toward their cars, holding on to hats, and purses, and each other.

"Holy hell. Let's get a move on, y'all!" my father yells to everyone.

Stefano screams and jumps at the next rumble of thunder. He leaps across the sand and away from the water. "Yeehaw. Giddyap," he yells over his shoulder to my father.

Daniel and I read each other with a smile. "Go," I tell my dad. "Take the girls, and we'll meet you at the restaurant."

Before the guests are off the beach, the sky opens up. Daniel grabs my head and pulls my mouth to his. In that moment, I don't care about anything but his lips on mine. We belong to each other, finally. He sweeps me up in his arms and makes a run for it. I squeal like the happiest girl in the world. And I am. It doesn't matter that my hair is drenched and stuck to my face like I'm a drowned rodent. My fingers are black from wiping streaks of mascara from my cheeks. My white dress is a sopping mess, and my bra is visible through it.

We're supposed to go straight to the restaurant, but that isn't going to happen. I know the minute we get into the car.

"I'm a mess."

"You're the most beautiful mess I've ever seen."

That look in his eyes never changes. With him, it's never as much desire as it is desperate need. He looks at me in the moment like he has so many times before, like he will die if he doesn't have me right then and there. We barely make it back to the beach house. He runs around the passenger side and scoops me out of the car to carry me inside. He insists, and I love him so much, I laugh and let him have his way. On our bed, the one we've spent hundreds of nights in, we become one as husband and wife. I want to say it feels like the first time, but it is so much more. I wipe away his tears as we lie side by side, speechless. Words are never necessary with him. We read each other like kindred souls. This is the best day of my life.

An hour later, at the restaurant, we toast, of course, with limoncello. No one but us gets the inside joke. That magical lemony elixir continues to make us smile.

I'd give anything to erase this past year from Ruby's life, but without it, Daniel and Grace wouldn't be here. I'm finally living the life I imagined—waking beside a man who adores me, all of me, despite my soft belly and stretch marks. His admiration is genuine, unlike Alex's. There's not an ounce of jealousy in his bones. When I complain about my figure, he stops me cold.

"Your body is amazing. You grew two humans, and I'm so proud of you."

"But look at you. You have abs of steel, and I have this." I pinch at my spare tire.

He chuckles. "Anytime you want to train, I'll get you out there running with me."

"Not a chance of me running. Not unless I'm being chased." I laugh and accept his flattery.

He shows me love with his actions, not only his words. I see it every day in the way he treats the girls, how he goes out of his way to do stupid and embarrassing things to make them laugh. Ruby often rolls her eyes at him, but she laughs too. And the way Daniel loved

Grace when he didn't know she was his says so much. Her eyes widen when she hears his voice or sees him enter a room. She coos, kicks her tiny feet, and flails her arms when he talks to her.

"There's my little sweet pea," he squeals.

There's so much love in our house. Each day, it overpowers the darkness a little more. Soon, maybe it'll be enough.

When Jack's mother heard Alex had been arrested, she immediately flew to Florida and regained custody. At first, Alex's parents put up a fight, but they backed down quickly when she told them she would call a press conference and tell the world how Alex had gained custody by threatening her. They knew bad publicity wouldn't bode well for his trial, so they conceded. She brought Jack to say goodbye to Ruby. I wasn't sure how I would react to meeting her face to face, but I agreed.

When I opened the door and saw her with hunched shoulders and watery eyes, I pitied her.

"I'm sorry for everything that's happened and for what I did all those years ago. I should have apologized to you long ago."

"Would you like to come in for a glass of sweet tea, to give Ruby and Jack a few minutes together?" I asked.

On the back deck, overlooking the ocean, she stared into her lap. "Please let me finish apologizing. It's important to me." She eyed me, her worry lines showing. "When I met Alex, I was so low. I'd just been through a bad breakup, and his interest flattered me. I should never have flirted back. I just never thought..." She takes a tissue from her bag and composes herself. "I never thought he'd do what he did to me."

At first, I assumed she meant his convincing her to take a job in Paris, but I realized I only knew Alex's version of the story. I put my hand on her arm as a kind gesture. "Lauren, what did he do to you?"

She stifled a sob, blew out a long breath, and told me her story.

The beginning part matched Alex's, but the night she conceived Jack was much different. "He asked me to meet him at his office to talk. I knew, considering what I'd done with him in the past, it was a bad idea." She sniffled. "But I was nearby, and I'd been seeing a therapist, so I was much stronger. I only went to tell him I was done with him."

Grace would be up soon, and I became uneasy with the direction our conversation was heading, so I hurried her along. "So what happened?"

"When I walked in the door, he kissed me." She shakes her head. "I shouldn't have let him, but I figured it'd be the last time. I told him it had been a mistake. Then I tried to leave..."

She looked out at the ocean, tears streaming.

My stomach dropped. I knew what she was about to say. "I don't understand. Why didn't you report him?"

"Who would believe me?"

She was right.

"If he hadn't..." She swallowed hard and wiped her nose. "Done what he did to you, I wouldn't have told anyone."

So she let the man who raped her come home to me? She let him have her son? "I don't understand. How did Alex end up with custody of Jack?"

She fumbled with her hands in her lap. "Through the years, he convinced me that while he was a *little* assertive that night, it wasn't rape. He said I knew what was going to happen that night if I showed up and that I deserved it." She put her face in her hands for a minute. "It was my fault. Once you found out about Jack, he said he was taking him and that if I fought him, I'd end up dead. He had this look in his eyes that told me he meant it."

She takes a slow sip of her tea. "I knew about you and Ruby through the years and how well you both raised her. I'd stalked you on Facebook and the papers. All the charities you help with. I knew you were a good mother and that Jack would be okay as long as you were there. It wasn't going to be forever." She stood, her mood shifting. "Please don't judge me. I had no way to support Jack without help. I was barely making ends meet. You know Alex. He would have killed me and gotten away with it. I know it. I just wish he was dead."

Crying baby Grace put an end to our discussion. Lauren and I lied, promised to stay in touch for Ruby and Jack's sake, but I knew we wouldn't. We all needed a future that didn't remind us of Alex Montgomery.

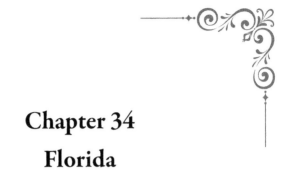

Chapter 34
Florida

On the stand, I give testimony to put Alexander Montgomery away. I relive the attack in front of the jury. In front of my daughter. In front of Daniel. Seeing the pain in Ruby's eyes and the rage in Daniel's causes me to fall apart. The judge calls a recess twice. Going in, I knew Alex was facing less than ten years. I also knew if I told the whole truth, he would go away for a lifetime, but I wouldn't speak those words. The damage to me had been done. There was no point in destroying my family any further. Alex would go unpunished for the rapes. For the first time, I am grateful for the Montgomery family's power in this town. I expected a full media circus, but as oftentimes happens in our county, the story is kept hushed.

I brace myself as the jury reconvenes. The verdict is read. Alex is found guilty and sentenced to eight of the possible fifteen years. The decision brings neither anger nor relief. I'm still imperviously numb. Dr. A says my feelings may take a while to surface. She tells me what to look out for and that denial is one of the beginning stages. Taking care of my family is my priority. The three of us are in therapy and will continue until healed.

BACK AT HOME AFTER an unnatural amount of thought and discussion, I decide to return to medical school. I'll reenroll at the

University of Florida in Gainesville and take most of my classes in nearby Jacksonville.

Daniel is thrilled. "I'm so proud of you, Doc."

We made so many plans to go back to Italy and to travel the world once Ruby left for college. "What about Italy?"

"Italy and the world can wait. We'll take off when everyone's on break or during the summer. Stefano and Luciana will keep an eye on the house for us."

With his arms on my shoulders and his blue eyes boring into mine, he says, "I've chased my dreams and seen so many places I never imagined. I've lived most of my life on the go, hopping from place to place. You haven't had the freedom or support from a partner to do what you wanted." He squeezes me. "But now you do. If you told me you wanted to fly to the moon, I'd do what I could to get us there. I swear to God I would."

And I know he's telling the truth.

WHILE DANIEL BATHES Grace and Ruby reads, I carry my thoughts outside and make my way to the end of the wooden walkway. Moonlight guides me along the path to the water. Before me, the vast ocean with all the world's energy rolls in, spitting bits of surf onto my cheeks. The sea, the moon, and the stars remain constant. No amount of heartbreak makes a difference. We are too small. My heart is no longer shattered or hardened. Instead, it's soft and full, despite the sadness of the past year and the tragedy of today. I am whole again, a little battered, but still in one piece.

I think of all I've learned in this precious lifetime of mine.

I think of how despite everything, my faith has been restored and I am stronger than ever.

I've forgiven myself for past mistakes and learned the importance of self-love.

Of all the things I know to be true, real love is so precious and rare those of us lucky enough to find it should hang on with both hands—never let it go, no matter the cost, whether it means being patient or fighting for it.

How do you know you've found it?

That's easy enough. Ask yourself—does this love make you a better person?

Does this love make you love yourself?

When you lie down next to this person—are you living in a moment you would die for?

For me, the answer is yes.

With Daniel, it has always been yes.

I know he's flawed, but I love that he encourages me to be whoever I want to be.

I love that he's patient and kind, despite his occasional outbursts, and that his heart and mind are wide open and vulnerable to everything, all of life's fleeting emotions.

I love that he gives me the space I need to grow and promises he always will.

I love that he lives big, grasps every opportunity, and knows without a doubt our time here is limited and uncertain.

I love that he's teaching me to live this way. Showing me that anything is possible, even if it means starting over and over, again and again, until it's right.

Before heading back up the steps, back across the boardwalk path, beneath the bright moon, I see him, barefoot and shirtless.

Silhouetted by the light behind him.

He is there, waiting for me.

The sight of him is so beautiful I gasp. My heart overflows with devotion so great my lungs hardly have room for air. With open arms, he holds space for me.

I step in.

He pulls me to him, exhales a long breath, a lifetime of worry and regret.

I cling to him—completely devoted, barely breathing.

"Never let me go," he whispers, in my ear.

"I never will."

Acknowledgements

More than a decade ago, I sat down on a beach at the base of a mountain along the Amalfi Coast and began the arduous process of putting my thoughts on paper. Those words would eventually come together to tell a story. Storytelling begins as a solitary project but rarely ends as one. For those who helped shaped my initial words into a polished novel, I am grateful.

Thanks to David Morgan, my first writing instructor at University of Richmond, and the first person to read my work and convince me I was a real writer. To my cousin Lisa Mitchell, who began down the long winding writer's path with me many years ago.

To the coffee shops who kept me fed and full of teas and lattes over the years:

DOS (St. Augustine, Fl)

Southern Grounds (Jacksonville, Fl)

The White Rabbit (Greensburg, Pa)

I am grateful to La Tagliata and the town of Positano, the inspirational place that changed the way I view the world. To my Italian friends, Francesco Monti and Christian Filippella, thank you for answers to my endless questions.

To the women of the WFWA (Women's Fiction Writers Association) and my smaller writing group, The Ink Tank, especially Robin Facer-Taylor and Sheila Athens, for their words of wisdom and motivation. To my editors, Sara Gardiner and Stefanie Spangler Buswell, for making the words shine.

Thanks to my eccentric mother, Joan, and my smooth-talking Texan dad, Nick, for giving me an unconventional life and an abundance of storytelling material. I am eternally grateful for my husband, Andrew, who loves me through thick and thin, and to my daughter, Jordan, my sons, Jimmy and Jake, and my sister, Chrisi, whose love for me is immense. I will always strive to make them proud.

About the Author

Tammy Harrow is an avid world traveler, writer, and photographer who has spent much of her life in the publishing industry, the first half in newspapers and more recently working for various magazines. Every couple of months, she tries to visit a new city or country in search of interesting stories to tell.

Her work has appeared in *Woman's Day*, *Budget Travel*, *Social*, and *Old City Life* magazines and on CNN, MSNBC, and National Geographic. She also has a bachelor's degree in journalism from University of Maryland.

Tammy lives in historic downtown St. Augustine, Florida, with her husband, teenage daughter, two cats, and a dog.

Read more at https://internationaltravelbug.com.

About the Publisher

Dear Reader,

We hope you enjoyed this book. Please consider leaving a review on your favorite book site.

Visit https://RedAdeptPublishing.com to see our entire catalogue.

Don't forget to subscribe to our monthly newsletter to be notified of future releases and special sales.

CPSIA information can be obtained
at www.ICGtesting.com
Printed in the USA
LVHW022344010622
720243LV00013B/1523